THE
OPEN
MARRIAGE

BOOKS BY VICTORIA JENKINS

The Divorce

The Argument

The Accusation

The Playdate

The New Family

The Bridesmaids

The Midwife

Happily Married

Your Perfect Life

DETECTIVES KING AND LANE SERIES

The Girls in the Water

The First One to Die

Nobody's Child

A Promise to the Dead

THE
OPEN
MARRIAGE

VICTORIA JENKINS

bookouture

Published by Bookouture in 2024

An imprint of Storyfire Ltd.
Carmelite House
50 Victoria Embankment
London EC4Y 0DZ

www.bookouture.com

ISBN: 978-1-83525-185-0
eBook ISBN: 978-1-83525-184-3

PROLOGUE

I can't take my gaze off the photograph that fills the television screen, the eyes staring back at me, silently accusing me.

'Did you know about this?'

I shake my head. The lie seems easier.

The word *Missing* runs in red across the bottom of the screen, repeated like a taunt. This wasn't how things were supposed to happen. No one was meant to get hurt. A police officer is saying something, but the words are drowned beneath my guilt.

'They must be presuming the worst.'

I get up and hurry into the hallway, barely making it to the downstairs toilet in time before the contents of my lunch make a reappearance. I feel the blood drain from my face as my stomach empties. Events of the past couple of weeks flood through my brain, a mental nausea that keeps me bound to the floor. I would have done anything to save my marriage. But now someone is missing, and I'm to blame.

ONE

I give myself a final mirror-check before leaving the bedroom: hair curled in loose beach waves, trusted black dress for all occasions; just enough make-up to make it obvious a more than usual amount of effort has been made. This much energy hasn't gone into my appearance since our wedding day, seven years ago to the day. The framed photograph on the bedside table sits as a reminder of the occasion: a small and personal ceremony, just a handful of friends and family present, the photographs taken in the park opposite the registry office. We were lucky to get them done before the weather turned, and by the time the rain came, we were already in the restaurant, where we shared a meal with our guests before coming home to the house Marcus and I had bought together only six months earlier.

We fell in love with the place as soon as we stepped through the door, and I think we'd been at the viewing for a total of six minutes when Marcus asked me if I wanted to make an offer. I'd always wanted to live in a new-build, something untouched and without history: a blank canvas we could make our own. This place was it. As I head down the stairs, I still remember the feeling I had when the estate agent opened the front door and we followed him into the wider-than-normal hallway. There was so much space and light. I felt for the first time in forever that I'd found a place where I could breathe.

A smell of garlic wafts from the kitchen. In the oven, bubbling thick and creamy, the tray of dauphinoise potatoes I prepared earlier is ready to be taken out. I check the time: 7.35. Marcus said he'd be home around 7.30, so I'm expecting him any minute. I'll put the steaks on to cook when he comes in: we both like them medium rare, so they won't take long. The pepper sauce I made is sitting in a saucepan waiting next to the griddle, and the salad I prepared is in the fridge: rocket and spinach leaves, peppery radishes, vine-ripened plum tomatoes.

I open a bottle of red wine and leave it on the dining table to breathe. When he hasn't arrived back by eight, I call his mobile, expecting to hear him on the road somewhere, nearly home. Instead, it goes straight to answerphone. The beeps click through, but I hang up, go to WhatsApp and send him a message.

Just wondering how long you're going to be. Food going cold xx

The potatoes have burned crisp at the edges despite the oven being turned off twenty minutes ago. I pour myself some wine and take it into the living room, switch the TV on and watch a woman grapple with a swan made out of meringue, the two-foot-high structure wobbling precariously as she carries it tentatively to a table of waiting judges.

The rain the forecast promised has started earlier than predicted, already lashing at the windows. Perhaps Marcus has got stuck in traffic, though rush hour is usually earlier on a Friday evening.

By the time I'm halfway through my second glass of wine, I

hear his car pull onto the driveway. It's 9.35. He goes straight through to the kitchen when he comes in.

'Lou?'

'I'm in here.'

'I am so sorry,' he says, coming into the living room, his hair wet with rain, his coat still on. 'I've only just now seen your message.'

He pulls off his coat and hangs it on the living room door handle, which annoys me more than it should.

'You said you'd be back around seven thirty.'

'Did I? Something came up at the meeting. This Isle of Wight thing's taking more planning than we realised.'

I don't know who 'we' is. Marcus is self-employed and has no fixed workplace: his meeting today was apparently in a hotel a half-hour drive away, but I doubt he's been there until now. He's had a lot on his mind recently, with his trip to the Isle of Wight coming up, but things are no different for me. The school has an inspection next month, and I'm still in the process of trying to clear out my mother's house ready for sale – a task I had massively underestimated the scale of.

'Who did you say the meeting was with?' I ask casually. I get up and pass him to go into the kitchen, where I pull the tray of congealed potatoes from the now-cold oven. 'I can stick them in the microwave,' I offer.

'I ate,' he says apologetically. 'I'm so sorry, Lou. You should have said you were planning something special.'

My fault, I think. 'That's kind of the point with surprises.'

I wait for him to acknowledge the relevance of today, but he doesn't. I had to leave for work earlier than usual this morning; Marcus had gone out for a run by the time I woke up, and I was gone before he came back. I typed out a text when I got to school, wishing him happy anniversary, but I deleted it before sending, waiting to see whether I got one from him first. It sounds petty, but I had a suspicion he'd forgotten the date. Now that suspicion is confirmed.

He comes over to me and puts his arms around me, pulling me closer. 'You look amazing, by the way. What's all this in aid of?'

I move away from him, the compliment instantly lost with the question. 'Nothing. I'm going to go and get changed.' I nod to the table, where the half-drunk bottle of red wine still waits. 'Get yourself a glass if you want.'

I go up to the bedroom and take off the dress, feeling ridiculous at the effort I made for no purpose. I choose a pair of pyjamas and get changed, then pull a make-up remover wipe from a packet in the cupboard in the en suite and clean my face of the foundation and mascara I applied hours ago.

When I go back downstairs, I hear Marcus's voice coming from the living room. I linger in the hallway, listening to what I think is a conversation with someone before I realise he's leaving a voice note. I try to squash the resentment that settles in my chest. He's only just got home after being out all day, but already his attention is with someone else, glued as always to his phone. We barely talk any more. Not about anything that matters. Marcus occasionally asks how my day's been. We sometimes talk about the most recent Netflix series we've watched, although even doing that together has become something that needs to be scheduled. We never have sex. I can't really remember the last time we touched each other in any way that involved more than a friendly hug.

When we first met a decade ago, we spent hours talking. No phones, no television screen; nothing between us to create any kind of distraction from one another. During that time we got to know all about each other. I learned about his career change from labourer to sound engineer, and about the break-up that had put him off relationships for years. In turn, I let him know details of my past of which few other people had knowledge.

Ambitions took shape. Secrets were shared. Plans were made. We were both in our thirties, but it felt like being a teenager again.

I shake myself from thoughts I know to be futile. Nothing stays the same. No one moves through the various stages of a relationship and maintains that honeymoon period you find within those first few months and years. It would be unfair of me to expect our lives to look now as they did then.

Marcus flips his phone cover shut when he sees me in the living room door.

'What's so funny?' I ask, having just heard him laughing.

'It was nothing. Here,' he says, standing to pass me the glass he's topped up for me. His phone starts ringing. He answers it as he passes me the wine. 'Mate,' he says, leaving to take the call into another room. 'That was insane.'

I drop onto the sofa, almost slopping the wine over the rim of the glass. The thought that we made the right decision not to have children pops into my head, sudden and intrusive. It unsettles me for reasons I can't be sure of. I've never regretted our choice. I just didn't expect to ever be so adamant it was the correct one either.

It occurs to me now that this resentment would have grown tenfold if we'd brought children into our relationship. It would have been my life that changed significantly. My career. Marcus's life would no doubt have stayed much the same, his time away with work unaltered by having a family to look after. I'd like to think that I might have fallen into the role of motherhood with acceptance and patience, when the truth is, I'm not sure I would have. I was uncertain, and Marcus shared my doubts. My relationship with my parents contributed to my ambiguity, and for this reason it always seemed the sensible option to keep our lives as we'd always known them.

Marcus's laughter rings out from the kitchen, and I know it's irrational that it irritates me so much. I have no objection to him being happy. I want him to be happy. I just wish that every now and then I was the source of that happiness, or at the very least included in some small part.

The paperwork that my mother's solicitor sent me last week stares at me from the glass shelf beneath the coffee table. I move a book over it, hiding it from sight, as though if it can no longer be seen, it no longer exists. I never imagined that when it came to it, I would be left to deal with everything, although why I thought any different I'm not sure. My brother could never be relied upon for anything.

'Who was that?' I ask when Marcus returns from the kitchen, phone in hand.

'Pete. He's going to be working on the show with us.'

The 'show' is a television production that Marcus is due to start working on next month: a detective series that's going to be filmed on the Isle of Wight. His job takes him all over the UK and occasionally overseas, often for weeks at a time.

'Wasn't he at the meeting tonight?'

'Couldn't make it. Wife's in hospital.'

If Marcus's laughter just moments ago is anything to go by, I'm assuming Pete's wife can't be that unwell. Either that or Marcus wasn't talking to Pete at all.

When he leaves his phone to go upstairs, I glance to find it still unlocked. Temptation gets the better of me and I do something I've never done before: something that's never even crossed my mind. I go to his messages. The last one, sent little over an hour earlier, is from someone called Lucy. I open the conversation and scroll back through the thread.

Thanks for tonight – it was so great to catch up with you. Forgot to tell you earlier, I finally got around to watching the documentary. Insane! Sorry it took me so long x

The words hit me like a punch to the gut. Wherever

Marcus was this evening – wherever this 'meeting' took place – he was there with this woman. *It was so great to catch up with you.* Not, *it was so great to meet up with you all.* But perhaps this Lucy sent the same message to a number of other people who were involved. Yet surely if that was the case, there might have been some kind of group chat set up.

I know it's juvenile, but the kiss at the end of the message bothers me. I don't know who Lucy is and what her connection to Marcus might be. I think of his recent projects, assuming the documentary she's referring to must be the Channel 5 series he worked on about extreme body modifications.

Good, isn't it? Marcus replied. *Bit of an eye-opener in places though!*

There's no kiss. It seems ridiculous that this should come as a relief to me.

Oh yeah, reads Lucy's reply. *That guy from Brighton. Definitely helped pull in the ratings haha x*

Best 6k he'd spent in his life, reads Marcus's response.

And then there's another from Lucy: *Not really my type though. I prefer someone older, with a bit more experience x*

Piss off, Lucy, I think. Whoever this woman is, she presumably knows Marcus well enough to know he's married. The message is suggestive enough to leave little room for interpretation: the older man she prefers is Marcus, and she's letting her availability to the possibility be known. But he hasn't replied, I tell myself. Not yet, at least.

I think of him laughing earlier before he disappeared into the kitchen. He might not have replied by text because he didn't need to. The conversation might have gone further over the phone. I go to his call records to find the last call. *Pete L* greets me from the screen. He was telling the truth about that at least.

There's movement on the landing, and I hear him coming back down the stairs. I hurriedly lock the phone and return it to where he left it on the sideboard, annoyed with myself for letting suspicion and insecurity get the better of me. I'm not this type of person. I've never checked a partner's phone – not during my marriage or in any relationship before it. I don't want to become this woman.

'That's better,' Marcus says, coming back into the living room. He's wearing a pair of grey joggers and a hoodie. I notice the first thing he does is look for his phone.

He hasn't done anything wrong, I remind myself. He said something had come up at the meeting about his forthcoming work trip, and this Lucy woman could have been involved in that something. He hasn't lied, has he? So as I watch him slide his mobile phone into his trouser pocket and reach for his glass of wine from the coffee table, why do I feel as though I'm losing him?

TWO

The following morning, Marcus is already up and out of bed by the time I wake. I went to sleep before him last night, leaving him downstairs to watch the end of a documentary he started bingeing earlier in the week. My first thought when I open my eyes is that I didn't drink enough last night to warrant the headache that's pinching at my temples, and it's only made worse when I get out of bed. I go down to the kitchen still in my pyjamas to see the glow of the gym's light at the bottom of the garden illuminating the stretch of lawn that lies in front of it. The rain that dances beneath its spotlight is like a cast of tiny ballerinas on a stage of grass. I wait for a glimpse of Marcus, knowing that if he was on the treadmill I'd catch at least the back of him at the edge of the window. More than likely he's sitting on the weights bench, phone stuck to his hand where it's always to be found.

Last night, after I'd gone upstairs, I couldn't sleep for thinking about those messages from Lucy. I kept telling myself that it was nothing more than a friendly exchange between colleagues, but then I started to wonder whether Marcus would have the same view if he'd read similar texts on my phone from a male colleague at school. They just seemed a little too friendly and overfamiliar; from her, at least.

I flick on the coffee machine and make a cup for myself and one for Marcus. If he's got something to hide down at the end of the garden in the man cave/gym he built himself a couple of years back, I may spot a glimpse of any guilt when I take this down to him. I slip my feet into the boots he has left by the patio doors and carry both cups out into the garden, trying not to slip as I hurry down to the gym. Marcus is near the window, now on the treadmill. I berate myself for taking so long preparing the coffees, wishing instead that I'd just gone straight out into the garden. When I open the gym door, having to use my elbow to push down the handle, the first thing I notice is his phone on the windowsill, never more than a few feet away from him.

He glances at the cup I place beside it. 'I've already had one,' he pants. 'Thanks, though.'

I say nothing and sit on the weights bench behind him, watching his calves as he runs. He was never much of a gym-goer when we met; this recent interest in working out is something that's only developed over the past couple of years. His midlife crisis, he calls it, but now, as I consider the time and privacy he has in this space exclusive to him, I wonder whether there's not another reason for it all.

He turns down the treadmill before slowing to a stop. 'Everything okay?' he asks, turning to me. I never sit here like this. I hardly ever come in here.

'You forgot, didn't you?'

He pulls a face. 'Forgot what?'

I thought about saying nothing, but I can't. It's not my intention to make him feel bad about what happened last night, but he should be aware that he forgot our anniversary. I don't want him to be under the impression I'll make an effort like I did last night just because it's a Friday.

'Our anniversary. Yesterday.'

I watch his face, his cheeks slightly pinkened with the exertion of his run, and see the realisation dawn in his eyes. 'Shit, Lou,' he says, stepping down off the treadmill. 'I am so sorry.'

I wonder just how many times he has uttered that last phrase during the past twelve hours.

'It's fine,' I tell him, shrugging it off. 'I just thought you should know why I'd gone to so much trouble.'

He sits beside me on the bench and places a hand on my knee. 'There's been so much going on. That's not an excuse, I know, but my head's been all over the place. Let me make it up to you tonight?'

'I've made it easy for you, though. The steaks are still there.'

'Even better then. I'll get some more red wine in.'

I sip my coffee and agree to let him cook tonight. As I leave to go back up to the house, thoughts of Lucy reappear for a moment before evaporating in the wet January morning air.

After getting dressed into my gym gear and taking two paracetamol for my headache, I drive to the leisure centre for the second of my twice-weekly yoga classes. By the time I pull into the car park, the rain has got lighter. The class is quite a large group, which suits me perfectly: I can hide at the back of the hall, where my lack of athletic prowess can go concealed behind a row of people far more flexible than I am. Despite coming to this class for the past eighteen months, I've managed to put on weight since last summer. After Mum's death, I stopped looking after myself, and I've always overeaten in times of stress. I drink too much wine, as well. Alcohol has always managed to soften difficult times, though unlike in my younger adult years, I now know when enough is enough.

I get there too early, while the woman who takes the class is still setting up her Bluetooth speakers. The fact that there's no one else in the hall makes me stop in my tracks in the doorway, wondering for a moment whether I've come on the wrong day.

'Morning,' she says cheerfully.

'Morning.'

I feel a bit rude placing my mat at the back of the room when there's no one else here, expecting her to make some kind of awkward joke about body odour. Fortunately for us both, she doesn't.

'Might be a bit quieter today,' she says, heading towards the door once her phone has connected to her speakers. 'What with the weather and everything.'

'Rain's just started to ease up,' I tell her.

I take off my trainers and kick them to one side before lying on my mat and closing my eyes, hoping not to get dragged into any further conversation. The headache that's been niggling at me all morning has started to subside, though it seems to have made way for an influx of anxiety. I wonder whether I should have come this morning. Maybe I'd have been better off staying home to make sure everything is okay between Marcus and me. But there'll be time for that tonight, I tell myself.

The door squeaks and a couple of women who always attend the group together head for the front of the hall, setting up their mats in front of the teacher's. It's occurred to me during these sessions that adults are really no different from children in so many ways. Among the regular attendees of this class, the same types that can be found in every classroom up and down the country are easily identified: the ones keen to impress; the ones who'd rather be elsewhere but have turned up because they feel they have to; the self-conscious; the overconfident; and then the group I belong to: the ones who hide at the back of the room where they hope they'll go unnoticed.

'We'll just give it another five minutes for any latecomers and then we'll make a start.'

I close my eyes again, losing myself to thoughts of Marcus and Lucy and work and inspections. I wonder why people rave about meditation if this is all it involves: just a long- drawn-out, torturous session of self-doubt and overthinking.

'Okay,' the teacher says, after what has felt like the longest five minutes of my life. 'If you're not doing so already, let's get stretched out on our mats and take a couple of moments to breathe deeply... in through the nose... out through the mouth.'

The sound of some kind of soft panpipes starts playing: the kind of music they play in spas. It's all quite nice until one of the women at the front of the hall manages to inhale through her nose louder than anyone I've ever heard. It begins to set my nerves jangling, but just as the music changes, the door opens again and a woman carrying a rolled-up mat to her chest edges into the hall as though unsure whether she's come to the right place.

'Sorry,' she mouths to the teacher as she makes her way to the middle of the room and unfolds her mat in the space between me and the women at the front.

'Welcome. Come join us, please.'

The woman's new to the class. I haven't missed a session in a couple of months now, and I've never seen her here before. I would definitely have noticed her; she isn't the type who could easily go missed. In her skin-tight Lycra and with her long dark hair pulled back into a high ponytail, she looks like a model from the cover of a fitness magazine.

She takes her time removing her trainers and placing her belongings at the side of the room, unflustered by the fact that she's come in late and is now holding up the session. When she sits on the mat, she somehow manages to glide into place, and I figure she must have done yoga elsewhere before: the first time I attempted the position we're currently in, I almost ended up popping out my hip.

As the movements become increasingly fluid and more technical, I find myself distracted by this newcomer, so apparently assured in herself. There may only be a handful of us here, but her confidence is enviable. I feel self-conscious as we move into a seated twist and I'm greeted by the fleshiness of my inner thighs, soft and wobbly beneath my leggings. The forty-four-year-old adult me realises the futility of comparing myself to another woman, but the awkward teenager that still lives within me can't help but do it.

I find the session harder than usual, my limbs heavy and tired. By the time we finish, I feel overheated with exertion, aware my face is flushed. The woman in front of me stands to roll her mat once we've all said our namastes, and my eyes can't help but follow her as she goes to her belongings and puts on her trainers. Her dark hair falls in front of her face as she leans down to tie her laces. Everything about her is angular and defined, from her lithe arms to her cinched-in waist. It's normal to see people who are attractive, but there's something striking about this woman: something truly beautiful.

I thank the teacher before leaving the hall, and when I get to the leisure centre's main entrance, I see the newcomer getting into the passenger side of a car that's waiting for her just outside the front of the building. The man in the driver's seat turns to greet her; I can't make out much of him, but I see her reaction to something he says: the tilt of her head as she laughs and leans in towards him affectionately. They kiss – an open-mouth kiss that even from this distance I can see clearly, so intimate I feel the awkwardness of having intruded on a private moment. I look away, embarrassed, hoping neither of them have seen me watching them. As I head into the car park and towards my own car, they pull away, and I'm left wondering when the last time might have been that Marcus kissed me like that – as a greeting and nothing else, rather than a precursor to something more.

The car is cold, and I sit with the heaters on, letting the blast of warm air uncloud the windscreen. I check my phone, but there's nothing from Marcus. There's no real reason for there to be, though a part of me hoped he might make some extra effort after learning this morning that he'd forgotten our anniversary. I wonder whether the man I've just seen in the other car sends texts to his wife for no other reason than to tell her he loves her. In the imagined world I've already created for this couple, he does, and I can't escape the feeling of having lost something: that once upon a time, somewhere in our past, this is how things were between Marcus and me.

THREE

The start of the week comes and goes without incident, which is rare for a school with over fourteen hundred students. Tuesday marks the six-month anniversary of my mother's death, though I'm the only person to seem aware of the date's significance. Marcus doesn't mention it at breakfast, though if he can't remember our anniversary, I don't hold out much hope of him recalling any other dates. I haven't heard from Cameron, but I didn't expect to. He and Marcus argued after the funeral: the last time either of us saw my brother. After school finishes and I've sent the last of the emails I need to get done before the work day is through, I drive to the supermarket to buy flowers, knowing I'm going to have to visit the churchyard. I meant to go once a month, but like my intention to clear out the house bit by bit every weekend, that plan only existed in my mind and failed to ever take fruition. Going back there seems too final, like having to acknowledge the funeral really happened and that my mother is really gone.

I'm not sure why I buy the flowers. It's always seemed to me a strange tradition, to place a bouquet where someone died or where a person is buried, especially so in the case where a relationship was so strained. Yet regardless of how difficult things with her might have been, my mother was still the person who did more for me than anyone else. I might not be able to understand why she did what she did, even now, but trying to forgive her may be the only way of allowing myself some peace over the memories of my childhood.

Mum is buried in St Anne's churchyard, in the same plot as my father. It was what she wanted, so I was in no position to argue against it or suggest otherwise. After his death, I naïvely thought she might begin to see things differently. Even though she'd been removed from him and their life together by his imprisonment, she was still tethered in the sense of being his wife: a responsibility in which she never faltered. When he died, I hoped she'd start to see things differently, for what they really were. Instead, she clung to the idealised version of him she'd created for herself, desperate to see nothing other than what she wanted to see. I understood it, to a degree. It can't be easy for anyone to face the fact they've lived a lie.

I chose a mass of white and pink tulips to place at her graveside: Mum's favourite flowers. I lay them carefully, arranging them in a spray of colour. Her headstone has been dirtied by the recent bad weather, flecks of soil and strings of wet leaves peppering the engraving. *Carol McNally, 8 April 1956–17 August 2023. Devoted wife to Jonathan. Loving mother to Cameron and Louise.* Her words, not mine. Despite a diagnosis of early-onset dementia while she was still in her fifties, she continued to live an independent life, and she made decisions about her funeral while she was still able to do so. She stayed in her own home for over a decade after her diagnosis, though towards the end she needed extra help. She told me on more than one occasion that she would rather die than be moved into a nursing home. *No one's ever taking me to the toilet, Louise,* she said to me one day, out of the blue as I was dyeing her hair. *When it gets to then, you'll help me, won't you?* And I knew what she meant, praying to a God I've always been uncertain of that we would never reach that stage.

As it happened, she never put that pressure on me to help her end her own life. She did it herself, with a fortnight's worth of medication consumed with a last breakfast of scrambled eggs and tomatoes. Her neighbour found her on the sofa, and when I went into the house after paramedics had removed her body, I noticed the plate and frying pan she'd used that morning had been washed and stacked on the draining board, the single knife and fork propped in the cutlery holder – a last attempt at order in a life and home that had been otherwise chaotic.

By the time I leave the churchyard, it's already dark. There's still over an hour until my yoga class, but as it's not really worth going home just to come back out again, I instead go and fill the car up with petrol and get a coffee from the take-away machine inside the garage shop. I park on a quiet street in a residential area and drink it while I linger over thoughts of Cameron and whether I should contact him to see how he's getting on. The argument at the funeral – bad taste from both him and Marcus – wasn't mine, and though I understand in principle why Marcus said what he did that day, I've never stopped feeling guilty about the way it made the gap between my brother and me even wider.

I put my coffee down in the holder between the driver and passenger seats and scrabble about in my handbag for my phone.

Just wanted to check on how you're doing. Hope you're okay.

I read and reread the message, not happy with it but not knowing what else to say to offer him an olive branch. I type a couple of alternatives, but they all sound too try-hard, and I eventually opt for the original. I wait as though expecting an immediate reply, but nothing is returned.

After driving to the leisure centre and parking at the back of the building, I go to the changing room to get out of my work clothes and into my gym gear. The room is quiet, just a couple of young women in their early twenties straight from the Latin dance class that's just finished in the main hall. Something is whispered between them as they retrieve their belongings from adjacent lockers, and they laugh, amused at whatever was shared. I feel self-conscious as I pull on my leggings, bought a couple of years ago and too tight since my recent weight gain. They cling in all the wrong places, and when I sit to change out of my work top, I feel the waistband cutting into my stomach.

The women leave, still laughing as they head out through the changing room doors, and I feel a sudden and foreign sense of isolation hit me like an Arctic blast. They seemed so happy, so carefree, and I feel a nostalgia for a time that never really existed. My young adult life was characterised by late nights and lost days, but none of them associated with the irresponsible abandon of youth. I spent years trying to find an escape: from my family history, from the legacy of my father's crimes, from myself.

Shaking myself from useless and futile thoughts, I leave the changing room to go to the hall. There are more people here today than there were at the last session, and already the room is half full. I'm laying out my mat when I feel someone approach me from behind, and as I stoop to pull my trainers off, I see the woman who was here at the last session standing beside me.

'Hi,' she says. 'Sorry... I hope you don't mind me parking up next to you.'

'Not at all.'

She smiles at me, a row of perfect teeth flashing between her lips. 'She's good, isn't she? The teacher, I mean. I've been to a few other yoga classes, but this one seems the best.'

It struck me at the last session that this woman wasn't a beginner to yoga: she has the flexibility of someone who may have been a gymnast or a dancer in her younger years.

'She's great,' I agree.

'What's her name?'

'Natasha.'

Music begins to play from the front of the hall, and we all settle ourselves on our mats to start. The noisy breather from the last session doesn't appear to be here today, or if she is, she's taken something to assist with her nasal congestion.

'I sent out some emails a couple of weeks ago,' Natasha says, about ten minutes in. 'I like to gauge what level we're at and what you need from these sessions in terms of challenge and recovery. Quite a few of you feel ready for something a little more complex, and we've discussed it before... so who's ready to try the crow?'

There are a few groans from the women at the front of the class, followed by laughter.

'As with every element of these classes, this is a choice,' Natasha stresses. 'Please don't attempt anything that causes any strain or discomfort.'

We watch as she demonstrates the position, and I'm not sure how she's physically managing to balance her knees where they now are, resting somehow on the back of her arms. 'Head up and face forward,' she instructs, as her back rises with the move, 'otherwise you'll face-plant your mat.'

There's laughter as some of the more athletic of the group attempt the position, while some less skilled but good-humoured individuals roll off on to their sides like upturned turtles. I don't even bother to try: there's no way my arms are strong enough to hold my body weight like that, and even if they were, I wouldn't trust myself not to break wind and embarrass myself.

Beside me, the new woman shifts into position, and I can't

help but watch as her toes push off the mat and her body glides forward so that she's elevated like a circus acrobat, effortless and beautiful. I watch in awe, caught in some kind of trance, as she holds her balance for a few moments, her gaze fixed forwards, before she removes herself gracefully from the position. She turns to see me watching her, and smiles.

'Beginner's luck,' she says modestly.

When the session ends, she waits to talk to me as I put on my trainers. 'Have you been coming to this class long?' she asks.

'About eighteen months.'

'No wonder you're so good at it.'

She's being nice: she's far more skilled at this than I am, regardless of how long I've been coming to the classes. 'I'm really not. I'm more of a wine and books kind of person.'

'Sounds perfect to me.' She pulls on her jacket. 'I'm Erin.'

'Louise.'

'It's nice to meet you properly, Louise. See you next time?'

It's posed as a question rather than a statement. 'Yes, I'll be here.'

I don't know why, but when she leaves, I feel the urge to follow her. I want to see if her partner picks her up. I want to see them together again. But with my work clothes and bag in the changing room lockers, I'm unable to leave straight away. I realise the strangeness of me wanting to observe her, yet there's something about this woman that draws me to her.

By the time I get my things and go to the car park, there's no sign of Erin or the car she got into on Saturday morning. An odd sense of disappointment settles in my chest. As I go to my own car, I find myself fantasising about this couple I know nothing about: where they might be headed now; what they might be doing later. By the time I've reached home, an entire conversation between Erin and the man I assume to be her husband has been played out in my head: an imagined exchange in which they plan the rest of their evening.

When I go into the house, the place is bathed in darkness. I check the garden, but Marcus isn't down in the gym either. When I go back to my bag to check my phone, there's a message from him.

Met with Pete for a pint. Don't wait up x

I text back to tell him not to drive home, though I know he never would after drinking alcohol. He'll probably just have a couple of drinks and ask me to drop him over to pick up the car before work in the morning. I grab something quick to eat – some leftover salad from last night – and go upstairs to shower. Under the flow of hot water, my mind drifts back to Erin. A series of intrusive thoughts come from nowhere: she and her husband in their bathroom together; her tanned skin pressed against the frosted glass of a shower screen. The image is so vivid that it sends a shock through me, and I turn the water off sharply, my hair still greasy with conditioner, my head and heart pounding with questions about why the thought of this woman won't leave me alone.

FOUR

The school day has barely started when I'm called to an incident in the art department. When I get there, two Year 8 boys are standing in the corridor, one either side of Miss Lewis's classroom. I see Miss Lewis through the glass-panelled door, still trying to settle the rest of the class. Maria Gatland stands between the two boys, poised like a football referee braced to break up a second scuffle. Admittedly, a very bejewelled one. I've never seen a woman wear as much jewellery as Maria, but she manages to pull the look off well: one of those bohemian types who can wear anything and make it look as though the outfit was designed for her.

One of the boys is holding a handful of bloodied tissues to his nose; the other has red flecks on his knuckles and an interesting pattern of scratches on his face. It isn't hard to work out what's happened here, but I ask anyway.

'I arrived after it was all over,' Maria explains.

'He started it,' the boys chorus.

'Corey,' I say to the boy with the bloodied nose. 'You go first.'

The other boy sighs quietly and lowers his head.

'He just went for me, miss. I was waiting to go into class, I didn't even say nothing to him.'

So now I know that whatever else happened, Corey said something to the other boy. I don't know his name. I recognise his face, but it's impossible to remember the names of every child in a school with so many students, and the sad fact is that the quiet kids get lost in the vacuum that exists between the gifted and the troubled. These are the ones we're not supposed to refer to as 'normal'. This other kid is one of those. Whatever happened before the punch, I'd put money on Corey having stirred things up somehow.

'And what's your version of events?' I ask the other boy, whose scratched face has turned deathly pale. He looks at me, but he doesn't say anything. Then he throws up over the floor, chunks of his breakfast spraying across my shoes.

A consolatory glance passes from Maria to me, just before she turns her head away and not particularly convincingly stifles a retch. She's never coped well with sickness, her phobia having worsened since her difficult pregnancy with her second child twelve years ago.

I glance at her classroom, which is empty. 'You on PPA? Would you mind taking Corey over to the nurse, please.'

Once they're gone, I send the other boy to the toilets to clean himself up and call someone to come and deal with the mess in the corridor. When the boy comes back, I ask him his name.

'Bobby.'

'Okay, Bobby. Now that he's not here, do you want to tell me what Corey said to you?'

He glances at the puddle of sick on the floor and his pale face flushes pink.

'Don't worry about that,' I tell him. 'Someone's coming to clear it up – no one else will see it. Do you want to tell me before they get here?'

Bobby stares at his shoes. They look just a few days from being worn through to his socks. 'He called me a...' he says, the last word lost in an inaudible mumble.

'You'll have to speak a bit louder, Bobby. I'm old.'

'He called me a cunt.'

Oh. Received loud and clear that time. 'Right,' I say. 'Well, Corey's always had a way with words. Ask his English teacher.'

Bobby looks at me, confused.

'But you can't go around punching people, no matter what they say to you.' I gesture to the scratches on his cheek. 'Do you need to see the nurse as well?'

He shakes his head.

'Come on,' I tell him. 'Come with me. I'm going to have to call someone from home, you know that, don't you? But we'll explain what happened.'

I tap at Miss Lewis's door, and she comes to speak with me in the corridor. I explain that neither Bobby nor Corey will be back in class. Behind her, the group quickly starts to become unsettled. Something flies through the air behind her, narrowly missing her head.

When I step into the room, the class falls silent. I see the reaction on Miss Lewis's face, a mixture of wonder and barely concealed resentment. It's taken years for me to get this response; it didn't just happen overnight. I remember too well being in her shoes, newly qualified and not much older than some of the sixth formers, and there were times I thought my teaching career was over before it had begun. It's been hard work, and much of the time thankless too, but it's all been worth it and I wouldn't change a thing.

With the class settled again, Miss Lewis gestures to the door. 'I thought you should know that one of the older kids filmed the fight on his phone.'

'Do you know who it was?'

'Jasper Healy. New boy in Year 11.'

'Okay, thanks. I'll deal with it.' I put a hand on her arm. 'You're doing a great job.'

She smiles gratefully, though I know she doesn't believe it. Not yet, at least.

After dealing with Corey and Bobby, I go in search of Jasper Healy's head of year. When I find him, he's busy taking an A level history class. Rather than interrupt, I go back to the office and find out which lesson Jasper Healy's in, then go to deal with it myself.

A tall, pale-faced kid with the generic skin-fade hairstyle worn by ninety per cent of teenage boys at the school lumbers reluctantly from the room, inconvenienced by the disturbance.

'We've not yet met, have we? How are you finding it here so far?'

'Same as every other school,' he says flatly, holding my eye with a premature defiance. I wonder how many schools he's already been to, and why he's been moved midway through his final GCSE year. I make a mental note to look into his details to find out.

'I understand you witnessed a fight earlier this morning, between two younger boys?'

'Did I?'

'Did you film it on your phone, Jasper?'

He pauses deliberately before answering the question. 'I don't know. Did I?'

I've worked with enough difficult teenagers to not be fazed by the attitude. In my experience, kids act out and play up for usually the same handful of reasons. Some crave the attention they're lacking elsewhere. Others are struggling to find an identity, or their behaviour is a reaction to change, whether physical or hormonal. Sometimes poor behaviour is a response to fear. In the saddest cases, it's a response to some kind of neglect or abuse.

'How old are you?'

'Sixteen.'

'Right. So old enough to know better then.'

He shrugs in the annoying way seemingly exclusive to teenagers: nonchalantly and barely moving, managing to communicate a 'fuck you' without opening his mouth.

'As you're not going to talk to me, I'm going to assume you weren't planning on keeping that video to yourself. I can't imagine that if you were involved in a fight you'd want it plastered all over social media, so I'm going to ask you to delete it now before temptation gets in your way. Is that fair enough, do you think?'

Jasper continues to say nothing. I feel like a detective conducting an interview in which the suspect remains insistent on repeating 'no comment', and the thought leads my mind to Callum Benton, one of only two kids I've worked with in my twenty-year career who didn't fit within the spectrum of 'normal' causes for bad behaviour. He came from a good family, with supportive and loving parents, and he was bright. Capable. But even as a child, he was rotten to the core – an anomaly that couldn't be explained or rehabilitated. He was born bad. In Year 7, he was caught handing out sweets to other kids: liquorice allsorts that had been individually filled with colour-matched drawing pins, a number of which had to be surgically removed from another boy's stomach after weeks of abdominal pain and vomiting. And just three years after leaving school, still a teenager, he received a life sentence for dousing an ex-girlfriend with petrol before setting her on fire.

'Show me the video, please, Jasper.'

'What video?'

I don't have time for this. I've got a meeting that starts in twenty minutes.

'There are two ways of doing this – you can show me the video and we'll sort it out here and now, just us, or I can go and phone one of your parents and they can come in and deal with you.'

Jasper exhales noisily through his mouth before taking his phone from his pocket. He unlocks it before going into his gallery, and then I hear the noise of the footage: raised voices, children cheering, an adult shouting at Corey and Bobby to stop.

'Let me see.'

His mouth twists as he reluctantly passes me the phone. He folds his arms across his chest as he watches me play the video. Whatever Corey had been expecting, it obviously wasn't the upper cut that was delivered by quiet little Bobby with precision accuracy. The fight had already started by the time Jasper began recording, so I can't see whether Bobby's claim is the truth. I delete the video from his gallery and then from the deleted items so it can't be reinstated.

'There,' he says, snatching the phone back from me. 'Happy?'

Delirious, I think. 'Thank you so much. Have you sent this to anyone or shared it anywhere?'

'No.'

He's probably lying. I make a mental note to check later.

'Get back into class.'

He turns and goes to the classroom door. 'Bitch,' he mutters beneath his breath.

FIVE

As I lie on the yoga mat with my eyes closed, barely taking in the softly spoken self-care spiel of the class teacher, I think not for the first time of how these few minutes are the only ones where I ever truly switch off. It's not even the case that there isn't time for me to do so: with Marcus often away with his job, time alone isn't unusual for me, and I make a habit of completing as much work as I can at school, trying to keep a balance between my home and professional lives. The problem – as my mother used to so frequently and enthusiastically remind me – is an overactive imagination: and yes, she used to say that as though it was a bad thing. I often wondered whether she'd have preferred a daughter who said little and thought even less; someone who would blithely accept everything that life sent her way, in much the same way I later realised she herself had.

The irony hits me as the lights are flicked on and the windowless room is lit with an artificial glare: despite acknowledging these past few minutes as a time to switch off from everything, I've managed once again to avoid doing just that. It's seemingly too much to ask for, my brain not in the habit of excusing itself.

I glance to my side, where Erin is still lying flat on her mat, soaking up the last few moments of shavasana. Post-yoga session, she still manages to look as though she's just finished getting ready to go out, the skin of her bare shoulders not even revealing a telltale sheen of sweat. I wonder how old she is. She's one of those people it's difficult to place an age on, her skin so clear that she could be as young as thirty, although I suspect she's probably closer to my age.

The rest of the class is already in a cross-legged sitting position, few having managed the effortless roll to rise demonstrated by the teacher, 'vertebra by vertebra', however that's humanly possible. Every time Natasha uses the phrase, I imagine myself dislocating like one of those plastic tube fidget toys little kids play with on plane journeys. Every attempt to roll gracefully makes me feel like an upturned chameleon that's just overindulged in its lunch. I put a hand to the floor and push myself up, grateful at least for the feeling of looseness in my hips that always follows the session.

'Is it me,' Erin whispers, 'or is this getting harder with every class?'

I smile. It didn't seem to me that she was having difficulty at any stage, and I'd have noticed: I've studied her pretty intently. That may make me sound weird, but she's the kind of woman who inspires awe in other women, her figure enviable and her personality instantly infectious. While the rest of the class nearly dislocated a hip getting into pigeon pose, Erin somehow managed to glide into the position, her limbs making the transition effortless. I've wondered whether her defined shoulders and lithe arms are a genetic blessing or if she's had to undertake a gruelling weights regime and restricted diet to achieve them, but it's not the sort of thing you can comfortably ask someone when you've known them only a couple of weeks.

'Let's all of us now close our eyes for a moment,' Natasha instructs us, her hands held together in prayer. 'Be aware of how different your body feels to when you entered the room. Take a moment to become attuned to your spiritual bosom.'

I can't see her, but I'm sure that by my side, Erin is sniggering slightly, the mischievous kid at the back of the classroom.

'Thank you for letting me guide you this morning,' Natasha continues. 'As always, love and light in all that meets you this weekend, and I look forward to seeing you all again next time. Namaste.'

The word is repeated in a chorus that's as enthusiastic as a Year 7 class uttering 'amen' at the end of an assembly prayer, and once we've stood to roll up our mats, Erin is straight over to me, lowering her voice to a whisper.

'How's your spiritual bosom looking?'

'Hanging south,' I tell her, 'the way of most things these days.'

She laughs lightly, the sound a tiny twittering of birds. Everything about her is delicate, from the slim fingers that hold her mat to the bare feet that can't be any bigger than a size four.

'Absolutely not true. My mother always used to tell me to never put myself down – there are plenty of other people ready to do that for you.'

I can't decide whether that's an uplifting life motto or a parent having subtly hinted at a child's lack of popularity, but either way I thank her for her words. We put on our shoes and leave the leisure centre together.

'Do you fancy catching up without the yoga mats one day?' she suggests. 'Wine... coffee if we have to. I'm not fussy.'

'Sounds good. Do you want to take my number?'

I give it to her and watch her tap it into her phone. I notice her engagement ring for the first time: an enormous princess-cut diamond bordered by tiny counterparts.

'Your ring is beautiful.'

'Thank you. He let me pick it myself. I wasn't messing about.'

She calls me so that I have her number ready to store in my phone, then we cross the car park together.

'Your husband not picking you up today?' I ask.

Her eyes meet mine and there's a moment in which a brief look of confusion is passed. As her expression changes, I realise I've just inadvertently admitted to watching her over the past few sessions.

'Not today,' she says, pulling her keys from her pocket. 'I've got the car.'

She presses a button and lights flash just ahead of us: the same car her husband picked her up in this time last week.

'See you Tuesday,' she says. 'Don't forget that catch-up, though.'

On the drive home, I find myself lingering unhealthily on the possibilities of what Erin goes home to: whether she and her husband will now spend time together – proper time, not just happening to be in the same room at the same time – or whether he'll be glued to his mobile phone in the way I know I'm likely to find Marcus when I get back to the house. Though I didn't see much of her husband last week, in my head I've created an imagined version of him: handsome, attentive; thoughtful. Pretty much, I realise, all the things Marcus used to be. The memory of that intrusive shower thought comes back to me, and I feel a stab of guilt at having pictured Erin and her husband in that way. Of having lingered on the thought when I should have pushed it from my head as quickly as it arrived. Yet still, when it comes back again, I don't do what I know I should, instead allowing it to linger like the memory of an almost-forgotten dream.

SIX

Marcus is in the kitchen when I get home, sitting at the table with his laptop open. He closes the lid as I enter the room, and my first thought is that he has something to hide. I don't want to check his phone again, or be scouring through his internet search history to catch him out. I don't want to become that wife. Yet I never thought he would become that husband.

I stand in the doorway and look at him for a moment, noticing all the things that stood out to me when I first laid eyes on him nearly a decade ago. He has a strong jawline. It sounds strange to say, but it was one of the first physical features that attracted me to him. He looked like a man who had strong opinions and confidence in his own abilities, all of which was somehow discernible from the way he carried himself when I first saw him walking through the lobby of the hotel where we were both staying: me for a senior leadership training course; Marcus on location with a film crew. He was with another man; I saw them talking together in hushed tones, watched as Marcus held the door open for him in a way that silently revealed not only his traditional manners but also his assuredness in his own masculinity. I saw him there on another two occasions over that next twenty-four hours, and on the third he approached me, asked me if I was there for business or pleasure. By the time I checked out to head home, we'd exchanged numbers.

'Hi.' I go to him and put a hand on his shoulder, and beneath my touch I feel him flinch, his body tightening as he instinctively moves away from me. The rejection stings like a burn. I try to tell myself that it wasn't as it seemed, that it didn't really happen, but it did. And the worst of it is that it happened apparently instinctively.

'What do you fancy doing today?' he asks, pushing his laptop away from him.

'I should go to Mum's.'

I can't put off going back to my mother's house any longer. I'd underestimated not only the scale of the clear-out but also the amount of paperwork involved in a person's death. When my father died, my mother dealt with the necessary legalities: the ones, at least, that hadn't been handled by the duty governor at HM Prison Chelmsford. I had no reason to involve myself with any of the preparations that went into planning his funeral, nor any of the legal matters that finalised the settlement of his finances, and I was grateful not to be asked for assistance with matters my mother knew I wanted no further engagement with.

Marcus grunts something that could be an acknowledgement, could be disapproval. It was so incoherent and barely there, it could have meant anything. It could have meant nothing.

'You need one of those companies,' he says.

'What companies?'

'Those companies that come and clear everything out for you.'

He turns his attention to his phone, so he misses the look I give him. He can be so insensitive at times, but I don't think he means to be.

'A lot of the things in the house are personal,' I remind him, a conversation we've already had. 'Documents, paperwork... all that stuff has to be looked through, it can't just be thrown out.'

'A lot of the stuff's junk as well.'

I go to the sink to get a glass of water. His attention remains glued to his phone. I feel like going over, taking it from him and launching it through the window, but the sudden surge of anger unsettles me. It isn't like me, and I don't want it to become me.

When did he start being able to make me feel this way?

I drain the glass before refilling it.

'Look,' he says, getting up now and finally putting his phone to one side. 'I didn't mean that. I'm sorry... it came out wrong.' He comes over to me and puts a hand on my arm. I wonder whether the gesture is an acknowledgement of his physical reaction when I did the same to him just minutes ago. 'I know it's important to you. What I meant was that it's too big a job for one person. Let me come with you.'

It's not the first time he has offered to help me sort through my mother's things, but as with last time, I reject the offer. Although he knew my mother, they were never particularly close. He never spent much time at her house because I never did: when I left there aged eighteen, I never intended to go back. It was only the circumstances of my mother's health that pulled me back to the place, and that became yet another element of my life that I chose to keep separate from Marcus, trying to preserve what we had to keep it healthy and pure, untainted by the history that scarred my family. By the time I introduced him to my mother, he and I had already been in a relationship for a couple of years. She didn't trust men, but having spent a lifetime with my father and then Cameron, I suppose no one could really blame her for that.

'I won't touch anything,' he suggests. 'I can just sit there and keep you company while you look through things, so you don't have to be alone.'

'I know you mean well,' I tell him, putting down the glass. 'But honestly... I need to do this on my own.'

Marcus exhales noisily, mumbling something as he turns away from me. He leaves the room, but not before retrieving his phone and laptop. I think about those messages from Lucy, wondering whether he might have by now decided to reply to the last. It occurs to me that perhaps my behaviour might determine that. What if by dismissing the idea of him coming with me today, I inadvertently push him closer to responding to her?

The first thing I would usually do after getting home from the leisure centre is have a shower, but there seems little point this morning: I know I'll feel grubby after an afternoon of going through my parents' possessions, so I'll do it when I get home later. I call goodbye to Marcus, who's now upstairs, but when I get no reply, I leave the house.

I have to push myself to make the trip out of Eastbridge to the nearby village of Pelton where I grew up. In all the hours I've so far put into clearing the place out, I've barely made a dent in the accumulation of five decades' worth of possessions. My parents were hoarders: my mother apparently for reasons of sentimentality; my father because it served as a demonstration to the outside world of the wealth he had generated – the outside world as well as his fellow occupants within, who were unaware of the true provenance of his riches. When I was growing up, my parents' house was always filled with guests: neighbours and friends who would gather for coffee mornings with my mother, and dinner parties at which my father could always be heard sharing lengthy anecdotes about his latest business venture. As a child, I wondered how anyone could bear to sit through such boring stories. As a teenager, it occurred to me that these people endured my father's shameless bragging either because they wanted something from him or because they were just like him.

The lane that leads to my childhood home houses just one

other property, about a quarter of a mile away, owned by the
widower who's lived there since I was a child. When I reach the
house, I sit for a while on the driveway, just looking at the place.
It's an imposing building: a detached red-brick Victorian former
schoolhouse that my father bought years before he met my
mother. He'd been left an inheritance from his paternal grand-
mother: a modest sum, but at the time a small amount was
enough to buy a flat, which he renovated and sold on for a
profit, and so it began. By the time he was thirty, he was a
millionaire. He'd taught himself the kind of manual skills his
own father had shunned as menial labour: from plastering to
plumbing, electrical work to tiling. He didn't mind getting his
hands dirty, although that attitude failed to extend beyond the
legitimate business that was registered for his tax returns.

The Virginia creeper growing across the front of the house
has been wild for some time now, left to stake its claim on the
brickwork like a curtain closing itself around the building.
Eventually the rest of the world will be cut off from the place.
When I eventually finish clearing out my mother's possessions
and manage to get it in a fit state to put it up for sale, whoever's
brave enough to take it on is going to have their work cut out.
Nothing has been updated here since the 1990s. When my
father was sent to prison, my mother stopped caring about the
things that had mattered before then. Windowsills were left to
grow mould where the damp crept in through the ageing
wooden frames. The paintwork on the front door is peeling in
thick chunks. The potted plants and flower beds that were once
so carefully tended have been left to die or grow wild. My
mother stopped cleaning, stopped cooking; stopped caring.

When I go inside, the hallway smells dank – that kind of
unlived-in odour that lingers in places untouched by human
life. I go to the kitchen at the back of the house and scour the
room for the roll of bin bags I left the last time I was here. As
always happens, the past greets me like a long-abandoned false

friend, taunting me with memories that over the years have changed shape and form. Cameron and me sitting at the table eating breakfast in our school uniforms, our parents whispering conspiratorially at the sink. The afternoons I would come home late after drama club to find my mother sitting alone in the living room, her eyes red with tears she blamed on her migraines. I wonder now whether those debilitating migraines she used to suffer from so regularly ever existed, or whether they were simply an excuse to distract from the real issues she kept to herself. Perhaps she felt she was protecting her children, though it was never the truth we needed protection from.

I had already moved away from home by the time my father was sentenced. Cameron was starting his final year of GCSEs, and he would later carry the excuse of our father's crimes as justification for his lack of achievement. I felt sorry for him, for a while. I met up with him and tried to help him, gave him money when he needed it, but it quickly became apparent that the only time he would ever contact me was when he needed a handout or a scapegoat, and I didn't want to be responsible for encouraging either. Our contact became less and less, until eventually it waned altogether. For a while, neither of us had any idea where the other lived, and it took my father's death to finally bring us back into contact.

My father owned a company that sold building supplies. He was well respected locally among tradesmen, but his business was hardly as lucrative as our imposing detached home would have people believe. To this day, I'm not sure of the assumption our neighbours and friends must have come to and can only presume they believed my parents to be the beneficiaries of a generous inheritance. Either that or they thought my father cut a lot of good deals. I'm sure he did, but they all benefited financially from the blackmail that took place alongside them.

I've never known why he wasn't made to pay back every single penny he extorted from the most vulnerable people he worked with. I suppose it would have been difficult for him to do so from behind bars, though a lot of the money remained in my mother's possession, and perhaps some legal loophole meant it was allowed to stay there. For years I believed she had been ignorant of my father's crimes. Then six months ago, she left a note, and two lines changed everything.

I knew. I should have said something, but I didn't.
I am so sorry for everything.

My mother had been aware of how my father was making his money. Maybe not right back at the start, back when Cameron and I were kids, but at some point she'd found out, and I've always wondered how long she had her suspicions before his crimes were exposed. How long she had them but ignored them, until it was no longer possible for her to do so. She left me with his blood money. It has sat untouched in an account, and I've still no idea what to do with it. If I could find the family of the man who took his own life, I would give it to them, though I doubt they'd want it. In the same circumstances, I'd refuse to have anything to do with it. I want nothing to do with it now, yet I've been left with the responsibility of deciding where it ends up, hopefully at a place where it can finally achieve some good.

I turn my attention to the sideboard and begin bagging unopened post and leaflets that have been shoved in drawers, never to be looked at again, wondering how many more weekends will be consumed by this immersion in the past. Had things been different, there might have been some comfort to be found here. I might have felt a painful but cathartic solace from searching through the debris of my family's history, our entire life together documented in the cards and bills and photographs and the utensils of our day-to-day living. As things stand, I can't find anything but lies. We lived in a house built on them, lie after lie stacked like bricks, the foundations shaken by a single allegation that brought the whole place crashing down around us.

The last of the junk is out of the third and final cupboard of the sideboard when I realise a piece of the back panel has dropped away. I pull the unit away from the wall, where a cluster of junk has fallen to the carpet: paper clips, pens, marbles from God knows how long ago, a stained teaspoon and an old supermarket receipt. There's also a photograph, age-worn and muted by years of abandonment in the dark space between the cupboard and the wall that looks as though it hasn't been vacuumed since my childhood.

I see the back of the photograph first: the carefully printed words written in my mother's hand. *Weston-super-Mare, June 1989.* When I turn it over, I'm greeted by the four of us: my mother, my father, Cameron and me. I was nine years old; Cameron just six. He's smiling a big gappy smile, his first tooth recently fallen out. I remember that day trip so clearly. Everything seemed normal. I was happy. We were all happy. Ignorance is bliss, after all.

My mother is smiling, but when I look now, I realise how painted on the expression is, posed and held for whoever was holding the camera. Beside her, my father sits stiff-backed, his hand held over hers in a way that to anyone else might appear protective. I'm sure that's how it must have seemed to me at the time, if I'd even paid it any attention. Children exist within a bubble of themselves until a certain age, and there are things I took for granted: one being that I thought of my parents as good. Reliable.

Looking at his face now, I wonder what he was thinking that day the photograph was taken. Days out like this, all four of us together, were rare: my father worked a lot, and he often came home after Cameron and I had gone to bed. Everyone admired him as hard-working and conscientious: a true self-made man.

What few people realised for a long time was that a majority of his income was made by extorting money from business partners and clients.

I still remember reading about that young family, the father of two young boys found dead in the bathroom by their mother when she got home from taking them to school. When my father was sentenced, a photograph of the man's wife at his funeral appeared on the local front pages. That image was burned onto my memory, a permanent reminder of where I'd come from.

I'm interrupted by my phone vibrating in my pocket. When I take it out, Erin's name greets me from the screen.

Hi Louise, just wondering if you're around tomorrow for that coffee/cake/wine? Just occurred to me that I've got a quiet day, but another time will be fine if you're busy x

Tomorrow is good, I write in reply. *Let me know what time's best for you x*

I am grateful to her for the distraction, and her timing seems in some strange way fateful, as though she could have somehow known that she was reaching out to me at a time it was most needed. I leave the bin bag where it is, not able to face this today. Perhaps Marcus is right after all: I need one of those companies. But what I need more than anything is to see and be with him: to focus on the things I need in the here and now rather than hiding from my problems by immersing myself in the past.

SEVEN

On Sunday morning I get up early. I can't lie in. It's either the routine of my day job or a result of my overactive mind, but once I've woken, I can't get back to sleep, and I wake every morning by 5.30 a.m. Going out for a walk on my own is something I do quite often on a Sunday morning, usually before Marcus is awake. I like the time to myself, and it gives me some exercise out in the fresh air. Marcus has never seemed to mind my need for solitary time, and if he's awake as early as I am, he usually heads to the gym at the bottom of the garden.

I go for a long walk through the woodland that backs onto the edge of the new-build housing estate where we live. My childhood home of Pelton lies on the far side of the woods, which were always off-limits when I was a child, my brother and I warned that if we ventured too far from home, there'd be dangerous men lurking among the trees, waiting to steal us away. For a while my parents did an effective job at keeping us scared and, in turn, keeping us near. Then we got older and learned that the real dangers lay closer to home.

Even at this early hour, the dark doesn't scare me. In fact, the likelihood is that the middle of the woods at seven o'clock on a Sunday morning is statistically safer than the town centre at midnight. There's probably no one else here, except maybe the occasional dog walker and the kind of fitness fanatics who get up at dawn to go cycling. It's peaceful being out at such an early hour. The silence settles over me like a heavy scarf, protective rather than threatening. The rest of life moves so fast that it feels good to escape, and walking and yoga are always the things that remind me there's more to life than data and deadlines and responsibilities.

It's nearly nine by the time I get home, and I've been out for two hours. When I go into the hallway, I catch a glimpse of my reflection in the mirror that hangs above the table. My cheeks are pinched pink by the cold air. I lean in closer, studying the fine lines that fan from my eyes like delicate moth wings. My appearance has altered more since turning forty than it did during the entire decade prior to that. I'm suddenly more aware of my skin's dry patches, the lines around my mouth, the slight sag of jowls that Marcus recently keeps telling me I'm growing an obsession with. Ageing is inevitable, but the thought of turning into my mother is one that leaves me cold.

Marcus is in the kitchen when I go through, still in the shorts and T-shirt he wore to bed. The house feels cold – somehow colder than it was outside – but I notice he hasn't turned the heating on.

'You've been gone a while,' he says, flicking the switch down on the kettle. He asks me if I'd like a cup of tea, and while he sets about making it, I start to prepare us some breakfast. We eat together, barely speaking. If I'm honest, I'm still bothered about those texts from that woman Lucy. I almost mentioned it last night, but I didn't want him to know I'd been looking at his phone.

'What do you fancy doing today?' he asks, spearing a piece of egg white with his fork.

'I'm meeting up with Erin for a coffee in a bit.'

He looks up from his breakfast. 'Who's Erin?'

In my head, I sigh. I'm sure I've mentioned her before, but he obviously wasn't paying attention. 'I met her at yoga,' I reply.

If he remembers, he doesn't say so. In fact, he doesn't say anything, just finishes his breakfast and then gets up and leaves the room, leaving his dirty plate on the table for me to clear away. I wonder what I've done to annoy him. Surely it can't be because I'm going out for an hour.

I decide to ignore him, but when I'm looking for my keys a little while later, he comes down to the hallway, lingering on the bottom step as he watches me rifle through the drawer.

'It's been lovely to see you this weekend.'

'What's that supposed to mean?' I ask, despite knowing exactly what it means. Yet another example of Marcus's insensitivity. He's made no effort with me at all recently, away with work for weeks at a time and playing golf with his friends upon his return. I'm still smarting from him forgetting our anniversary last week, despite his efforts to make it up to me the following evening. We had a nice night together, but it always feels as though there's something missing: some spark that once burned but has now fizzled to less than a glow.

'Well, you went out yesterday, so I thought I might get some time with you today.'

'I came back early,' I remind him. 'You'd gone out.'

'What was I supposed to do, just sit in and wait for you all day?'

This doesn't sound like Marcus; he's never this needy. 'I'm going out for a couple of hours. I'll be home for lunch – we'll have the rest of the day together.'

His face changes. 'I'm sorry,' he says, coming over to me. 'I'm being an idiot. It's just because I'm going away again soon, that's all. Go and have a nice time with your friend. I'll see you later.'

He kisses me on the cheek and pulls me in for a hug before I leave. The physical closeness feels nice, but the strangeness of Erin and her husband appearing in my mind again makes me pull away sharply. Marcus eyes me, wondering what he's done wrong.

'Everything okay?'

'Fine,' I lie. 'Sorry. Bit of a headache, that's all.'

He goes to the sink, takes a glass from the draining board and fills it with water. He passes it to me before leaving the kitchen, returning with a strip of paracetamol. 'Take these,' he says, pushing two from the blister strip and handing them to me. 'Let's have a quiet afternoon when you get back, shall we? Watch a film... cosy up on the sofa?'

'Sounds perfect.'

I find my keys and put on my jacket before leaving the house. The town centre is just a short walk away, so I head there on foot. Eastbridge is a small town, thirty miles or so south of Bristol, essentially little more than a high street but a pretty one at that. There are a few pubs that have managed to remain independently owned, and the rest of the businesses consist of coffee shops, hairdressers and boutiques selling jewellery and clothing. There's a church a mile or so away, just up the road from the local primary school. It's picturesque in its rural surroundings and popular for weddings. The neighbouring villages are small, and with Eastbridge the only comprehensive school within a ten-mile radius, it has a high intake.

Erin is already in the coffee shop when I arrive. She must have only just got here, as I see her taking off her coat as I push open the door, her attention absorbed by the titles on the bookcase in the corner. She wears skinny jeans and a grey sweater that hangs casually off one shoulder, managing to look glamorous on a Sunday morning, an achievement I can't relate to.

'Hey,' she says as I take the seat opposite. 'This place is so cute.'

'Nice, isn't it? They sometimes do open evenings here – poetry readings, book signings, that sort of thing.'

Erin browses the drinks board behind the counter. 'I don't know what I fancy. What are you having?'

'I can recommend the hot chocolate. It's probably ludicrously calorific, but it's delicious.'

'I'll try the same then.' She pushes her chair back. 'Let me get them,' she says. I go to object, but she puts a finger to her lips. 'My treat.'

I watch her approach the counter and order our drinks. Her figure is enviable, but I've gone beyond the stage of wishing for what other people have, finally gaining an acceptance of myself that was alien to me in my twenties and thirties. No amount of punishing workout regimes or restrictive diets could ever give me a body like Erin's. Some people are just genetically blessed, and I've made peace with the fact that I'm not on that list.

'Nice weekend?' she asks when she returns to the table.

'It's been okay. You?'

'Just a quiet one. Cleaned the house yesterday. Ran a few errands. Living the dream.'

'I'm in the process of trying to clear out my mother's house. Well... I've mostly been putting it off really. She passed away six months ago.'

'Oh Louise. I'm so sorry.'

I don't tell her that she ended her own life. I realise I've already cast a shadow over what should be just a casual catch-up.

'I'm sorry,' I say. 'I didn't mean to dampen the mood.'

'You haven't. If you want to talk about it, you can. If you don't, that's fine too.'

A member of staff comes over with our drinks.

'Wow,' Erin says with a laugh. 'I think I've gained four pounds just by looking at it.'

'Well worth it, though.'

She looks at my hand as I reach for my mug. 'Your ring is beautiful too,' she says, her fingers reaching over to mine. It's weirdly intimate, her touch lingering too long. 'Did your husband pick that?'

'Yes. I was impressed as well.'

'How long have you been married?' She sips her drink and wipes a smear of whipped cream from the corner of her mouth.

'Seven years. We'd been together for three before we got married. How about you?'

'Together twelve, also married for seven.' She takes another sip, a creamy moustache left on her top lip. 'Hard work, isn't it?'

'Marriage?'

She slides her tongue across her lip. 'Yep. Bit weird when you think about it. In what other context do you commit yourself to the same thing for life? No one stays in the same job for forty years any more. No one eats the same dinner every day until they drop dead. Imagine seeing someone live the same daily routine every day for seventy-odd years. What a waste of a life. Yet here we are, metaphorically tethered to the same men we said some really odd vows to. Weird. Did you do the "obey" bit?'

'For the wedding vows? God, no.'

'Me neither. No one seriously says that any more, do they? Yeesh.' She glances around the room before lowering her voice. 'To be honest, Kieran and I hit a rough patch. We're okay now,' she adds quickly. 'But I think life sells us a lie, doesn't it? You know the way most people say "fine, thanks" when someone asks how they are, even if they've got a raging migraine and they've just been declared bankrupt? That's kind of how I see it with marriage. We're all supposed to say we're happily married, even when we're not, because let's face it, nobody can be happy *all* the time.'

There's something about Erin that's different to anyone else I've met, and it's hard not to love her for it, no matter how brief a time I've known her. I sometimes find small talk difficult. If I'm honest, I often find it boring. Erin's gone straight to something bigger, more meaningful, and she's done so without apology. She speaks like the woman I probably could be if I were a little bit braver. A lot braver.

'So what about you?' she asks. 'Are you and your husband still in the honeymoon phase?'

'After ten years together?' I say with a smile. It would be disloyal to say anything negative about Marcus, and as much as I like Erin, we've not known each other for long. Maria knows a little about the problems Marcus and I have had recently, but she's attributed a lot of those to the pressures of caring for my mother and then mourning her since her death, the circumstances of which were particularly difficult. She's right in a way, but I know there's more than that, and I don't expect her to be able to see it. For a start, there's those texts from Lucy. I doubt Maria has to worry about that kind of thing. Her husband, James, is one of those rare anomalies among human beings: practically perfect in every way – the Mary Poppins of fathers. He works full-time, yet when the boys were younger, he was always there in the evenings to take them to football practice and swimming lessons, to bath them and read them a story before bed. He cooks and cleans as regularly as Maria does, which in a society that boasts equal rights but in reality rarely delivers sadly makes him one of the few.

'He's a good man,' I tell Erin.

'Of course he is. You wouldn't have married him otherwise.'

I laugh. 'True.'

'But...'

'But what?'

'There's always a but. He's a good man, but...?'

I shrug. 'Same as any marriage, I suppose. Familiarity. Routine. I wonder sometimes whether I'm enough for him.'

'Why would you wonder that?'

'I don't know. As you said, marriage is difficult sometimes. Life's difficult.'

Erin leans across the table and lowers her voice conspiratorially. 'Kieran and I hit rock bottom once. Like, heading for the divorce courts territory.'

'But you rode it out.'

'Exactly.' She glances around, making sure no one's close enough to hear her. 'Take a guess what saved our marriage.'

I wait a moment, expecting her to tell me before realising she's actually waiting for me to guess.

'Therapy?' I say, taking a sip of my drink.

'Sex with other people.'

A line of whipped cream almost ends up in my nostrils. Erin laughs and sits back. 'That's the best reaction I've ever had. I don't go around telling everyone, by the way.'

I take a moment to compose myself, realising she's being serious. 'That wasn't a joke then?'

'It's just sex,' she explains, a little too loudly. 'We don't date other people or anything.' She lowers her voice again. 'Honestly, Louise, it was the best thing we ever did.'

'Wow,' I say awkwardly, wishing my hot chocolate mug was big enough for me to hide behind. 'That wasn't the answer I was expecting.'

'I had my doubts at first. It wasn't something we just jumped into. So to speak. We've learned through trial and error that the key is to find another couple you trust completely. What's your husband's name?'

'Marcus.'

'Do you have kids?'

I shake my head. The truth is, I never saw myself as a mother, and that hasn't changed. I love working with young people. I gain an immense satisfaction from watching children achieve and seeing them develop, and in knowing that in some small part I've had a hand in shaping their futures. But I've never wanted any of that beyond my role as a teacher. My mother once called it a product of my resistance to commitment. This was before Marcus and I got married. I'd never seen marriage as a part of my future, and I'd responded by telling her I didn't want to be emotionally and financially tethered to any man in the way that she'd been to my father. We never talked about it again after that day.

I notice Erin doesn't react to this in the way most people do, with a sympathetic look or a vacuous comment such as 'oh, you poor thing', as though not having children hasn't been a conscious choice. Particularly among older women there's the assumption that there must be something wrong with me, and my life is seen as somehow less fulfilled – an attitude I've learned to ignore. My life is happy. I have plenty of purpose. I contribute to society in a way that's meaningful, and I've never regarded having children as the only means through which a person can leave behind some kind of legacy – surely the most ridiculous reason to procreate.

'How about you?'

'Two. Jay's sixteen, and Iris would have just turned ten.'

Would have. The words ring in my ears. I want to make sure I've understood them correctly before I respond, not wanting to inadvertently say anything insensitive or inappropriate. Though I'm unsure how I could have misinterpreted them in any way. Iris is no longer with them.

Erin gives me a sad smile. 'She was born with a rare heart defect,' she explains, sensing my awkwardness. 'We'd known since the pregnancy that her life expectancy would be short. In the end, it was longer than they'd predicted.'

She looks down at the table, at the cream that has melted and lies dispersed on the surface of her drink. I feel selfishly uncomfortable at the sight of the tears that have filled her eyes.

'I'm so sorry,' I say, the words echoing with their emptiness.

Losing a parent is hard, but losing a child is a pain that's unimaginable.

'Thank you.' She doesn't look up from her drink. 'We were lucky, despite everything. They were the most special six years.'

The coffee shop seems to have shrunk around us, the walls closing in, everyone else evaporating so that there's only the two of us, caught in this moment of absolute trust. My guess is that she hasn't lived around here for long: Eastbridge is a small place where everyone seems to know each other, and her eagerness to talk to me at the yoga sessions suggests she's been looking to make a friend. I wonder now if Iris's death was the reason for their move.

'Here,' she says, unlocking her phone before scrolling to find a photograph. 'This is her.'

She shows me a photograph of a little girl with striking blue eyes and a strangely sad smile. She doesn't look much like Erin, so I'm guessing Iris must have been more like her dad.

'Please don't mention her to Kieran when you meet him,' she says, wiping the corner of her eye. 'My husband. It broke him.'

'Of course. God, Erin. I can't imagine.'

She stares down at her drink for a moment longer before shaking herself with a sad smile. 'I'm so sorry.'

'Don't be,' I say, clearing my throat as I try to put thoughts of my mother to one side for the moment. 'It's healthy to talk about things.'

Although a part of me wonders why I'm the person she's chosen to confide in. She barely knows me, but perhaps that's the draw. Sometimes it's easier to open up to a person who's unconnected to your life. Isn't that why so many people seek the help of therapists?

'What do you do for work?' she asks.

'Teaching. And you?'

'Paediatric nurse. Though I've not worked much since Iris died.'

We sit in an awkward silence for a while until the conversation is diverted to the selection of cakes on display behind the counter, and we spend the next half-hour avoiding the subjects that have gone before. I give Erin a brief tour of the high street after we leave the coffee shop, introducing her to the menu at the Boar and suggesting a lunch there one weekend.

It's only after we've said goodbye and she's walked to catch her bus home that I realise she must, even if only subconsciously, have plans for the four of us to meet. Or for me to meet Kieran, at least. *When you meet him*, she said. Not *if*. But that could have meant anything, I tell myself. She could just have meant if I happen to go to their house one day and he's home while I'm there. It didn't mean anything more than that. Unless, of course, it did.

EIGHT

I'm a couple of streets away from home when it starts to rain. By the time I get in, I'm already soaked through, my jacket not appropriate for the unexpected downpour. In the kitchen, Marcus has prepared lunch. The table is adorned with what we've always referred to as 'picky bits': a selection of cheeses, some cold meats, salad, coleslaw, olives and the special sun-dried tomato bread that he must have gone to the supermarket for while I've been out.

'What's all this in aid of?' I ask.

'Does there have to be a reason for it?' He slides a chair out from the table like an overly enthusiastic waiter hoping for a generous tip. 'I've got some making-up to do, though.'

I assume he's referring to last weekend, rather than anything hidden up his sleeve that he's feeling guilty about.

'You already did that,' I point out.

'How was your friend?'

'Erin,' I remind him. 'Fine. She's lovely. We had an interesting chat.'

'Interesting?'

I laugh awkwardly. 'Yeah. She told me some things about her marriage, actually.'

Marcus hands me a plate before sitting in the chair opposite. 'Go on. Don't leave me in suspense.'

I stall for a moment, wondering how to just casually drop Erin's open marriage into a natural dialogue, as though it's on a conversational par with the weather or what's for tea tonight, but I need to say something about it so I can get on to the subject of Lucy and those messages. I know if I don't deal with it, it'll keep niggling away at me.

'I'm not sure how much longer I can wait for this reveal,' he says, cutting a wedge of Brie and transferring it to his plate.

'They have an open marriage.'

I spoon some salad onto my plate, feeling Marcus's attention on me.

'She just told you that today, over coffee?'

'Hot chocolate actually, but yes.'

Marcus's left eyebrow rises. 'Each to their own, I suppose.'

'She reckons it saved their marriage.' I meet his eye now, trying to gauge his reaction. He looks a bit puzzled, and I don't think he has the first idea that I'm attempting to suggest that our own relationship might be in trouble.

'Shagging other people?'

'That was my first thought, but apparently... yes.'

He pops an olive into his mouth, and I can't explain why I find the way he does it so annoying. 'Sounds like a recipe for disaster to me,' he says, his mouth still full.

'Who's Lucy?'

He stops chewing and looks at me. My eyes follow his, watching for any signs of guilt. But there's nothing. He doesn't seem to have a clue what I'm referring to.

'I don't know. Lucy...'

I already wish that I hadn't mentioned her. Marcus will know now that I've been looking at his messages; either that or

I'll have to find a quick excuse to try to work myself out of this without him realising the truth.

'She didn't give a surname. She called the house phone – said it was about work.'

He doesn't believe me. He looks down at his plate, pushing a lump of coleslaw around with his fork. 'That'll be Lucy Burgess. She works for Skyline Productions – we've been in talks about a project.'

I make a mental note of both names, planning an internet search later, when Marcus isn't around.

'I don't know how she got the house number. She usually contacts me on my mobile.'

I feel my cheeks colour, ashamed now at my suspicions. I'll probably google this woman later and find that everything's legitimate, and I'll look like the suspicious wife I seem to have become.

We sit for a while in silence while we finish eating. It's not the kind of peaceful silence between a couple who are comfortable in the absence of conversation; more, it's the uneasy discomfort of two people who know something needs to be said but neither can find the right words.

It's Marcus who eventually breaks the silence.

'Do you fancy a bath before we watch that film we planned? I'll go and run it for you.'

For a ridiculous moment I thought he was suggesting we take a bath together. We haven't done that kind of thing in years, not since the early days of our relationship, when we wanted to do everything in as close proximity to one another as possible.

'Thank you.'

He goes upstairs, and I hear the water running while I clear the dishes from the table. When I go up to the bathroom, Marcus is sitting on the edge of the tub. He's lit candles around the tap end, and steam rises from the thick bubbles that await me.

'How was your morning?' I ask, realising I've not yet asked him what he got up to while I was out with Erin.

'Good. Just been finalising the plans for the Isle of Wight.'

'It's going to be great. I wish I could come with you.'

Years ago, whenever an event that Marcus was working away at fell within a school holiday, I would go with him. I've spent a lot of time at music festivals, listening to bands and browsing stalls while he worked. They were good times, but they feel foreign now, part of another life that we long ago left behind. I can't imagine him ever inviting me to an event these days.

'I don't think it's going to be that exciting, to be honest.'

He leaves the bathroom, the conversation abruptly over. I wonder whether I've upset him by asking about Lucy, although I think I may have got away with the phone call excuse, just.

I stay in the bath for over half an hour, languishing in the silence that's only broken when Marcus calls up to say he's putting the kettle on. I get out and dry my hair, then dress for comfort in a pair of leggings and an oversized T-shirt. Marcus is in the living room, two cups of tea waiting on the coffee table and the fluffiest blanket we own on the sofa.

'What do you fancy?' he asks, the remote control in his hand. He gestures to the television, where a screen of Netflix options waits. I always find the amount of choice overwhelming, and there have been many evenings we've been too tired to watch anything by the time we've finally decided what to try.

'You pick something,' I say. 'Give me two minutes.'

My phone is by the microwave, where I left it earlier. I go into the kitchen and retrieve it, going straight to the internet search engine. I type in *Lucy Burgess*, followed by *Skyline Productions*. She appears immediately, and when I go to the image results, I wish I'd just stayed in the living room with Marcus.

Lucy Burgess can't be older than thirty, and she's beautiful in an Instagram-influencer kind of way: wavy blonde hair, big eyes, full lips, and skin as clear as untouched paper. I can't imagine many men turning down her advances – particularly not my forty-seven-year-old husband, who is apparently the subject of her interest in older men.

I delete my search history and lock my phone, leaving it in the kitchen when I go back to the living room. Marcus is underneath the blanket, still browsing Netflix titles.

'Your new friend might be on to something, you know,' he says, his attention remaining on the television. 'Three quarters of these shows seem to be about affairs.'

I sit at the opposite end of the sofa, stealing half of the blanket to cover my legs. 'They don't have affairs. That's kind of the point.'

I hear my abrupt tone as Marcus must, and he glances at me questioningly, probably wondering what he's done in those brief few minutes I was in the kitchen.

'Affairs that have been okayed then,' he corrects himself.

I open my mouth to contradict him, but then change my mind, wondering what the point is. He's as good as dismissed what I've told him about Erin and her husband without bothering to listen to any of the details. His indifference bothers me, yet every ounce of common sense I possess tells me that this must surely be a good thing. Perhaps he isn't interested in having sex with anyone else. Isn't that exactly what I should need to know? Or, my brain taunts me, maybe he just isn't that interested in looking at possible ways to save us.

NINE

Eastbridge Comprehensive is a sprawling modern slab of concrete and glass built in a triangular shape. I've always imagined that from above it must resemble a giant V, flicking an insult to the sky with the ambivalence of half the students within its walls. Before I got the job of head teacher here, the school had been failing, making frequent news headlines for its poor academic results and a string of pupil-related offences that meant a succession of yearly intakes saw drastically reduced numbers. It was a difficult slog to raise it from the reputation it had gained, but the team here now made it possible and, in the end, worthwhile.

When I first arrived, I was given a set of keys, with the instruction that every door was to be locked behind me. I felt like a warden working in a prison, and it didn't take long to see why most of the staff and students were afflicted by a permanent sense of despondency, embarking on each new day with a promise of failure before the registration period had even taken place. The keys were ditched the day after my arrival. So were trainers and hoodies, and the reintroduction of a more formal uniform had exactly the effect so many critics of tradition had argued was no longer attainable. I'm not suggesting that a uniform alone was responsible for turning things around, but it was a solid start, and it turned out that was all that was needed. That's not to say the school no longer has it challenges, though, and as I pass the hall ten minutes after the bell for end of day has sounded, I'm reminded of some of them.

Five tables with a single chair at each are lined up in a row, a disinterested teenager sitting at each. One of them is Jasper Healy, his head lowered, shoulders slumped. Supervising the detention session is Maria Gatland, who's by now familiar with the new boy. I watch as she passes him and says something to him, but he doesn't so much as raise his head to acknowledge her. Paper and pens are handed out. Maria notices me at the door, and once the task for the session has been set, she comes out into the corridor to speak with me.

Maria is one of those people everyone seems to warm to, staff and students alike. Even the most troublesome of teenagers never gives her much bother, and she's gained a track record of excellent academic results from students other teachers might have written off.

'What's he done now?' I ask, nodding towards where Jasper sits, his pen and paper untouched.

She pushes a curl behind her ear. 'Which one?'

'Jasper.'

'Called Mr Williamson a prick.'

'Sounds about right. Jasper, I mean, not Mr Williamson.'

Maria laughs, but its afterglow quickly falls from her face as she studies mine. 'Are you okay?'

'Fine,' I tell her. 'Just been a long week.'

'It's Monday,' she points out.

I smile. 'Is that all?'

'Nice plans for the evening?'

'Not really. There's a bottle of wine waiting in the fridge, but now that you've just reminded me we're not even at hump day, I'd probably better leave it there.'

'Drink it,' she instructs, like an *Alice in Wonderland* sign trying to lure me further down a rabbit hole. 'I've got a football match to endure this evening. The first of three this week. The sooner James finishes these evening shifts the better. They're all outdoors, too – I bet it pisses down all evening. Wish me luck.'

She heads back into the hall. Glancing past her, I see Jasper Healy looking up from whatever work he's been given, watching us. His eyes meet mine, and he holds my gaze, defiant. I don't look away. I wait for him to: the first unwritten rule of dealing with a child who believes he can unnerve you. Not just a child, in fact. Anyone.

I return to my office to deal with the rest of the day's emails, and just as I'm writing a response to the last, I hear my phone ping in my handbag. I finish what I'm doing before going to see who it is. Cameron. My heart flutters without even having seen his words. Unless I open his message to find he's typed the words 'piss off', this means he's accepted the olive branch I threw him.

Things are okay. Just started a new job. How are you?

The fluttering in my heart morphs into a swell of relief. A response means he's okay. It means he's alive. There was a time when Cameron's life had spiralled into such a mess that for a while I lived on tenterhooks, fearing the sound of my phone ringing: constantly anticipating a call from someone contacting me to tell me my brother had been found dead.

No matter what Marcus thinks of him, he didn't know him before. A memory comes back to me, long forgotten: the day we found a toad at the bottom of the garden. We kept it for a while as a pet, making it a makeshift pond using a plastic lemonade bottle we cut with a pair of craft scissors and building it a house with the bricks that had been left over after work was done on the garage. Cameron cried when the toad was one day gone, and the memory sparks a chain of thoughts that remind me that my brother wasn't always the way I've known him in adulthood. He made a cross using cardboard from a cereal box and worked it into the ground beneath the apple tree at the end of the garden, despite knowing the toad was likely still alive and had simply decided it had had enough of being fussed over like a household pet.

My brother was once sensitive and capable of empathy, able to care for another life. Along the way, something changed him, and the only thing that something could have been was our father. I wonder to what extent the woman I might have become was also altered by him. Like my mother and like Cameron, there was a before and after version of us all.

It's so good to hear from you, I type. *All okay here. Where are you working?*

I press send, and as I'm clearing my desk ready to leave for the day, my phone pings again. I expect another message from Cameron, but it's from Erin.

Saw this and thought of you xx

Attached to the text is a link. I click on it, and it opens up an internet article: 'The Joys of an Open Marriage'.

I skim the opening couple of paragraphs before messaging Erin back, thanking her and telling her I'll read it in more detail tonight.

Show Marcus xx, she texts back.

TEN

When I get home from work, I'm surprised to find Marcus, for once, not glued to either his laptop or his phone. Instead, he's hanging some of the frames I've been nagging him to put up for ages, making a collage up the stairs of a collection of photographs we've taken on various holidays over the years.

'What do you think?' he asks, stepping back to admire his handiwork, just two remaining framed photos resting at the bottom of the staircase.

'Looks great. Thank you.'

Yesterday's doubts about Lucy and the possible state of our marriage somehow manage to look different as I watch him now, halfway up the staircase with a drill in his hand and a look of smug satisfaction stamped on his face. Would someone in the midst of an affair or even considering the possibility of one be making this much effort to personalise our home? It doesn't seem plausible, yet it also seems the perfect guise beneath which to conceal a sordid secret.

'I'm going to put the kettle on,' I say, dumping my handbag on the hallway table. 'Fancy a cuppa?'

'Yes please. This'll only take me a few more minutes.'

I go to the kitchen to make tea, and when Marcus is finished, he comes to join me. After inspecting his completed project, as requested, we go into the living room together.

'I thought I'd get those shelves up in the gym,' he says. 'Makes sense now I've got the drill out.'

'Can that wait? I wanted to talk about yesterday.'

Marcus sips his tea. 'What happened yesterday?'

'Nothing happened. I just want to talk about us.'

His eyes widen. 'Oh,' he says, dragging the word across three syllables. 'You mean this new friend of yours? The swinger.'

The word makes me cringe. It evokes images of pervy old men and seedy gatherings, and I try to erase the intrusive thoughts that have popped into my head to set me off balance.

'She's not a swinger.'

'I'm pretty sure it's the same thing.' He looks at me over the rim of his mug.

'She said it helped them, though, when their marriage was in a bad place.'

'Is that what you think about us? That we're in a bad place?'

'Aren't we?' I say, deflecting the question back at him.

'No marriage is perfect, Lou.'

'I know that. I just... If there was a way to make it better...' I leave the insinuation hanging in the air, and Marcus, as I knew he would, instantly grips onto it.

'You're not considering it, are you?'

'I just wanted to talk about it.'

'Yeah, of course. We can talk about anything, can't we?'

Can we? I think. It hasn't felt like it recently. But I suppose I should be grateful that he's willing to now; that he even, for once, seems to be absorbing what I'm saying.

'I'm just surprised, that's all.'

'Because you think I'm boring and conservative.'

He tilts his head, his mouth twisting with disapproval. 'I didn't say that.'

'You didn't need to.'

'You are actually considering this for us then?'

I laugh, but even I can hear how awkward it sounds. 'That's not what I said. I just said I wanted to talk about it.'

I don't want you to start looking elsewhere, I think, the flawless image of Lucy Burgess appearing in my mind.

'I don't want to make this bigger than it is,' I say, putting my tea on the coffee table. 'I just think we should talk about things, that's all. We've not had sex in ages.'

It's actually been six months. I remember it because that same morning, not long after I'd got out of bed to make coffee, I got a call from my mother's neighbour to say he'd found her dead in her living room, lying peacefully on the sofa as though she was taking an early nap. The guilt at not being there with her that morning has never gone away. I don't think it ever will.

'And your new friend thinks this is a problem?'

I feel my cheeks burn. He keeps referring to Erin in a way that manages to suggest I've got some kind of fascination with this woman I barely know. At least, that's how I'm taking it. He's never actually said anything of the sort, so it must be me. Perhaps that's the effect she's had.

'I haven't been talking about our sex life,' I say, although I suppose this isn't entirely true.

'It's fine. I'm not bothered if you have. Are you worried about it?'

'About what?'

'The fact we never have sex.'

'Are *you* worried?' I ask.

'I miss it,' Marcus says. 'But I'm not worried about it. You never answered my question, though. How do you feel about it?'

'I worry a bit, I suppose. I wonder whether it's me.'

He pulls a face. 'What do you mean?'

I want to tell him that I noticed how he reacted to my touch last week, when I put my hand on his shoulder. But I know it'll start an argument, so I don't.

'Are you still attracted to me?'

'Where's all this come from?'

'Nowhere. It's just what happens, isn't it? People become familiar. Things go stale.'

'You think we're stale?' he asks, and he can't keep the hurt from his face.

'Aren't we?'

Silence settles. Marcus sips his tea, so I reach for mine, both of us drinking without looking at the other, uncomfortable truths making eye contact difficult.

'I'm sorry,' I say, not really sure what I'm talking about.

'You don't need to say that. You've got nothing to apologise for.' He puts a hand over mine and looks at me intently. 'You want to shag someone else then?'

'Marcus...' But I laugh, because his serious expression has morphed into a grin, and this is how he deals with everything, as infuriating as it can be. For as long as I've known him, he has played the clown as a defence mechanism. I wonder whether this developed after he found out about his ex's affair. Alexis broke his heart, but whenever I tried to talk to him about it, he'd make a joke before changing the subject. He hides his pain under a mask of humour. Sometimes it seems to work, but I'm not sure it's always the healthiest of things. I don't want this conversation to be a thing that hurts him, or something either of us feels we need to hide from.

'I'm not trying to make light of it,' he says. 'Sorry. This Erin seriously thinks it was a good thing for her and her husband then?'

I give him the details of everything she shared in the café, including her views on monogamy. Then I show him the article she sent me earlier, not telling him it came from her.

'Wow,' he says when he finishes reading. 'Progressive. Or marriage suicide.'

'Would you want to sleep with another woman?'

It hasn't passed me by that he never gave an answer to my question of whether he still finds me attractive. I know he'd find Erin attractive. I can't imagine any man *not* finding Erin attractive.

'I haven't thought about it.'

I raise a cynical eyebrow. 'Come on. You must have thought about it at some point, at least since I've mentioned the idea of an open marriage.'

'How would *you* feel about it?'

'About you sleeping with another woman?'

I don't know how I feel. I assume the idea of it should make me feel jealous, but it somehow strangely doesn't. I wonder what that says about me. All I know is, I don't want to lose him, and those messages from Lucy have sown a trail of doubt that refuses to be swept away.

'If you want to,' I say, 'then I'm happy with it.'

'Happy?'

'What do you want me to say?'

Marcus reaches for the side of my face, his eyes fixed on mine, and tucks my hair behind my ear. It's a simple gesture of affection, yet his touch manages to feel strangely alien. I can't remember the last time he did something like that, and it's sad to think that such everyday affection should have become a rarity.

'If you want to try it,' he says, 'I will. For you.'

'For us,' I correct him. 'Seriously, though... it's a stupid idea, isn't it? I mean, someone along the line would regret it. Or even worse, decide the alternative is a better option.'

'Erin and her husband don't seem to regret it.' He shrugs. 'And neither of them has run off with anyone else.'

'You're serious? You want to consider it?'

'You can fill out a risk assessment first, if you like.'

'Marcus. Just lay off the jokes for a minute. A fantasy is a fantasy for a reason.' I narrow my eyes, waiting for some kind of sarcastic comment. But it doesn't come. 'Do you mean it?'

'Do *you* mean it?'

But I already know he's not messing about now. He's really willing to give this a go.

He gets up. 'Give me a minute.'

When he comes back, he's carrying his laptop. 'Just hear me out,' he says, sitting next to me and opening the lid. 'If this is what you want – what we want,' he adds, before I have a chance to correct him, 'we should do it properly. Do you fancy looking at some sites?'

'Sites?'

'I don't know,' he says with a shrug. 'I assume you just have to fill in some details and then you're able to find other couples?'

I allow him to do just that, the whole scenario a surreal experience in which I feel myself detached from the person I really am, like I'm hovering over a version of us in some parallel universe, watching without being able to intervene. Within minutes he's registered an account and we're able to gain access to photographs of couples looking to meet other couples.

'Oh my God.' I almost choke on a mouthful of tea. 'Look at him!'

Marcus raises an eyebrow.

'Not like that,' I quickly add. 'I mean... the pose. It's quite something, really.'

'Next,' he says, with the tone of someone ushering a line of queuing travellers through an airport scanner. He swipes a finger across the screen. 'Ooh,' he says, his head tilting to an almost ninety-degree angle as he studies a photo of a man with biceps the size of watermelons and a woman dressed in the kind of hot pants worn by ring girls at boxing matches. 'No.'

'I think we're looking at the wrong website. I assumed there'd be more normal people like us.'

He glances at me. 'Normal?' He swipes through a few more couples, the scenario made even weirder every time he reaches for his cup of tea. It feels as though we're browsing a furniture website in search of a new sofa. 'I don't think any of this is normal.'

I put a hand on his arm to stop him. 'You're right. It isn't normal. Just put it away – this is ridiculous.'

He puts the laptop on the sofa beside him. 'I don't want to do anything you're not certain about.'

All I hear in his words is that if I was certain, he would be more than up for this. He wants to have sex with someone else. So now I have a choice: either he does it with my knowledge and my blessing, or he's tempted behind my back; if not with Lucy then with someone else he meets through work or on one of his trips away.

'I'm certain,' I say, not allowing myself time to swallow the words back down before they can be spoken.

'It's them, though, isn't it? If we try this, you want to try it with Erin and her husband.'

I put my face in my hands, feeling my cheeks burn with the awkwardness of this whole thing. I wish now that I'd never mentioned it. 'I don't know. Maybe it would be safer. I know her, after all.'

'You've not known her long.'

'No, but I know her more than I know some stranger off the internet.'

'What does her husband look like?'

'No idea.'

'Look them up on Facebook.'

'I don't know her surname.'

'Then ask her for a photo.'

'I can't do that!'

'Why not? She's more or less suggested it to you, hasn't she? Go on... text her.'

'Now?'

'No... next week.'

I roll my eyes and pick up my phone from the arm of the sofa. I've no idea how to ask Erin for a photo of her and Kieran without sounding like a total weirdo.

'What do I say?'

'Hi, Erin, I'd like to try out your husband, but Marcus wants to rate you first, so—'

'Marcus!'

'It's a joke,' he says, raising a hand. 'It's a joke. Where would you rate her out of ten, though?'

Ignoring him, I tap out a message.

Hi Erin, hope all is well with you. I've been thinking about what you said at the café, and Marcus and I have talked and think maybe you might be able to help us. This all feels really weird though xx

I press send before I have time to talk myself out of it.

'What did you write?' Marcus asks.

'Just asked whether they might be able to help us.'

'She's already given you that answer! Did you ask for a photo?'

'No, I can't just do that straight away. I'll wait until she messages back. You're starting to sound a bit too keen on all this.'

'I'm just curious, that's all. Like you.'

My phone vibrates in my lap.

Seriously, this is so exciting! Erin has replied. *I'm so glad you guys have talked about it. If there's anything you want to ask, go for it xx*

Marcus glances over at the message. 'There's your invitation, I guess.'

Still not quite believing I'm really doing this, I ask Erin if she could send us a photo of her and Kieran together, as Marcus has never seen her and I've never met Kieran. Within moments, the phone vibrates again. The photo shows the two of them sitting on what looks like a harbour wall, a grey sky threatening rain in the background. She looks as attractive here as she does in person: dark hair, dark eyes and tanned skin, her features entirely symmetrical. Kieran is equally good-looking: slightly older than her, maybe mid forties, with the kind of greying hair that manages to make men look even better. He has nice eyes, an unusual shade of blue unless the camera has distorted their natural colour.

'She's gorgeous, isn't she?' I say, handing Marcus the phone and taking a swig of tea while I try to suppress the flicker of jealousy that shifts through my chest.

'She's attractive, yeah. I mean... so's the husband.'

I shrug. 'He's okay.'

'Okay? He looks like a Next model. You know... one of those midlife ones who always has a sweater slung over his shoulder while he gazes into the distance.'

'What do you think, then?'

I'm surprised when, for once, he doesn't come back with some flippant quip or sarcastic comeback. Instead he puts the phone on the coffee table and moves closer to me, putting his hand on my leg. 'If this is what you want, we'll try it. Just one rule: we be honest about everything, okay?'

'We always are.'

Though I wonder whether this is true of us any more. It used to be, but somewhere along the way we got lost. Perhaps that's the same for everyone, though. If we were all honest with our thoughts and feelings all the time, everybody would hate everyone.

ELEVEN

This is definitely one of the strangest things I've ever done, and as I get out of the Uber that drops me at the door of the bar, I feel acutely self-aware, as though I'm wearing my thoughts on my forehead for everyone else to see. I wonder at the possible reactions of the strangers sitting near the window were they to know why I'm here tonight. To anyone else, Erin and I will appear like any other couple of friends on a night out, sharing a bottle of wine and the week's gossip, the people at the table next to us oblivious to the fact that we are meeting to discuss the benefits of an open marriage.

My cheeks flush with the thought as I straighten my dress before entering the bar. I see Erin within moments of scanning the room, sitting alone at a high table beneath one of those low-hanging brass lights that seem so fashionable these days in any place that serves alcohol. She looks stunning: more beautiful than I have ever seen her. Her warm skin glows beneath the lamplight, and the off-the-shoulder dress she's wearing – ruby red and figure-hugging – is a look I would never be able to pull off. I feel a pang of uncharacteristic jealousy punch me in the gut, and I silently berate myself for the childishness of it.

'Louise,' she calls, waving as I weave between people making their way to tables carrying drinks, not caring who glances over at her overly enthusiastic welcome.

'You look amazing.' The words spill from my mouth, and her face beams at the compliment.

'Thank you. So do you.' She gestures to my feet. 'Those boots are gorgeous, where did you get them?'

'Verona. In what now feels like another lifetime.'

'You can tell you got them abroad. You never get quality like that over here.' She taps her cocktail glass with a perfectly shaped fingernail. The peach-coloured drink is already half gone. 'What are you having? Try this. Honestly, go on, it's so good.'

She pushes the glass my way and I try a sip. Whatever it is, she's right, it's delicious: fruity and fizzy, if not a little bit too strong.

'Help yourself,' she says, standing up. 'I'll get us two more.'

'I'll get them,' I say, but as I reach into my bag, she puts a hand on my arm to stop me. 'Please don't. I'd like to. You can get the next round in, how does that sound?'

I thank her and sit down, watching as she makes her way over to the bar. The room is busy tonight, packed with young groups and older people still in their work clothes, come straight from their offices to end the week with a few drinks. I wonder whether Erin is a big drinker. In my late teens and early twenties, I drank too much, reliant on alcohol to mask the social awkwardness that stemmed from the notoriety my father's crimes had brought with them. I never knew how to act in big groups or what to say to the people I did know, let alone how to behave around strangers, and so I used the only escape I thought I had available to me, and drank until I forgot who I was, and who my father was: until the world around me shrank to something that was manageable and made some kind of sense. I did a lot of things during that time that I'm not proud of, but I've tried to atone for them since.

I watch Erin return with our drinks and notice the heads that turn as she passes. I wonder if she's used to being looked at wherever she goes. Why would Kieran be interested in sleeping with other women when he gets to go home to her every night?

'Madam,' she says, placing the cocktail glasses on the table before gesturing with an exaggerated flourish of the hand, like a magician's assistant with an invisible handkerchief. 'Enjoy.'

She uses her little finger to tidy a smudge of lipstick at the corner of her mouth. 'So,' she says, eyeing me with a knowing glance, 'you and Marcus have spoken then?'

She smiles at my immediate awkwardness: the tension in my shoulders must be visible.

'We have... yes.'

'And you want to try it?'

I look around me, aware that anyone at the nearby tables could overhear our conversation. 'We're open to talking about it.'

Erin nods slowly. 'You're in then.'

'I didn't say that,' I reply with a laugh.

'You didn't need to! Come on, you wouldn't be here now if you didn't want to try it, would you?' She puts a fingertip on the edge of her glass and traces it in circles. 'What do you think of Kieran?'

'He looks nice,' I say casually, feeling myself cringe. I can hardly admit to her that her husband is exactly the kind of man I'd be attracted to if I wasn't already married.

'He thinks you're hot. He's always liked blondes.'

I feel myself blushing, for God's sake. I'm a forty-four-year-old woman with a career and a mortgage and a pair of varifocals – I'm not even sure what I'm doing in this bar, let alone sitting here having this conversation. The rational part of my brain tells me this whole proposal is ludicrous, yet there's something so intoxicating about the idea. There's something so intoxicating about Erin.

'This is very exciting,' she says.

'This is very crazy.'

She shrugs nonchalantly. 'Crazy is okay. It's allowed sometimes.'

A part of me has wondered whether this is an element of the attraction towards Erin's proposal. For so many years now, I have been proper and professional: the hard-working head teacher, the caring daughter; a consummate giver to other people. There's no resentment on my part for any of it, and I wouldn't change a thing. But I've wondered whether in trying to escape my former self – the girl who drank too much and partied too hard and had too many one-night stands with strangers – I've managed to abandon all the components of myself that were the fun bits. I lost myself somewhere along the way, and I wonder if that's why Marcus seems so often far removed from me.

'When was the last time you enjoyed yourself?' she asks, with an insight that's almost eerie. 'And I don't mean at a yoga class. Exercise isn't enjoyable, I don't care what anyone says.'

Such a simple question, yet I find it difficult to answer. The truth is, I don't know. I can't remember, and that tells me everything.

'Oh dear,' Erin says, when the pause before answering becomes too lengthy. 'That long.'

'We all find enjoyment in different things,' I say, a little defensively.

'Of course. But enjoyment doesn't have to be rationed, does it? And being in a profession doesn't mean your life has to be strait-laced and serious all the time. You're allowed a personal life. It's okay to let your hair down. And by the way,' she adds, reaching across the table to touch the waves that sit on my shoulders, 'it looks gorgeous when you do.'

'How would it work? Marcus and I are bit naïve about all this.'

'Well, what happens is, the man has a penis and the woman has a—'

'Erin!' I'm suddenly aware for a moment of the room around us.

She laughs. 'I make a joke of everything, I know. I'm sorry. It's the only way I can get through life.'

We fall into silence as Iris's invisible presence settles between us.

'We'll book hotel rooms,' Erin explains. 'We'll arrange a day and time, we'll have a drink or two in the bar first, and then we'll go upstairs. You've nothing to feel awkward about. We've done it all before.' She reaches for her glass. 'And when I say "all"...' She winks at me over the top of her drink.

'I'm still not sure,' I admit. 'It's just... when you've only been with one person for so long, it's a weird thought to, you know...'

'You know what I think? You seem to be under the impression that you and Marcus have problems, but actually you must be pretty strong. There are too many misconceptions about open marriages. People assume it must mean that one person doesn't love the other enough, or that the relationship is failing. But really the opposite is true. Only a strong couple can talk about this kind of thing without jealousy. Only emotionally mature people can accept that no animals, humans included, were designed to be attracted to only one person for their entire lives.'

'You and Kieran have a strong marriage then?'

She nods. 'I realise that now. But it wasn't always that way. After...' She stops abruptly and looks down at her drink. 'You know what we went through. It almost broke us. If we can come back from that, we can survive anything. We're at a place where we understand each other now. That's when you know you'll be okay.'

Sitting here listening to Erin speak, the rest of the room seems to have evaporated. Despite all the noise and movement around us, I only see and hear her. She has a mesmerising quality about her, something soothing in the way she speaks.

'You know this kind of thing is way more common in relationships between two men, don't you?'

I'm not sure why I'd know this, but anyway. 'Really?'

'Absolutely. Men are better able to separate sex and love. Women tend to look for an emotional connection where they seek a physical one, whereas men just see sex in the same way that most other mammals do. I hate to say it, but when you think about it, men have kind of got it right on this one. Sex and love are not the same thing, are they? I can sleep with any man, but it doesn't mean anything. And the same applies to Kieran. I don't feel jealous when he has sex with someone else. It's just sex. I know he loves me, and I love him. He's the person I share my secrets with. He's the one I want to sit and watch TV with after a long day. He's the father of my kids, and I would never want another for them.' She falls silent for a moment, and I know that both our thoughts have returned to Iris, the little girl with the beautiful eyes and the sad smile. The way she always talks about her using the present tense is heartbreaking.

'He's the person I want to spend my time with,' she concludes, before sipping her drink and adding, 'I mean... not *all* my time, but you know what I mean.'

Erin churns out so much sexual psychology that it's a wonder she hasn't taken to training as some kind of therapist, and the soft intonations of her speech would make her perfect for the role.

'I mean, besides all that, Kieran's really good in bed. It would quite frankly be an act of public disservice not to share him.'

I laugh. I like Erin. She's warm and funny and not quite like anyone I've met before, and I admire this difference in her. She says what she feels and she doesn't seem to care what anyone thinks of her, yet paradoxically she makes me feel that what I think of her does in fact really matter.

'I'll leave it with you for now,' she says. 'There is absolutely no pressure from us. But when you're ready, let me know.' She taps her newly emptied glass. 'Ready for another?'

TWELVE

A week after I met with Erin, Marcus and I drive north to the Cotswolds, to the hotel she and Kieran have booked for the night. It's not too long a journey but far enough away that we're unlikely to bump into anyone we know. There's no reason why anyone should think we're anything more than two couples meeting for dinner, but I can't shake a feeling of paranoia about the whole thing, and going further afield helps to ward off some of my doubts. But not all.

'Are you sure we're doing the right thing?'

Marcus stops at a set of red lights and turns to me. 'Do you want to go home? We can back out of this any time. I don't want you to do anything you don't want to do.'

The truth is, I do want to do it. The thought of it has been with me all week, presenting itself at the most inappropriate of moments – once, during a PTA meeting when I had to excuse my momentary mindful absence with the pretence of a migraine. I know I should feel differently; that by now, talking myself through everything that might go wrong, either on the night or afterwards, should have been enough to change my mind about going through with it. But it hasn't been. And there's more to it than simply wanting to do it. I feel excited by it.

It feels strange to have not yet met Kieran, although I remind myself that Marcus knows neither of the couple yet. I know that Erin is his type. I imagine she's every man's type, and I doubt she and Kieran have ever struggled to find men willing to engage in their extramarital activities. I didn't want to admit it to Marcus, but I found Kieran instantly attractive from his photograph: tall, with dark hair and piercing eyes, the same icy blue as their daughter's.

'What are you thinking?' Marcus asks.

'Nothing,' I say quickly, discarding the fantasy that filled my head, because the logical part of my brain tells me that everything that's just flitted through my mind like the pages of a flipbook is too many degrees of wrong. 'Everything's good. I want to do this.'

'But...?'

'I just keep thinking about someone at work finding out.'

'How would anyone at work find out?' He reaches over and squeezes my knee gently. 'And what would it matter? You're allowed a private life.'

He's right, though it would definitely matter. Erin may also have been keen to remind me that professional people still have a right to have fun, but when you're a teacher, there are boundaries on what kind of fun is deemed appropriate. Partner-swapping at hotels is highly likely to feature on the list of don'ts, although Marcus has a point: how would anyone find out?

We arrive at the hotel first. I get a message from Erin just after we reach the car park to say they're running ten minutes late, so we go to the bar for a glass of wine. I order a large, needing the alcohol to take the edge off my nerves, and it goes straight to my head.

'You look amazing,' Marcus tells me, for the third time this evening. I can't remember the last time I made this much effort or wore this kind of dress. I'm usually dressed conservatively for work, 'demure' an unofficial uniform. After my mother's diagnosis, I stopped going too far or having more than a single glass of wine, too worried that I'd get a call and need to drive over to her house at a minute's notice. I rarely went out, so there was nothing in my wardrobe that was suitable for today. I ordered the dress I'm wearing especially, wanting something sexy but not too much. Not too little, either. There's a zip that runs the length of the back, so it's easy to remove.

Under the table, Marcus runs a hand up my leg. His fingers push the dress higher before slipping beneath it and finding the inside of my thigh. I feel my skin pimple with goosebumps. I know he's doing this just to reassure me, but it doesn't stop me from feeling mildly ridiculous. The whole thing is starting to feel insane, like I'm watching myself from outside my own body and doing nothing to stop myself walking into a disaster.

'Louise.'

I hear Erin's voice before I see her. When I turn, she and Kieran are approaching us. She's wearing fitted jeans and a black top; I feel so overdressed I could crawl under the table to hide. Kieran is even better-looking in person than he is in the photograph Erin sent us, though this shouldn't surprise me: a woman as attractive as Erin was never going to have an average-looking husband.

Marcus's hand slips from my leg, and he stands as they reach our table.

'This is Marcus,' I say, fumbling over the words like an idiot. Erin reaches over to shake his hand before putting her arms out to hug me. 'You look amazing,' she says quietly in my ear, as the men introduce themselves with seemingly little awkwardness.

'Louise, this is Kieran,' Erin says, pulling away from me. Her husband takes my hand. His fingers are strangely cold. He barely makes eye contact with me, but I'm grateful for it.

'Would either of you like a drink?' he asks, gesturing to my empty wine glass. When he finally looks at me, those piercing eyes send a thrill of anticipation flowing through my veins. I imagine him unzipping my dress, and I feel my face colouring at the thought.

'Not for me, thanks,' I say. I'd better not drink too much before we get upstairs. I want to remain in control.

'Let me get them in,' Marcus offers.

I watch him go to the bar with Kieran, while Erin sits in the empty chair next to me. This close, I can see how perfect her skin is, young and unblemished. I realise I've never asked her age.

'That's a lovely dress,' she says.

'Thank you. I wasn't really sure what to wear. I feel a bit overdressed now.'

'Stop overthinking everything,' she says with a smile. 'It'll all be fine. Better than fine. It'll be good, I promise.'

When the men return with the drinks, there's an uncomfortable moment in which nobody seems to know what to say. Someone then breaks the ice with a comment about the hotel's surly receptionist, and we exchange generic pleasantries about the weather and the traffic, so that no one who passes our table would suspect we're all about to go upstairs and see each other's spouses naked.

'We've not talked rules,' Erin says, lowering her voice. 'I mean, we're pretty easy-going. You might have decided your own. But if we do take things further after tonight, my one non-negotiable is that nothing ever happens in our homes. As long as everyone's transparent and honest about what's going on, everything's good. That fair?'

No one says anything, the awkwardness tangible. Marcus mumbles something that sounds like 'fair enough', and then Erin downs the last of the wine in her glass.

'Why don't you and Marcus take your things up,' she

suggests, passing me their room key across the table. 'Louise, you take this... you can go to our room.' She meets my eye and smiles, and I hear the unspoken words she's managing to say with just a look: that Marcus should go to our room and wait for her there. 'Kieran and I will finish our drinks and then we'll be up.'

I glance at the key fob, checking the room number. Erin seems to sense my hesitation and smiles at me encouragingly, a reassurance that everything will be okay and we haven't made a massive mistake in coming here. We leave them in the bar and head up to the first floor. Marcus stops with me at the room Erin and Kieran booked. He comes in with me and closes the door behind us.

'Fuck,' he says. 'This is really happening.'

I sit next to him on the bed, trying to push off the feeling of nausea that has settled in my stomach.

'Are you okay?' he asks.

'Fine,' I lie. I am not fine. I am nervous as hell and feel slightly sick, but I'm not sure whether it's uncertainty or expectation. 'She's beautiful, isn't she?'

'Erin? She's attractive, yeah. But she's not you.' He kisses my neck. I appreciate his attempts at reassurance, but I know he's downplaying just how pretty she is – in much the same way I haven't made mention of how attracted to Kieran I am.

'I should go before he gets here,' Marcus says, standing from the bed. We hug awkwardly before he leaves.

Moments later, there's a knock at the door. I open it expecting to find Marcus having forgotten to tell me something, but instead Kieran is standing there, even taller than I realised now he's standing right in front of me. He's holding two glasses of wine. He can barely make eye contact with me still, even though there's now only the two of us here.

'Come in,' I say, moving out of his way. It feels odd inviting him into his own room.

'Don't drink it if you don't want it,' he says, handing me a glass.

'No, that's lovely. Thank you.'

We stand near the bathroom, neither of us knowing what to say or do. I wonder if he's always this awkward in this situation. I assumed he'd be the confident one; the one to take charge. I realise now I was relying on it, to take the pressure off me having to think too much or know what to do.

He's standing close to me, so close that I can smell his after-shave. His stubble is greying at his jawline, and I wonder what he looked like when he was younger. I imagine he's one of those men that gets better-looking with age.

'Cheers,' he says, raising his glass to mine.

'Cheers.'

Our glasses clink, and then he moves away from me, going further into the room. He sits on the bed. I stand for a moment until he invites me to sit beside him.

'Are you okay?' he asks.

'Yeah. Just a bit nervous, you know.'

'You don't need to be.'

I'm not really sure what he means by this, but I assume it's an attempt to reassure me. With my free hand, I pull my dress down my thigh where it's risen as I sat down. I notice the way his eyes follow my hand and linger on my bare skin.

He's too good-looking. There's something about his eyes, and when he looks at me it feels as though he's somehow able to see past my awkwardness, like he can read my thoughts. I'm close enough to make out every blemish of his skin: the small dry patch on his left cheek, the fine lines fanning from his eyes, the inch-long scar at his right temple. The fingers of his free hand move to my face and gently push my hair behind my ear. It feels too intimate. Too intense. Sensing my reaction, he moves away. He stands and puts his wine glass on the dressing table.

'I'm sorry. I shouldn't have done that. Look... we can just talk, okay? Or I can go and get Erin – they may not have...'

He stops suddenly, not knowing how to finish the sentence. I wonder whether he's picturing his wife with my husband. Perhaps he wants to go and put an end to something that may not yet have had a chance to start. I should feel the same.

I put my glass on the bedside table and stand from the bed.

'Don't go,' I say, the words leaving me before I can keep them inside.

He lingers near the bedroom door. I've sent him all the wrong signals. He doesn't think I want to do this.

I go to him and take his hand, his fingers still cold against mine. I picture him pulling off my dress. I see his mouth on mine, his bare chest pressed against my skin, his body covering me as we sink into the bed.

'Just say the word,' he tells me.

And so I do.

THIRTEEN

A shard of early-morning light pushes through the gap in the curtains and falls upon a sleeping Marcus, the curve of his body covered by the duvet. I've been awake for over an hour already, aware of the sun making its lazy ascent beyond the houses that stand behind our garden. I should be out of bed and getting ready for work by now; instead, I've been lying here fretting, worrying. Panicking that although Marcus has seemed fine since Saturday night, something at the core of what we are might have been irreversibly altered.

He lies with his back to me, his face turned to the door. I wonder how he's able to sleep so easily when my mind has been tripping on the assault course of what happened over the weekend.

He stirs as though able to hear my thoughts. Eyes still closed, he turns and reaches to me, his hand finding my waist.

'Are we okay?' I ask.

He opens his eyes to look at me. 'Why wouldn't we be?'

'You know. After what happened.'

'What did happen?' he asks, his lip curling into a smile. 'Do you want to tell me all about it? In detail?'

'Marcus,' I say, with mock reprimand. 'Try to be serious for once. Please.'

The grin falls from his face. 'I wasn't making light of it,' he says, putting a hand on my bare shoulder. 'Even though that's what we should be doing.' He studies my face, looking for a hint that he's said the wrong thing. 'Isn't that what we should be doing?'

'I just need to know that we're okay. That it hasn't changed anything between us.'

'Has it changed anything for you?'

'No,' I tell him, because I want to mean it. It was something we felt we needed. Something we felt we wanted to do. But it hasn't altered how I feel about Marcus or our life together. It hasn't affected how I feel about *us*.

Yet I can't stop thinking about that night. About how different it made me feel.

'Do you regret it?' he asks.

I don't know what the right answer is here. If I say no, does it suggest I want to do it again, that I enjoyed it too much? I don't want to make Marcus feel that he isn't enough. Should I just say yes, even though it's not the truth?

A flush of heat rises to my chest as the memories of those hours creep back.

'You're overthinking things,' he says, his hand falling from my arm. 'You've got nothing to feel bad about, Louise.'

His hand moves under the duvet, his fingers finding the inside of my thigh. He kisses my mouth before moving on top of me, his mouth now finding my neck; I feel him hard against my hip, the most turned-on he's been in as long as I can remember. Other than at the weekend, that is. I feel Marcus's tongue against my skin, but when I close my eyes, all I see is Kieran. It's Kieran's hands I feel on me, the memory of Saturday night alive and tangible.

I reach for Marcus and pull him up to me, stopping what he's doing.

'What's the matter? You okay?'

'Nothing's the matter,' I lie. 'I'm fine.'

He kisses me again, and I go with it; if I don't, he'll know something's wrong, and I can hardly tell him I want him to stop because I can't stop thinking about someone else.

When he's finished, he gets out of bed and goes to the en suite. I hear him turn on the shower, whistling as he steps beneath the flow of hot water. I stay under the duvet, trying not to overthink. Yet trying not to overthink only ever leads to more thinking, and the more thoughts that race through my brain, the worse I feel. This was supposed to help us. Where Marcus is concerned, apparently it has. It's brought us closer together, in the physical sense at least. And yet I feel such a fraud. I should feel happy that we've had sex for the first time in six months. But I can't, because the guilt of thinking about sex with Kieran overwhelms everything else that I might be able to feel good about.

Ten minutes after he went into the bathroom, Marcus comes back out, his hair dripping wet and a towel wrapped around his waist. He goes to the wardrobe and I watch him flick through hangers, choosing what to wear for his journey to the Isle of Wight. We won't see each other for at least three weeks now, depending on how well the filming goes.

He pulls on a pair of boxers before using the towel to dry his hair.

'Have you spoken to Erin since Saturday?' he asks.

Even hearing her name feels somehow wrong, for reasons I'm not sure of. I told myself I wouldn't be jealous, and I don't think that's what this is. I don't feel resentful of her; how could I, when I was a willing participant in what happened between us all?

'We've texted each other.'

'And she's fine with you?'

I nod.

'There we are then. Everyone's fine. You'll see her at yoga tonight, won't you?'

'I'm not going. We've got a parents' evening.'

He comes back over to the bed. 'You regret it, don't you?' He sits down beside me. 'I'm sorry, Lou. Let's just put it behind us, okay?'

He puts his hand over mine and moves his thumb back and forth across my skin – something he always used to do when he knew I was feeling agitated. His way of reminding me I'm not alone.

'I don't regret it. We always said we'd never look backwards, didn't we? Everything happens for a reason, and all that.'

He reaches for his phone from the bedside table and lights the screen to see the time. 'I'm sorry, I'm going to have to get going or I'll be late for the ferry.'

I go downstairs and make him a coffee for the drive to Southampton while he finishes dressing and puts his bags in the car. When I take it to him, he's in the hallway pulling on his coat.

'I'm going to miss you,' he tells me.

He zips up his coat before taking the coffee from me. I doubt the statement is true; he'll be unlikely to have time to miss me, and even if he wasn't going to be so busy, pining for each other during periods of separation has never been a habit for either of us. The set-up has always suited us. Before we met, I'd spent most of my adult life alone. When I met Marcus, I wasn't ready to say goodbye to the freedom and space I'd grown used to. I didn't want to have to answer to anyone or be responsible for someone else's happiness, and thankfully he wasn't the sort of needy partner my ex had been.

'You liar,' I say teasingly.

He steps towards me and pulls me into a hug. 'We're fine,' he reminds me, one last time. 'Better than fine.'

'Hope it all goes well.'

I wave him off before going back into the house to get ready. I stand in the shower with the water too hot, my eyes closed, face tilted to the jet as I allow it to scald my body, my skin tingling beneath the heat. I think of Marcus. The sex we had. How happy he seemed this morning, with everything between us so normal. And then my brain takes me back to Saturday night, to Kieran's hands on my body, and I know I shouldn't be thinking about him as much as I am.

FOURTEEN

The rest of the week passes quickly. On Friday evening, I've just poured myself a glass of red wine and taken it to the living room when the doorbell rings. I go to the door expecting it to be a delivery driver; I'm still waiting for the chest of drawers I ordered for the spare bedroom over a fortnight ago, and although it's gone 8 p.m., it's not unheard of for things to be delivered this late. When I open the door, I find myself instead staring at the ghost of Christmas past.

My brother raises an eyebrow, as though to say 'Surprise!' and he's right, it certainly is. The python tattoo that snakes up his neck peeks from the top of his parka, its tongue lapping just below his ear.

'Louise. You're looking well.'

I truly wish I could say the same. Cameron looks ashen and too skinny – even more so than when I last saw him. His trousers hang loose around his hips and he's wearing a hooded top with the name of some obscure band printed on it, alongside the image of a dead crow. The scrawny emo look might have suited him at seventeen, but as a forty-one-year-old man, the effect only manages to make him look a bit desperate.

'Can I come in?'

I hesitate on a response, knowing exactly how Marcus would react to me letting Cameron inside our home. But Marcus isn't here, I remind myself.

'I won't stay long. Is Marcus home?' He glances at the space on the driveway where Marcus's car usually stands before looking back at me.

'Ten minutes,' I tell him, stepping aside to let him into the hallway.

'It was good to hear from you.'

'Do you want a cup of tea or anything?' He looks as though he needs a good meal rather than a cuppa, but offering him dinner would be a step too far.

He shakes his head. 'I won't stay long. I don't want to cause any trouble for you.'

I know he's referring to Marcus. At my mother's funeral, the two of them almost came to blows over the inheritance she had left. I was furious with them both for causing a scene at such an inappropriate time, though I could understand the frustrations on both sides. Cameron wanted a share of what he believed he was entitled to. Marcus was just defending me. He's never forgiven my brother for shunning responsibility for our mother, and he saw first-hand the effect that caring for her and having to watch her condition worsen had on me. We knew her capabilities were leaving her faster than even the doctors had anticipated, and yet still I didn't push for her to move into sheltered accommodation, where she would have had someone always close at hand to check on her. She'd wanted to stay at home for as long as possible, but if I'd encouraged otherwise, she might still be here now, and I've lived with that guilt for the past six months.

'Congratulations on the job,' I say. 'You didn't get back to tell me where you're working.'

'It's only packing work in a factory.'

'A job's a job. Good for you.' I don't mean it to sound patronising, but it does.

'We need to talk about the money.'

'We've already talked about it.'

'You can't seriously still be thinking about giving it all away?'

'It's blood money, Cameron. People's lives were ruined as a result of what that man did. Would you really be able to take it and enjoy using it to enrich your own life?'

I already know the answer to that one. This is the man who as a fourteen-year-old boy took my mother's credit card from her purse and withdrew the largest sum the cashpoint would allow him. When my father confronted him about it, he lied, claiming the new trainers he'd suddenly acquired had been given to him by a friend at school whose parents had bought the wrong size. My father disciplined him for the theft and the lies, but it was only after his own crimes were exposed that I realised the irony of him punishing his son for being just like him.

'Where's it all going to go then?'

'I haven't decided yet. Someone worthy.'

'I've got nothing, Lou. I'm on my arse. I live in a rented bedsit I can't afford to heat. I had to sell my car to buy food. Am I not worthy enough?'

It would be futile to point out that Cameron's dire financial circumstances are a result of his addictions and bad life choices; he knows all this, but he doesn't want to accept responsibility for it.

'If either Mum or Dad had wanted you to have it, it would have been left to you,' I say.

'And what about the house? Even in the state it's in, it's worth at least eight hundred grand. You can't buy a garage for less than fifty in that area. It's my home as well.'

'*Was* your home,' I remind him, my frustration growing. 'You know, perhaps if you'd shown any concern for Mum's health at any point while she was unwell, you'd have been included in that will. You can't contribute nothing and expect something back – life doesn't work like that.'

'Thank you for the lesson, miss. Jesus, you're so condescending. No wonder Marcus spends so much time away from this place.'

The words sting, but I won't let it show that he's got to me. He knows nothing about my marriage and nothing about Marcus.

'I've been speaking to a solicitor. He agrees it isn't fair that you get everything.'

'This isn't about fairness. It was Mum's choice – that's the end of it.'

'It isn't the end of it, though. I'm going to challenge it. I'll take you to court if I have to. I've just as much right to that house as you have.'

'You're going to have to leave,' I tell him, hating that it's come to this: that once again, everything has come down to money. When he told me he'd got himself a job, I hoped he might have turned his life around, but he's still clinging to the idea that someone else will bail him out of the mess he's made of everything.

'Help me,' he says pleadingly, stepping closer. 'You're my sister, for fuck's sake. Family's supposed to help each other out.'

'Like you helped me out with Mum?' I spit, losing my patience. 'Where were you when she was screaming, terrified out of her mind by the men with machetes in her bedroom? Where were you all the times she cried like a child, calling over and over for her mother? Where were you when she was lashing out because she thought I was a stranger in her house?'

My vision blurs with tears, the memories of those months stark and all too real. It was horrifying to witness a once so capable woman reduced to the confused and often psychotic state that at times overcame her. I had Marcus back at home, yet I had never felt so lonely.

Cameron looks at me blankly, feigning ignorance of any of this. He was never there, for me or our mother. He knew about all these things when they were happening, but it's easier for him to convince himself that he was oblivious to it all.

'Go home, Cameron.'

'Home? I've lost everything, Lou.'

He lost his wife because he failed to sort his life out, despite being given chance after chance. He lost his daughter for the same reason. He lost his home because he lost his job and he lost his job because he lost his self-respect and his dignity. But I don't remind him of any of these things, because he already knows them all, and I don't want to cause him any more hurt than he's already enduring.

'I'm sorry I came here,' he says dejectedly, turning to go back into the hallway. He reaches the front door and opens it.

'I'm not,' I tell him quickly, before he leaves. 'I'm not sorry I've seen you.'

He turns back to me and smiles sadly. 'Just watch your back, Louise. Bad things happen when you least expect them.'

He pulls the door shut and I go into the living room, watching from the window as he leaves the driveway and heads for the end of the street. I've no idea what he meant by his parting words, or what threat they intended, if any. All I can really be sure of is that while Cameron is still hell-bent on getting his hands on that money, we will never be able to have any kind of relationship. I need to get rid of it as soon as I can, so it's no longer an issue for either of us.

FIFTEEN

On Saturday morning, I drive to the leisure centre. By the time I get there, my palms are sweaty on the steering wheel, my heart racing at the prospect of seeing Erin face to face for the first time since last weekend. I'm already dressed in my gym gear, so I go straight to the hall. Erin is already there, and she sees me as soon as I reach the doorway.

'Good morning,' she says, smiling as I lay my mat out close to hers, because as much as I'd like to pitch up at the opposite side of the hall, I'm not sure I can really get away with it. 'You've been quiet this week.'

'Busy with work, that's all.'

'I've missed you since last weekend. We haven't had a chance to talk about things properly yet... you know, without the men there.'

My mouth feels dry. I reach for my bottle of water and take a sip, running my tongue over my cracked lips. 'We can't really do it here,' I say, lowering my voice to keep my words from the three rows of women already sitting in front of us.

'Well I know that,' she laughs. 'Come over to my place for a glass of wine soon, what do you think?'

I think it's a terrible idea. Kieran might be there, and even if not, I'd be surrounded by the thought of him. 'Sounds great.'

'I've got a date with my sister tonight. Let's arrange something for next weekend, if you're free.'

I force a smile, but I can't look at her. I've been thinking on and off about her husband all week, dwelling for longer than I know is appropriate on the memory of his naked body pressed down on top of mine. I'm grateful when Natasha starts speaking, drawing the rest of the room to a hush. I lie back on my mat and try desperately to relax. For the next hour, I barely take part in the session. I miss cues and I fail to hear instructions; I'm here, but I'm not an active participant, simply making up the numbers while I will the time away.

When the session ends, I can't roll up my mat quickly enough.

'Are you okay?' Erin asks. 'You seem flustered.'

'I think I'm coming down with something,' I tell her, shocked by the ease of the lie. 'I need to get over to my mother's house too – get on with the clear-out.'

She looks at me with sympathy and puts a hand on my arm. 'You need a break from it all, Louise. Leave the house – it's not going anywhere. Take some time to concentrate on you for a while.'

We walk out to the car park together and say our goodbyes, then I head to the local supermarket to pick up some groceries before taking them back to the house. I make pasta for lunch, then follow my Saturday-afternoon routine of going over to my mother's house. Her old radio is still in the kitchen cupboard; I plug it in expecting it to no longer work, grateful when it does. I tune into a local radio station and try to block out my thoughts with the idle chit-chat of the show's presenters, interspersed with music probably favoured by the teenagers at school.

The following few hours are more productive than any previous Saturday has been, and by the time darkness has fallen outside, I've filled ten bin bags from the kitchen and the dining room: some for the charity shop, but most for the tip. I find the roll of bin bags I left propped on the dish rack and rip one loose, taking it to the cupboard under the stairs. Years ago this would have been a pantry, but my mother used it to store all her cleaning products, the ironing board and the vacuum cleaner. As none have been used in years, everything is thick with dust and cobwebs, and as I start to pull things out at random, I disturb a spider the size of a saucer. It's so big it makes me start, and as I jump back, I turn and catch my face on the corner of a shelf, knocking a grimy can of furniture polish to the floor.

I put my fingers to the soft skin just beneath my eye, feeling the dampness of blood where the sharp, unsanded edge of the wood grazed me. The spider has tootled off somewhere, too fast for me to catch and rehome in the garden. I go into the kitchen and look for a clean tea towel in the drawer, before dampening a corner and pressing it to the cut beneath my eye. My cheekbone feels bruised, though I was lucky I didn't catch it a centimetre higher, at least.

Abandoning the task at hand for a moment, I sit at the kitchen table while I continue to press the tea towel to my face. My temples are throbbing, and I know it's not caused by the blow to my face alone. I think of Marcus somewhere in a hotel room, wondering whether he's alone. This agreement to an open marriage has surely given him licence to do whatever he wants while he's away on work trips. We never agreed that Erin and Kieran would be the only people we slept with. We never established any rules beyond those set out by Erin.

Feeling nauseous, I turn the radio off. I need some water, but I don't want to drink from any of the glasses or mugs in this place, not when they've been untouched and unwashed for so long. Admitting defeat, I lock the place up and go home.

It's gone 7 p.m. by the time I get back, and the dark sky is heavy with the threat of rain. Being in the house and rooting through things that haven't been touched in so long – not to mention being surrounded by memories I now know to be lies – has left me feeling grubby, so I'm looking forward to a long soak in the bath with the book I've been trying to get through for the past couple of months.

Before I even unlock the front door to my own home, I sense something is wrong. There's a feeling in the air somehow, something static and charged, and I have a horribly unsettling sense that someone has been here not long before me. I take a step back, as though the keyhole has just mouthed a silent warning to me, and when I look in through the living room window, I get a preview of what awaits me inside.

The room has been ransacked. The bookcase at the far end of the room is empty, its contents strewn across the floor. The ornaments that sat on the mantelpiece are smashed on the rug, which is stained, like the sofas, a deep red. Like blood.

With fumbling hands, I go back to the front door and turn my key in the lock. The hallway table has been tipped onto its side, the drawers hanging open, bills and statements, keys and receipts littering the path through to the rest of the house. I step carefully over the mess, my body braced at the thought that someone might still be here. At the far end of the hallway, the kitchen appears to be untouched; from what I can see of it, at least.

I stand in the living room doorway and look at the chaos in front of me: the smashed ornaments that litter the floor; the cream rug beneath the coffee table mottled with an abstract pattern. Wine, not blood. A warning, perhaps. This time, at least.

Cameron's words ring in my ears: *Watch your back, Louise.*

Does the inheritance mean this much to him? Is he so willing to accept money that was gained through violence and extortion that he's prepared to do this to his own sister? And if this is where he's starting, where might it end?

I can't even begin to think about cleaning up the mess. I don't deserve this. All I've ever tried to do is my best, even though I know there have been plenty of times my best has been far from the mark. I've never done anything to hurt anyone or inflict suffering. As so often during my life, it feels that I'm paying for someone else's crimes.

I go into the living room and stoop to pick up a fragment of cream porcelain: the elbow of a figurine given to Marcus and me as a wedding present by one of his elderly aunts, who passed away just a year or so after we were married. It was a couple embracing, their silhouettes encircled with a heart-shaped frame, and I recognise the elbow as that of the female – smaller than the male's and slightly more angular in shape. I can't see the bodies, and assume that the piece must have been dropped or thrown with such force it's now beyond repair. It strikes me as oddly symbolic somehow, but I try to shoo the thought away like a fly swatted from my face.

I stand and look at the mess that surrounds me, wondering whether I should care more than I do. It's not the broken things that bother me – it's the thought of Cameron being responsible for it all, and the disappointment that flows with it. Despite everything, I still love him. He's my only remaining family member, and no matter what he may have done, I've never believed him to be bad. His own worst enemy, certainly, but never cut from the same cloth as our father.

I go into the hallway, dejected. Cameron is no longer my responsibility; he hasn't been for a long time now. Yet once again I'm left to clear up after him.

I stand silently at the bottom of the stairs, waiting to hear a noise from upstairs or from the kitchen. Time seems to slow, and it feels an age before I find my legs unweighted enough for me to move again. I go to the kitchen slowly, as silently as possible, bracing myself for the possibility of finding Cameron sitting at the kitchen table waiting for me. But he isn't here. I take a knife from the block near the cooker, feeling the handle tremble between my fingers with the ridiculousness of the scenario. Even if there was someone upstairs, I don't think I have it in me to hurt them.

I go back to the staircase, reminding myself that there are no signs anywhere of a break-in, and anyway, the chances of being broken into at random just a day after Cameron's threat seem slim. It leaves the question of how he got into the house, but at the moment I can't think about that. I just need to make sure he's not upstairs. That I'm here alone.

I've always held onto the hope that Cameron can be saved from himself, that if someone just continues to believe in him, he'll eventually stop the destructive, self-harming ways that have come to characterise his adulthood. And despite everything, there's still a part of me that makes allowances. There is someone good in there somewhere. Someone better than this. There's still time. But just how much time does one man need? And how many mistakes become one too many?

By the time I get to the landing, my heart is pounding in my chest. I feel dizzy and light-headed, probably because I've not eaten or drunk anything since breakfast. I move from room to room, pushing each door open with my foot, the knife gripped in my hand as a warning to anyone who might be behind them. But there's no one here. I'm alone, as I hoped, yet the feeling of isolation isn't as comforting as I thought it might be.

I sit on our bed for a while as my heart rate settles again before going back downstairs to search my handbag for my phone. I pull up Marcus's mobile number and call him, but it goes straight to answerphone. I hang up before it connects. It's not like Marcus not to have his phone on: he relies on it so much for work, and he's often answering texts and replying to emails late into the evening, as annoying as that can be. All the months of lockdowns and the cancellations of events and live television put him out of work for a long time, and he's been making up for lost opportunities ever since. Not being busy was something he quickly discovered he couldn't cope with, and with me still at school with the children of key workers, he came to realise that he'd taken for granted his previous freedom to work.

I try his number again. Again it goes straight to answerphone. Perhaps his signal is bad.

In my WhatsApps, there's a message from Maria, sent last night. I open it to a photograph of a broken-heeled shoe – the pair she wore to work yesterday, I'm guessing – caked in mud, with the simple caption *I love football* followed by the steam-coming-out-of-the-nose emoji. She hasn't been online since, according to this, but I try her number anyway, hoping for the sound of a friendly and familiar voice. It rings and rings until it clicks through to her answerphone greeting.

Scrolling through details of people I barely know or haven't spoken to in ages, I try to settle upon someone I can call for some reassurance. I just need to hear a familiar voice, to feel a little less alone. I stop when I reach Erin's name, even though I've only known her such a short time. I won't tell her about what's happened here, or even mention my brother. I don't want her to taint our new-found friendship with my family's problems.

I call her number, but a man answers.

'Kieran? It's Louise. Is Erin there?'

'No. She's out tonight. Forgot her phone.'

And now I remember: her date with her sister.

'Oh. Okay.'

'Has something happened?'

'No,' I say too quickly. 'It's fine.'

'I'll let her know you called when she gets back.'

'Yeah, okay. Thanks.'

I'm about to hang up when he asks, 'Are you sure everything's okay?'

The concern in his voice destroys my resolve not to tell anyone what's happened.

'There's been a break-in at my house.'

'Christ, are you okay? Where are you?'

'I'm here, at home.'

There's a lengthy silence in which I start to wonder whether he's still at the other end of the call.

'Are you on your own?'

'Yeah. I mean, Marcus is away with work, but I'm all right.'

'I'd offer to come over, but Erin has taken the car. I could get a taxi—'

'No. I mean, the place is chaos anyway,' I tell him, not wanting him here. Having him in my home would feel too strange.

I should have called the police, but I can't bring myself to do it. I'll have to mention Cameron, and though he'll have brought it on himself and it's no less than he deserves, there's still a part of me that doesn't want to see his life become any messier than it already is.

'I just...' I trail off, not knowing what to say. 'I'm sorry. I shouldn't have called.'

There's a long pause. 'You can come here, if you like,' Kieran offers.

I picture him between my legs, his chest pressed against mine, the smell of his aftershave breathed into my lungs. I don't want the images there, but they refuse to leave me. I try to distract myself by thinking about Marcus somewhere in a hotel on the Isle of Wight, perhaps down at the bar with the people he works with. He's chatting to someone, laughing; surrounded by familiar faces. The thought makes me feel suddenly very alone.

'I'll text you our address,' he says.

SIXTEEN

Erin and Kieran's house is a semi-detached new-build on an estate across the other side of town. The driveway is empty, the black Kuga in which I saw him pick her up from the leisure centre absent, gone with Erin to meet with her sister. Now that I'm here, I wonder whether I've done the right thing. I just don't want to go home. It doesn't feel safe, and the silence manages to deafen me.

I drive past the house and turn the corner at the end of the street, parking at the kerb near a small children's playground. I don't know why I do it, but some instinct tells me not to park directly outside. As I walk towards the house, Kieran sees me through the front window, and he points me around to the side of the house. He's waiting for me at the side door when I get there.

'You okay?' he asks, as he steps aside to let me into the kitchen.

There's a smell of lemon cleaning spray mingled with bleach in the air, so strong it catches in my throat as I reply. 'Just shaken up.'

'I'm not surprised. Would you like a cup of tea? Are you sure I'm not putting you out?'

'No,' he says, flicking the switch on the kettle. He goes to the cupboard and takes out two mugs. 'So what happened? How did they get in?'

I don't want to mention my brother to him: if anyone finds out that Cameron was there, it might get back to Marcus, and if Marcus finds out what he's done, I dread to think how he might react.

'Looks as though they broke in through the back door.'

I stand by the doorway in silence as he makes us tea, only speaking to me to ask if I like it strong and whether I take sugar.

'We can take them into the living room,' he says, handing me a mug. 'It's a bit comfier in there.' He stops talking when he notices the bruising under my eye, more apparent beneath the kitchen's bright lighting.

'What happened to your face?' He puts the fingers of his free hand gently to my cheekbone; this afternoon's muted green bruise has become an angry dark flower blooming on my pale skin. Instinctively I pull away.

'I'm sorry. I didn't mean—'

'It's fine,' I say, too quickly. I feel myself flush as visions from that night at the hotel skitter through my mind, an X-rated flip-book of naked limbs and sweat-sheened skin. I can still smell the aftershave he wore; can still taste the wine on his tongue. I don't want to be reminded so vividly, but the memories refuse to fade.

'I hit my face on a shelf,' I tell him.

He looks at me with narrowed eyes, suspecting a lie. 'You weren't at home during the break-in?'

'No. It happened at my mother's house. The bruise, not the break-in.'

We go into the living room and sit at opposite ends of the sofa, both awkward at the close proximity of the other.

'She died.' I don't know why I say this. Something to fill the uncomfortable silence that hangs in the room, although anything else I might have chosen to say now seems more appropriate than that. 'Six months ago,' I add.

'I'm sorry.'

I think of Iris and realise for the first time that there are no photographs of the little girl anywhere, on the windowsills or the mantelpiece. In fact, there's nothing personal to really make the house look like a home. They may be renting. They may not be planning to stay here indefinitely. There's so much that Erin and I haven't talked about, yet every conversation will seem different now, after last weekend.

I recall Erin saying how Iris's death had broken Kieran – so much so that she asked me not to mention their daughter to him when we met. Perhaps having photographs of her up on the wall is too painful for him, and I suppose if they've chosen not to have her face on display, then they've also decided that their son's photographs shouldn't go up either. I wonder how Jay must feel, living in the shadow of his younger sibling's death.

'Have you reported it to the police?' Kieran asks, stirring me from my reverie.

'The break-in? Not yet.'

'You need to, while there's still evidence. They'll be able to take fingerprints.'

I know that if Marcus was home, this is exactly what he'd also be telling me. He would have already called the police himself. He'd already be over to where Cameron lives, if we even know that any more.

Kieran reaches for his phone, checking the time. 'I'm not sure when Erin will be back.'

I sip my tea. He's put sugar in it despite me asking for just milk, but I'm grateful for the sweetness as it hits my tongue. The thought brings another image from that hotel bedroom racing back to my mind in high definition, and I feel a flood of colour burn my cheeks.

On the table beside me, Kieran's phone starts ringing. The sudden sound startles me, and my hand shakes, tea slopping over the rim of the mug. 'Shit.' It seeps straight through my thin leggings, burning my skin.

'I'll get you a cloth.'

I stand as Kieran crosses the room to go to the kitchen, and somehow, despite all the space in the room, we manage to nearly bump into each other. He apologises awkwardly before leaving the room. I glance at the call he's ignored, an 0300 number lighting up the screen. He returns with a tea towel and an ice pack from the freezer. He wraps the pack in the towel and passes it to me.

'I'm sorry,' I say, sitting back down. 'I'm so clumsy.'

'Bloody nuisance calls,' he says, checking the now silent phone. 'I get them all the time.' He looks at me with concern. 'You should probably take off your leggings.'

There's an uncomfortable silence. I keep my head lowered, focusing on my leg, but the cold hasn't reached through the tea towel and my clothes yet, and the burning sensation on my skin is intensifying.

'I didn't mean... I meant you could go to the bathroom. It's just up the stairs.'

I need to use the toilet anyway, so I mumble a thanks and go upstairs, finding the bathroom through the first door. I peel my leggings down and sit on the toilet. The skin of my left thigh is scalded pink, and I hold the ice pack against it for a while.

I've just washed my hands when there's a knock at the door. I unlock it and peer around. Kieran is standing there, his eyes refusing to meet mine. 'Do you want me to take a look?'

'It'll be okay. Thanks.'

But I don't close the door. I just linger there, not knowing what to do or say, realising, as I know he does, that the attraction between us is unsettlingly strong, as it was that night. I look up from my leg to find him watching me now.

'There's some cream for burns somewhere. I think it's in the cupboard.' He gestures behind me, so I move aside to let him into the bathroom, not comfortable with the idea of searching through his and Erin's things myself. The thought of her makes my breath catch in my throat for a moment, but even that's not enough to prevent what I know is about to happen.

He doesn't make it to the cupboard. He moves closer to me, that same aftershave he wore at the hotel filling the air between us, and I don't stop him when he puts his hands on my shoulders and pushes me back against the wall, his knee pushing between mine as it did at the hotel, the urgency of his desire melting my uncertainties. And when he takes me by the hand and leads me to the bedroom, I forget everything else.

I remember Erin when it's over, when her husband and I are lying half dressed beneath their duvet, as though for the past hour she ceased to exist. Guilt floods my throat like bile. This is what Alexis did to Marcus. Now I'm putting him through it all over again. I'm putting Erin through it too.

'Are you okay?' Kieran turns towards me, his bare leg touching mine in a way that is too intimate. Too familiar.

'Fine,' I say, moving away from him. I think of the one rule we all agreed upon: no sex in one another's houses.

'I'm sorry if I...' But he trails off, the sentence unfinished, and I'm not really sure what he's apologising for. I'm as guilty as he is. This was a massive, horrible mistake, and the last thing I want to do now is talk about it.

'I'd better go.'

'Give me a minute.' He gets up and goes into the en suite. I hurriedly pull on my underwear and leggings, the room looking suddenly so different from the way it did less than an hour ago. I shouldn't be here. I need to go home.

I'm wondering where the hell I left my bag when I hear a noise downstairs. Moments later, there are footsteps on the stairs. Erin is home. I think of my shoes by the back door; my coat lying on top of them. I wonder now whether my car keys are in my pocket and if I even had a bag with me. If she goes into the kitchen, she'll see them straight away. I move carefully to the door, not wanting to make a sound. There's someone on the landing. I realise there's no way out of this. The only way to leave the house is by going downstairs. I'm going to have to face her. I'm going to have to admit what we've just done.

The bedroom door isn't fully shut; there's a wide enough gap for me to look out onto the landing. When I do, I see someone standing further along the hallway, at the door next to the bathroom. He has his back to me. Erin and Kieran's son. I take a step back into the bedroom, moving from view as the boy turns. I hold my breath as he looks towards his parents' bedroom, and it's now that I see his face. The surly expression he wears as an accessory. The hair shaved too close at the back of his skull. I know this teenager. Erin's son Jay is Jasper Healy.

I wait motionless as he goes into his bedroom and listen for the sound of the door clicking shut. All I can think of in this moment is that I have to get out of here before anyone sees me. Before Jasper sees me. I move as fast as I can without making a noise, edging to the top of the staircase. Every step seems to creak beneath my bare feet as I make my way downstairs. I can still hear water running in the en suite, and I have to leave before Kieran comes looking for me.

As I step onto the hallway floor, I look at my feet and realise I was wearing socks when I arrived. I can't think now what colour they were or whether they had a pattern, but I know I've left them upstairs, and I don't have time to go back for them. I go to the kitchen door where I left my things, put on my shoes and coat, and slip out as quietly as I can, pulling the door closed behind me. I check my phone: a missed call from Maria and a message on WhatsApp: *Phone was on silent. Everything okay?*

I walk quickly to the side street where I parked my car, and when I turn back to the street, that's when I see her. Erin, in the Kuga, nearly at her driveway. My heart pounds as I run to my car, get in and lock the door. I have no idea whether she saw me.

SEVENTEEN

When I get home, I ignore the chaos of the living room and go straight upstairs to shower, trying to wash the smell of Kieran's aftershave from my body, hating myself for everything I've just allowed to happen. Afterwards, I go into the bedroom and get dressed in a pair of pyjamas. I can't get into the bed. I look at Marcus's side, at the indentation of his head still visible on the flattened pillow, and the guilt swallows me like a monster in the darkness, momentarily crushing the breath from my body. We said we would be honest with each other. This wasn't part of the arrangement.

I get a blanket and go downstairs to the living room, where I set up camp on the only end of sofa that hasn't been soaked with wine. I could sleep in the spare bedroom, but there's no television in there, and I need its presence to make me feel less alone. With the television on – its muted sound and warm glow making the room seem less threatening – I eventually manage to drift off with the carnage of Cameron's visit still lying around me, and when I wake before 5 a.m., it's the first thing that greets me.

I go through a series of motions before calling the police.

Shower again, brush my teeth, dress, apply make-up. I make coffee and eat a slice of toast, then sit in the kitchen and stare out at the lawn, turning last night over and over in my mind. I feel sick at the memory of seeing Erin last night; of knowing that she was so close to home while I was there with Kieran. Would I have heard something from her by now if she'd spotted me? Did Jasper see me there, and has he told his mother everything?

I wonder what Marcus is doing. I wonder whether he's picked up my missed calls – he surely must have by now. I've no idea what I'm supposed to say when he calls me back. He'll know there was something wrong yesterday, and he isn't easily fobbed off; he knows me well enough to know when I'm with-holding something from him.

The police arrive at just gone 12.30, nearly three hours after I called them. They have to step over the mess in the hallway to get into the house, the upturned table still standing at a tilt with its drawers hanging open.

'Have you touched anything?' one of the officers asks.

'Plenty.'

I talk them through everything that happened, from explaining why I was at my mother's house to getting home and finding the place ransacked. I make them tea, and we sit at the kitchen table while I give them the details of the inheritance and my brother's visit just a couple of days ago, knowing if I don't tell them now, it'll only likely surface later, and the police will then wonder why I withheld information from them.

'Any signs of forced entry?'

'No.'

'Has your brother ever been given a key to the house?'

I shake my head. He's never even been loaned one, so it's impossible that he might have had one cut. But then I remember the spare key in the hallway drawer.

'Wait there,' I say. I go into the hall. I pick things up from the floor: letters and statements; keys and random batteries and hair slides and elastic bands. 'It's not here,' I say, thinking aloud. 'The spare key.'

The officers come from the kitchen.

'Did your brother have a chance to take the key from the drawer when he was here on Friday evening?'

'I think so. I mean, yeah, he must have. It's not here now.'

'And the break-in happened yesterday, before you arrived home at seven p.m.? Can I ask why you've only now contacted us?'

I can hardly tell them that I've been too consumed with the guilt of sleeping with my friend's husband, so I feign a state of shock instead. 'He's my brother,' I say. 'I didn't want to get him into trouble.'

Despite what Kieran said last night, there's no forensic search of the house; no dusting of the place for fingerprints. I'm not sure what I expected really: there was never going to be an influx of white-overall-clad specialists; it's not as though a dead body has been found in my living room. Instead, I make a statement and give them my brother's details and then off they go, leaving me to deal with the mess.

Marcus calls me a couple of hours after the police have left.

'I'm so sorry I haven't got back to you until now. The signal down here's terrible, especially at the hotel. We're at one of the film locations now – it's only since we got here that your missed calls have come through. Is everything okay? Has something happened?'

I stall for a moment, deliberating over whether to tell him about Cameron. Marcus is miles away and can't do anything to help the situation. Telling him will only cause him unnecessary worry. I don't think Cameron will come back, not after what he's done. He'll be too ashamed to show his face again for a while. I can manage the mess on my own, no matter how long it might take. I've already made a start, using the task to try and distract my mind from what happened last night.

There's no reason for Marcus to know about the damage done, and would it really matter if he never found out Cameron had been here? What he doesn't know won't hurt him.

My chest tightens at the thought of Kieran. I could also keep what happened between him and me to myself, though I already know I'll never forgive myself for the secrecy.

'Nothing's happened. Sorry... I just wanted to hear your voice, that's all.'

'I had a text from Ron to say police were at the house earlier.'

Shit. Ron is the octogenarian who lives a few doors up and across the street and has reached a stage where he's not got much better to do than look out of his window and watch what's going on in other people's lives. His hearing is terrible, but only selectively, and his ability to use a mobile phone is apparently as good as anyone else's.

'Yeah,' I say, realising I can't lie now. 'Look... Cameron came here on Friday night.'

'What the fuck for?'

'What do you think?'

'Jesus, when's he going to let it go?'

'I'm not sure he is. I mean, not if last night was anything to go by.'

'What happened last night?'

I pause.

'Louise?'

'He trashed the house.'

'He did what?!'

I can almost feel the burn of Marcus's fury down the phone.

'It's fine,' I tell him. 'The police have been... It's all been dealt with.'

'But has *he* been dealt with?'

'It's with the police.'

'Oh, there we are then. So fuck-all will be done about it, you mean.'

I bite my tongue. Trying to talk to Marcus when he's in a mood like this is pointless, though I know he's only reacting this way out of concern for me. Kieran's face appears in front of me, flashes of his naked flesh taunting me. I feel his hands in my hair; his weight pressing me down into the mattress.

'How did he get in?'

'I'm not sure.' I don't want to tell him that it looks as though Cameron took the spare key from the drawer while he was here on Friday. He'll only worry about him coming back, and he'll be angry with me for allowing my brother the space and time to get to that drawer in the first place. I feel pretty confident Cameron won't try to use the key again, but I'll look into getting the locks changed anyway.

'I must have left the back door unlocked,' I tell him, knowing I need to offer some kind of explanation.

'For fuck's sake. I'm sorry, I don't mean you. I mean him. Prick.'

'I'm fine,' I tell him. 'Everything is fine.'

Another explicit image of Kieran fills my head.

I am so, so sorry.

'I just feel a bit useless here, miles away.'

'You don't need to worry about anything.'

'Will you let me know what the police say when they get back to you?'

'Of course. I'll call you.' Although I don't expect that to be any time soon. I doubt a domestic dispute between feuding siblings is going to rank high on their list of priorities.

'Okay. Look, I've got to go. Filming's about to start.'

I wait for him to tell me he loves me, but he doesn't.

'Good luck,' I tell him. 'Speak to you soon.'

When the call is ended, I sit on the sofa and stare at the mess, no motivation to get back to what I was doing before

Marcus called me. Phone still in my hand, I go to WhatsApp and open my chat with Erin.

Are you free today? I type. *I need to see you.*

I stare at the message, reading and rereading it, then delete it, too much of a coward to deal with the consequences of what I've done. I change my mind; type it again, word it differently.

You free to chat today? X

It sounds casual, not too desperate. It doesn't suggest there's anything urgent that needs to be discussed; it's more a friendly request for a relaxed catch-up, and she said only yesterday that we needed one. I stare at the words for too long before pressing send. Then I spend the rest of the day anticipating a reply that never comes.

EIGHTEEN

Monday morning has barely started when I get a call from the head of the science department to say that Jasper Healy has been involved in what he vaguely refers to as 'an incident'. When I get over to the biology labs, Jasper is standing in the corridor, a teaching assistant beside him, presumably making sure he doesn't try to make a run for it. The boy spends so much time being accompanied by teaching assistants that he's starting to look as though he has a bodyguard with him everywhere he goes.

'What's happened now?' I ask, hardly managing to conceal my frustration. It's not just this. I barely slept last night, dreading coming into work today. In theory, the school is big enough for me to avoid bumping into any given individual, although I knew my recent luck would make the chance unlikely. More than Jasper, though, I'm worried about Erin. She always replies to my messages, and usually pretty soon after I've texted. The only reason I can think of for her not doing so yesterday is that she knows about what happened between Kieran and me on Saturday night and she's biding her time before she confronts me about it.

The teaching assistant looks at Jasper, prompting him to offer an answer before she has to. When he says nothing, she tells me he threw a chair at another student.

Without saying anything, and without making eye contact with Jasper, I go into the classroom. The students have settled into a silence that is eerie, nearly all heads lowered as they copy something from the textbooks in front of them. At the teacher's desk, Mr Owens sits with a boy who's holding a bloodied tissue to his forehead.

'Can I see?' I ask the boy, gesturing to his head.

He moves the tissue away.

'That might need glueing,' I say to Mr Owens. 'I'll call his parents. Can you send him over to reception in about ten minutes?'

I go back into the corridor.

'Okay,' I say to Jasper, still unable to look at him. 'You need to come to my office with me.'

I expect him to cause a scene about it; instead, he picks up his bag from the floor and follows me like a sheepish puppy. I think about seeing him on the landing of his parents' house, and feel my cheeks flush with shame. What if he saw me there? He's such a cocky little shit that surely by now, if he had, he would have said something. He would have taken a warped pleasure in letting me squirm in the embarrassment of my sordid secret being out in the open.

He didn't see you, I tell myself. Everything is going to be fine. I know he didn't see me. He couldn't have. There would have been a reaction on his face to the sight of me in his parents' home, in his parents' bedroom, but there was nothing. He went straight into his own room, oblivious.

But Erin might have seen you, I remind myself.

'Why did you do it, Jasper?' I ask as we step out of the science block and make our way past the canteen.

Like someone under police questioning gripping onto his right to remain silent, he doesn't reply.

'Alfie's head might need glueing. He's definitely going to need a visit to hospital. You realise they'll ask how it happened.'

Still he says nothing. God, this kid is exasperating. It's almost impossible to imagine that he's Erin and Kieran's child. His mother is so friendly and upbeat; nothing like this surly young man who ambles along lazily beside me. He's nothing like his father either, not in looks or personality. I think of Iris and feel a knot of sympathy in my chest. I've no idea what this boy has been through.

The thought of Iris and then of Erin makes my stomach churn with sickness. Though we haven't known each other for long, I consider Erin a friend. I'm sure she thinks of me in the same way. If I asked for her forgiveness, I wouldn't deserve it. The same applies to Marcus. I imagine him setting up for the day's filming, excited by the buzz of the location and the rest of the crew. Oblivious to what's going on back at home, and to what I've done to us.

'Something must have happened,' I say, as much as to distract myself as to get some kind of sense from Jasper. 'Did Alfie say something to you? You wouldn't have just lost it like that for no reason.' Nothing. 'When you're ready, you can talk to me. Not everyone's against you, Jasper. I just want to understand.'

We reach the office, and I ask the secretary to contact one of Jasper's parents. The thought of having to face either of them in person today fills me with a sinking dread, and I'm not sure which would be worst. If I see Erin, she might bring up the subject of Saturday night, forcing a confession in the most humiliating way and in the worst of places. If it's Kieran who comes, we're going to have to act as though everything is normal: just a head teacher and a student's father, completely removing ourselves from what happened between us.

I leave Jasper sitting outside reception and go into my office. Little over half an hour later, a knock at the door rouses me from my thoughts. Beneath my blouse, my heart thumps with a restlessness that's both unprofessional and ill timed. If Kieran's here, I don't want him to see how unsettled I am by what's happening. This is about Jasper, I remind myself. It's no different a conversation than were this to involve any other student.

The secretary's face appears around the door. 'Jasper Healy's dad's here to see you.'

My heart sinks. I thank her before following her out to the reception area. Kieran is standing near the front desk, his hands shoved into his pockets as he stares out of the window at the lashing rain. Jasper sits beside him, but they don't appear to have acknowledged one another. Perhaps he's already had words with his son before I came out of the office, and for now at least there's nothing more to be said.

'Mr Healy,' I say, reaching out a hand to greet him. 'Thanks for coming in.'

He says nothing, but takes my hand in his, his fingers cold. It reminds me of when we first met in the hotel bar, the thought of that evening here again, an intrusive thought that quickly embeds itself in the forefront of my brain, playing on repeat. He follows me into the office. Once the door is shut and the secretary is on the other side of it, out of earshot, I'm safe to drop the act.

'Didn't you think to tell me you have a son at this school?'

'It's Foster.'

'Pardon?'

'Kieran Foster. Jasper and I don't have the same surname.'

'Okay. Apologies for that.'

It occurs to me now that I'm not even sure what Erin's last name is, but plenty of women keep their maiden name when they marry, and perhaps Jasper shares that with her. Then I remember her telling me her son was sixteen, but she'd been with Kieran for twelve years. I hadn't really thought anything of it at the time, my focus instead on poor little Iris.

'So,' I continue. 'You didn't think to mention him?'

'He's only just started at the school. And how was I supposed to know you work here?'

'Surely Erin said something?'

'Did you tell her you were head teacher here?'

I realise that no, I didn't. I try to recall whether I've ever mentioned the school. I know I told her I work in teaching, but that must have been as far as the conversation went. We were too busy talking about other things – our marriages, mostly.

'We've only recently moved here,' Kieran continues defensively. 'It wouldn't have occurred to us to give you the details of our lives when we barely know you.' His expression changes. 'Why am I justifying myself to you?'

I bite my tongue, trying to remain as professional as possible under the circumstances. And let's be clear: these are the worst circumstances I've found myself in during my twenty-year career. 'Let's just keep the focus on your son, shall we? Jasper's behaviour since joining the school has been unacceptable. He was given a warning after an incident when he filmed a fight on his phone, and another after swearing at a staff member. This latest incident has to be met with a greater punishment, I'm afraid. Another child has been injured. It's likely he'll need hospital treatment.'

'Is he okay?'

'Cut to the forehead. Might need glueing.'

Kieran shakes his head and looks down at the floor, exhaling audibly. 'You're going to suspend him, I'm guessing.'

'We have to set an example to the other students.'

I don't miss the way his right eyebrow rises slightly. I'm aware what the look says. Who am I to talk about setting an example, in light of everything I've done? I don't like the way he's silently judging me when he's guilty of the same. We are both to blame here.

'Are you okay now?' he asks, his voice softening. 'After what happened to—'

'Not here,' I say abruptly.

'I was just going to ask about the house, that's all.'

'It's fine. Everything's fine.'

He nods slowly. I wish I wasn't so attracted to him. I wish he wasn't standing so close to me.

'How long?' he asks.

How long what?'

'Jasper's suspension.'

'One week. I'm afraid I don't have any other option.'

He nods and goes to the door. I follow him, and we reach for the handle at the same time. Our fingers brush each other's, both of us pulling away as though burned.

'Have you said anything to Erin?' I ask.

'No.'

I wonder why she never texted me back yesterday. She must have seen my message by now, though it still hasn't double ticked on WhatsApp. Why hasn't she received the message?

'I saw her,' I tell him, my voice lowered to a whisper. 'Outside the house.'

Kieran won't make eye contact with me. Now that he's this close, I realise how tired he looks. I wonder whether they've argued. I keep thinking about that pair of socks left somewhere in their house, presumably in their bedroom. He's acting strangely, but then it's likely that to anyone else I appear that way too. It's difficult to act normally when you're racked with guilt.

'Are you okay?' I ask.

He looks as though he's about to say something but changes his mind. His complexion is grey; he looks washed out. He's probably feeling as terrible about what happened as I am.

'It was a mistake,' I tell him. 'No one need find out. There's too much at risk for all of us.'

He nods. 'It should never have happened. I'm sorry.'

There's a knock at the door, which startles us both. When the secretary opens it without waiting to be called in, Kieran and I dart away from one another like two magnets repelling.

'I'm sorry,' she apologises. 'I tried to stop him, but Jasper's gone.'

'Shit,' Kieran mutters beneath his breath. 'I'd better go look for him.'

The secretary steps aside to let him pass. 'All okay?' she asks, after he's gone.

'Fine.'

She returns to her own office, leaving me alone to go over and over the conversation that's just been had, trying to gauge Kieran's behaviour towards me. I'm pretty sure he regards Saturday in the same way I do: a huge mistake, never to be repeated. If Erin doesn't already know about us, I'm pretty sure he won't say anything to her. There's only a few months until Jasper's GCSE exams. It's unlikely he'll stay on for A levels, although plenty of teenagers opt for it over having to look for a job. Hopefully by the summer there'll be no need for me to ever see Kieran again.

Though there's still Erin, I remind myself. She considers me a friend, but I'm not sure we can stay that way unless I keep this a secret for ever.

I sit at my desk, head pounding as I think of Marcus. This was supposed to bring us closer. It was supposed to save our marriage. It was only meant to be about sex. Now he's away with work, at least I've got a little while to work out what I'm going to say to him. But when he gets home, how am I supposed to look him in the eye when I can't stop thinking about someone else?

NINETEEN

When I open the front door after getting home early that evening, the first thing I see are Marcus's shoes in the hallway. His coat is hanging at the end of the banister, and a rich smell wafts from the kitchen – onions and spices. He shouldn't be here – he should be on the Isle of Wight, where he was when we spoke yesterday – yet here he is, and he's making a curry. Marcus doesn't rate himself as much of a chef. He once tried to tackle a Sunday roast when his sister came to visit us from Scotland, the results of which were a dried-out chicken, cremated potatoes and then, once the gloop from the gravy pan had been dealt with using a chisel, a takeaway from a local pizza place. One thing he's brilliant at cooking, though, is a curry, and I'd recognise the aroma of his signature dish anywhere.

He has his back turned to me when I go into the kitchen. I stand in the doorway for a moment, watching him stir the contents of the pot on the cooker top. The radio is on, a Queen song playing, Marcus contentedly singing along about having such a good time. I wait quietly, saying nothing, reminded of the night ten years ago when I went over to his flat for the first time. He was living with a friend when we met: I'd seen him on his way out when I arrived, so he'd let me in, Marcus not realising I was already there. I did the same then as I'm doing now: stood in the kitchen doorway and watched him, oblivious – only that time he was prancing around in just a pair of boxers, his skin still damp from the shower, a remote control held to his mouth in lieu of a microphone. He jumped half a mile when he turned to find me there, yet there was no embarrassment or self-consciousness: he just laughed and covered himself with a tea towel, and I fell a bit in love with him right in that moment, because he was so carefree and happy and so unlike everything that had come to define me.

Somewhere during the past decade, we've lost what we once were, and I feel an aching for it in my chest that burns like a bereavement.

'Hey.'

'Shit, Lou.' His hand flies to his chest as he turns sharply. 'I didn't hear you come in.'

He rushes straight over to me and pulls me close, my face on his shoulder, his hand smoothing the back of my head. I don't deserve his kindness.

'Are you okay?'

'I told you I was fine on the phone. I can't believe you've done this.'

'It's only a jalfrezi.'

'Not the curry – I mean I can't believe you've come home in the middle of a work trip. This is exactly why I didn't want you to know about the weekend.'

'I'm glad I know.' He narrows his eyes; he's caught sight of the bruising beneath my eye, paler now than it was on Saturday, but still visible. 'Did he fucking do that?'

'No, Marcus, he didn't do it. I hit it on a shelf when I was over at my mother's house.'

His eyes study mine, seeking a lie. I couldn't feel worse in this moment. I might be telling the truth about the bruise, but the big untruth sits between us, the elephant in the room only I can see.

'You promise?'

'I promise.'

He pulls me close again. Each time he holds me feels worse than the last, the guilt threatening to swallow me whole. If he finds out about Kieran, he'll never forgive me. *Why couldn't you have been like this sooner?* I find myself silently asking. *Why couldn't you have been more attentive, more caring?*

'You shouldn't have come home,' I say.

'Okay. And what sort of husband would that make me?'

'You've worked so hard towards this production. So much preparation has gone into it. Don't let Cameron spoil it for you.'

'I don't care about him,' he says, kissing the top of my head. 'I just want to make sure you're okay. I'm here for you, not him.' He moves away from me, his hands resting on my shoulders. 'I did some thinking yesterday, after we talked on the phone. I've been away too much. Since the lockdowns ended... I don't know, my priorities have been all wrong.'

'You've been making up for lost time. That's understandable.'

'I was making up for lost money,' he corrects me. 'Time's the important thing, though. After I left on Tuesday, I thought about our conversation that morning in the bedroom and I realised something needs to change. That night at the hotel wasn't the problem. Maybe it's just me.'

'It isn't,' I say, the guilt inside me bubbling as it threatens to boil over. 'It isn't you. This is nothing to do with what happened at the hotel. Cameron's done this.'

'Forget Cameron for a minute. What about everything else... us?'

'We're fine. Aren't we? Aren't we fine?'

But even I can hear how unconvincing I sound. Panicked, even.

'We're fine, Lou,' Marcus says with a laugh. 'As long as you're fine, I'm fine.' His eyes narrow. 'Has something else happened?'

'No,' I say, too quickly. 'I'm just tired. I didn't really sleep at the weekend.'

'Go and put your feet up,' he instructs me. 'Put some junk on the TV. Dinner won't be long.'

'Let me set the table,' I offer.

'Louise,' he says, putting his hands on my shoulders and turning me towards the kitchen door. 'For once, just let me look after you. Please.'

I go into the living room. The mess of the weekend has been cleared up, but there are still pink marks on the rug that refuse to be washed away, as well as wine stains on the sofa that are going to need a professional cleaning company to get rid of. There are patches and lines where I washed down the walls. Redecorating feels too big a task to even consider at the moment. I put the television on, turning the sound up to try to drown out the echoes of my earlier meeting with Kieran. Marcus can't find out about Jasper being at the school. It's just too complicated, and somewhere I'm likely to trip over a lie and expose myself.

I stare at the screen as a group of contestants answer questions in the hope of winning fifty thousand pounds. It won't make you happy, I think. The nice house, the nice car; even the husband who cuts work trips short and comes home to cook dinner. I have everything, and yet it's not enough. Or it wasn't, at least, until I was at risk of losing it all.

And yet I can't ignore the fact either that Marcus was never this attentive before these past couple of weeks. I wouldn't expect or want this from him all the time: it would be claustrophobic, exhausting. Had there been more of it earlier, though, I wonder if we'd be in this situation now.

'Louise!'

I go into the kitchen, where the table has been adorned with a banquet: a bowl of steaming curry, two types of rice, a selection of vegetable side dishes and a tray of chutneys.

'You shouldn't have done all this.'

'Do you want a beer?' Marcus asks, going to the fridge and taking a bottle from the bottom shelf. I shake my head. I've had a tension headache since yesterday, and alcohol will only make it worse.

'Tuck in,' he says, sitting opposite me.

I have no appetite – in fact, I'm feeling a bit sick – but he's gone to such effort that I can't tell him this. I stab a samosa with a fork and slide it onto my plate.

'How was work?' he asks.

'Okay,' I say, realising this is the first time in a long time he's asked about my day.

'Nothing happened then?' he asks with a laugh.

'It's just been hard to concentrate, you know. After the weekend's… incident.'

He reaches across the table to hold my hand. 'I was thinking, if it'll make you feel safer, we'll get the locks changed. I know you said you might have left the back door unlocked, but I'm happy to get it done if it'll put your mind at rest.'

'I thought the same, actually. I'll call someone tomorrow.'

'I'll sort it. You've got enough to think about with work.'

I watch him spoon jalfrezi onto his plate, wondering why it's had to take something like Cameron smashing our house up for Marcus to act this way towards me. The thought that if evenings such as this were more commonplace between us perhaps things might be different creeps back into my consciousness. We might never have felt the need to spend that night with other people in a ridiculous attempt to push ourselves back closer to each other. None of what followed would have happened.

We sit in silence for a while. He looks at my plate, at the

food I've barely touched. 'Don't you like it?' he asks, disappointed.

'No. I mean, yes, it's lovely... It's me. I'm sorry. I'm just a bit off my food. My period started yesterday,' I fib. If I tell him this now, he won't try to instigate anything later. If he touches me, I'm not sure I'll be able to look him in the eye and maintain the lie.

'I can put it in the fridge and you can try again later, when you're ready. It'll keep until tomorrow anyway. Go back and put your feet up. I'll do you a hot-water bottle.'

Stop being nice to me, I think. I don't deserve it. I don't deserve any of it.

I sit with Marcus while he finishes eating, and once the plates have been loaded in the dishwasher and everything's been put away, he tells me he's going to go for a shower. I wait to hear the water run upstairs before I find my phone and send Erin a message on WhatsApp.

Everything okay? Give me a call when you're free x

I wait to see a double tick appear beside the message, but it doesn't. Taking the phone with me into the living room, I sit on the sofa and turn on the television again, needing the background noise as a distraction from my thoughts. I hear Marcus's footsteps upstairs; hear him singing once he's out of the shower. When the message still hasn't double-ticked, I call Erin's number. It goes straight to answerphone, and I know something's wrong. No matter what Kieran told me, I suspect he's lying. Erin knows.

TWENTY

At work the following day, I struggle to stop thinking about Erin. I've been around her enough times to know that her phone is rarely far from her hand, and I've never known her to have it switched off. Perhaps she's doing this to make me suffer – drawing out the uncertainty so that when she finally confronts me, I'll have been set up to break instantly. I need Marcus to go back to the Isle of Wight. My brain feels overwhelmed; I can only deal with one thing at a time. I need to speak to Erin before I tell Marcus about what happened.

'Penny for them.'

Maria's face appears around the door. When she comes into the office, she's carrying two mugs of coffee.

'You're showing your age with that phrase,' I tell her, watching as she kicks the door shut behind her. 'I doubt anyone under the age of forty knows what it means.'

'Deflection,' she replies, handing me a mug. 'You can't fob me off that easily.'

She pulls a seat over and sits opposite me at the desk, left eyebrow arched in a question mark.

'I'm fine,' I tell her.

'Hmm.' She sips her coffee, her bracelets jangling; her focus fixed on me through the steam that rises from the mug. 'You were AWOL during assembly this morning. I mean, not to anyone else, but I know you.'

I can't help but smile at that. Maria's right: she knows me better than anyone here. I should have known this morning that my detachment wouldn't go undetected by her; I was acutely aware of it myself, almost deaf to the recitals about climate change that were being delivered by a handful of class 8B students.

'Are you still worrying about the house?'

When she says 'the house', what she means is my mother's place. Like Marcus, Maria has made several offers to help me with clearing out, but I've declined each time. It just feels too personal. I used to think that as soon as it was sold I'd be able to move on, but I wonder now whether that will prove true. Bricks and mortar mean nothing. It's the pressure of everything else that's keeping my head below the surface.

'No. It'll obviously be a weight off my shoulders once it's gone, but I'm not dwelling on it. There are more important things to worry about.'

'And those things are...?'

Sex with a student's father. The end of a friendship. The death of my marriage.

'I wonder if I did the right thing with Jasper Healy.'

Maria's mouth twists into a corkscrew. 'He threw a chair at another student. That's bad enough, but the poor kid ended up needing his head glued. Jasper was lucky to get away with a suspension, if you ask me. The other kid's parents could have pressed charges.'

She sips her coffee. She's still watching me, and I know she doesn't believe that Jasper Healy is really the issue that's bothering me. I've had to suspend students on plenty of occasions, and I've never dwelled over a decision before.

'There must be a reason why he's behaving the way he is.'

I think of Iris, and how her death must have affected Jasper. Of course, I can't mention this to Maria when it was told to me in confidence.

'You sound as though you're defending him,' Maria says, unable to keep a note of criticism from her tone.

'Not at all. I just want to understand it.'

'He's just been pulled out of another school during the most important year of his education. It's no wonder he's struggling to settle. But he's old enough to know that lashing out at everyone else isn't the way to deal with it.'

We sit for a moment in silence. I feel claustrophobic beneath the pressure of the secret I'm carrying, all born of a single decision: one that now, with the wisdom of hindsight, seems to have been doomed from its inception at the coffee table that night I discussed it with Marcus. If I'd never passed on Erin's suggestion, I might never have met Kieran. And if I had met him at some point, it would have been under very different circumstances.

'Do you think there's bad in everyone?' I ask, the question slipping into the air before I have a chance to draw it back in like a lizard snaring a fly with its tongue.

She studies me for a moment, still wondering where this is really all coming from. 'To a degree, yes. I mean, no one's perfect, so there must be.' She reaches over to rest her coffee cup on my desk. 'What's all this about, Louise? It's not work, is it? Are you and Marcus okay?'

'Fine,' I say, a little too quickly. 'I was just thinking about this place, you know... the inspection. All the hard work everyone's put in to turn the school around. I don't want anything to mess it up for us.'

'And what could do that?'

I could, I think. I know I'm not myself at the moment. My

personal life is causing too many distractions at a time when I can't afford not to be at my professional best.

'Louise, if this is about Jasper, we can make sure he's not in any of the classes that get observed by the inspectors. There are plenty of ways to keep him out of the way if you think he's going to cause problems.'

I've seen it happen in other schools; I've known students to behave at their very worst in a deliberate attempt to sabotage reports when they know the teachers are under scrutiny. But I can't tell Maria that none of my concerns really relate to any of this.

'There's good in everyone too, though, isn't there?' I muse, trying to distract myself from my own brain.

Maria smiles at me, head tilted, gently mocking my naïvety. 'No, Louise, not necessarily. You think that way because you're a good person, but let's be honest, some of these kids are dickheads. I know,' she says, gauging my reaction, 'you think I'm the Mother Teresa of all teachers. I'm not supposed to say that, am I? You know, statistically, if you have a thirty-year teaching career, you'll at some point work with an average of two murderers and at least three paedophiles. That's a fact, it's not just me being cynical. So I think it's fair to say that in certain cases, there's no good to be found. It's a wasted effort looking for it.'

I think of Callum Benton, the anomaly who defied explanation. Perhaps Maria is right: some people are just rotten to the core. But I can't bring myself to believe it of Jasper, no matter what he's done. He's lashing out at someone, angry at the world. I wonder whether he holds someone responsible for his sister's death.

I wave a hand dismissively, shooing away my own train of thought. 'Ignore me. One of those days.'

Maria glances at her watch. 'Duty calls,' she says, realising that period five is due to start in ten minutes. She picks up her empty coffee cup. 'Listen to me,' she urges, in that way she has that always manages to get even the most disrespectful of teenagers to pay attention to her. 'What we've done here in terms of turning this school around is pretty phenomenal, even if I do say so myself, and much of that is due to you. It would take something catastrophic to undo all that good work, so there's one less thing you need to worry about.'

'Thank you.' I get up to follow her to the door, her words making me nauseous. I don't deserve her praise. I'm a fraud.

'Let's have a proper catch-up outside of school soon,' she suggests. 'Well,' she adds, with an eye-roll, 'as soon as football allows me a night off. The sooner James is off these evening shifts the better.' She stops and turns to me with a look of cynicism. 'When you're ready to tell me what's really going on, you know where I am.'

As soon as she's gone, I close the door behind her, shutting myself off from the rest of the school and the rest of the world. My head is throbbing so intensely it's affecting my vision, and I wonder whether I'll be safe to drive home in a couple of hours' time. I get my phone from my bag and type Kieran's name into the internet search engine, not wanting to do so on my office desktop. The results throw up countless matches, from a building firm in Newcastle to a poet in County Antrim. When I condense the search by adding our location, I find him halfway down a list of Facebook profiles, his photograph taken in a pub somewhere, face turned from the camera as he raises a pint.

His profile is set to private, so little else is available to me. A couple of old profile pictures, one of him with Erin. They look quite a bit younger; my guess is the photo must be at least six years old. Before their daughter died, I think. Before their life as they'd known it was so cruelly ripped from them. Erin smiles back at me from the screen, beautiful and oblivious. The guilt that tears through me is sudden and strong. Though I've known her only a brief time, she's been a good friend to me, supportive and understanding. I've repaid her kindness in the worst possible way.

I wish I'd never met Kieran. I wish I could undo the past few weeks; undo the conversation with Marcus that led us to this mess. If Erin had never joined that yoga class, none of this would have happened. I click back out to the search results and type in Erin's name, first using the surname Healy, then using Foster. I never asked her surname, and it occurs to me now that I never asked her why they moved to the area either. Now, knowing that Jasper is her son, I'm even more curious. Moving a child to a different school halfway through the academic year is a big upheaval, with grades likely to be affected. It must have been something big to make them do it, but I never asked because it felt intrusive to do so.

As the search results on Erin Foster are thrown up on my screen, the breath is sucked from my lungs and the words swim in front of me. I click on an article from a local newspaper, dated today. Its headline glares at me from the phone.

Local Woman Reported Missing

TWENTY-ONE

I don't recall a single detail of the journey home from work. I drive on autopilot, my mind consumed with thoughts of Erin and what might have happened to her. Kieran's strange behaviour at the school yesterday when he came to collect Jasper looks different now. He must have known by then that Erin was missing. Perhaps he had already reported it to the police. If Jasper knows his mother is missing, it would explain his behaviour. So why didn't Kieran mention anything to me?

It's nearly six o'clock by the time I get home. I could have finished earlier, but I chose to stay at school, delaying the inevitable. I'm going to have to tell Marcus about Erin. If he doesn't already know about her disappearance, it's only a matter of time before he sees or hears about it somewhere else. Bad news has a habit of travelling quickly.

He's in the living room when I get in. The television is on and he's sitting on the sofa with his laptop. He flips the lid shut when he sees me. 'Good day?' he asks.

'Fine.' I pull my coat off and dump it on the arm of the chair. 'I've got a headache. I'm going to go upstairs for a bit.'

'Can I get you anything?'

'No. Honestly, I'm fine, it's just been a busy day.'

I'm grateful when he doesn't make more of a fuss, but I'm only halfway up the stairs when he shouts my name, calling me back to the living room. When I go in, he's standing by the coffee table, his focus fixed on the television. Erin's face stares at me from the screen.

Marcus turns up the sound.

'The thirty-nine-year-old mother of one was last seen on Sunday,' the newsreader says.

I can't take my eyes off her photograph, her eyes silently accusing me.

Marcus turns to me. 'Did you know about this?'

I shake my head. The lie seems easier, because if I tell him now that I read about it earlier today while I was still at work, he's going to wonder what I was doing running internet searches on Erin in the first place. The lies are stacking up like blocks on a game of Jenga. When they finally tumble, the fallout is going to be catastrophic for us all.

He turns his attention back to the television.

'Anyone with information about Mrs Foster's whereabouts can contact police anonymously on the number shown below.'

'They must be presuming the worst,' he says quietly. 'They don't put out things like this for people who've just gone AWOL.'

I feel sick. None of this makes sense, and yet one explanation shouts louder than any other, forcing itself to be heard. Erin found out about Saturday night. She knows about Kieran and me. Perhaps she confronted him over it. She found those socks. They fought... he hurt her. He's tried to cover his tracks. Maybe this is why he never told me yesterday that she was missing. Why he was behaving so strangely in my office.

I go into the hallway, to the downstairs toilet, barely making it in time before the contents of my lunch make a reappearance. I feel the blood drain from my face as my stomach empties.

'Lou,' Marcus says, at the other side of the door. 'Are you okay?'

I clench my teeth. I don't want to have to say the words 'I'm fine' yet again, when that's the only answer I seem capable of offering. I flush the toilet and splash cold water over my face. When I open the door, Marcus is standing in the kitchen doorway waiting for me.

'Have you picked something up at work?'

'I suspended their son from school yesterday.'

His face creases with confusion. 'Whose son?'

'Erin's. Kieran's.'

'They've got a son at your school?'

'It was news to me as well. He only started a month or so back. He's been causing trouble ever since he arrived.'

I think of Jasper walking beside me from the science block to my office yesterday morning, refusing to say a word when I spoke to him. The frustration I felt towards him now seems unfair. I've no idea what this kid has been going through for the past couple of days. He must be worried sick about his mother.

A headache begins to pound at my temples, brought on by the sickness and the shock. I follow Marcus into the kitchen. He gets me a glass of water and hands it to me.

'You can't feel bad for suspending the kid. You didn't know anything about Erin, did you?'

'Of course not.'

I sit at the kitchen table, barely able to make eye contact with him. I've felt guilt before, after my mother's death, eating at me from the inside out, yet somehow this manages to feel different. Worse. Ending her life was her choice, regardless of how much I wished I could have changed her decision. But it's different for Marcus. He's oblivious to everything.

'You should eat something,' he says. 'You've gone white as a sheet.'

He takes a slice of bread from its bag and pushes it into the toaster. 'What did he do?' he asks, his back to me as he waits for the toast to pop.

'Who?'

'Their son. Why did you suspend him?'

'He threw a chair at someone. The other boy had to be taken to hospital to have his head glued.'

Marcus goes to the fridge to get the butter. 'But he didn't say anything to you about his mother?'

'He doesn't talk to me. He doesn't seem to talk to anyone unless it involves swearing at them.'

'Did you see Kieran then? At the school?'

I taste bile in my mouth, thick and cloying on my tongue. Every time his name is mentioned, visions of his skin on mine pop into my head in a quick-fire succession of intrusive thoughts. Now I realise I have no idea who this man is. I have no idea what he might be capable of.

'Yeah,' I say, feeling heat rise in my chest. 'He came to collect him.'

The toaster pops. I watch Marcus buttering the slice of toast, and this simple domestic act alone threatens to reduce me to tears. I took this life for granted. I took us for granted. Were things really that bad between us? Wasn't it just a lull in our marriage that would have passed on its own, without intervention? Without me fucking everything up? What is wrong with me? In searching for a route back to what Marcus and I once had, I unlocked a door that would lead me away from all of this: this life we created where we had everything we could ever have wanted.

'Christ,' Marcus mutters. 'Poor bloke. He must be worried sick.'

Or worried he's going to be found out, I think. It said on the news that she'd been missing since Sunday, but perhaps that was only what Kieran had told them. Maybe something happened between them on Saturday night.

Or maybe Erin is doing this to make him suffer. Maybe she found evidence that I had been to their house, they argued and then she left. It may truly be the case that Kieran is genuinely concerned about her whereabouts. But this scenario seems unlikely when there's Jasper to consider. No mother would leave her son to think she could be dead, and Erin would never allow a police hunt to go ahead just to spite Kieran for doing something they do regularly. I'm clutching at the most desperate of straws by trying to convince myself she's fine.

I should tell Marcus about what happened between Kieran and me. Even though it will cause chaos, I should do it now, get it out in the open. I should be honest and just accept the consequences, no matter how terrible they might be. This is my mess. And now, inadvertently, I may have put Erin's life in danger.

'There's something I need to tell you.'

He hands me the toast on a plate and looks at me expectantly. When I say nothing more, he raises an eyebrow, waiting for what comes next.

I went to Erin's house on Saturday night. I had sex with Kieran.

'What is it? Louise... are you okay?'

However I word it, the result is the same. The truth of it remains irreversible, and his response to it won't be altered no matter how much I try to sugar-coat it. Some things can't be varnished to make them shinier. And if Kieran has already done something to Erin, a confession from me won't change what's happened.

'Louise. You're worrying me now.'

I realise I can't do it. I'm a coward. I can't face the repercussions of a confession. I don't want to lose him.

'Maria and I have been talking about maybe going away for a weekend somewhere. You know, just a girls' trip – spa, a few drinks, that sort of thing.'

'Sounds a brilliant idea. You could do with the break. When are you going?'

'Nothing's been agreed yet. We just talked about the possibility, that's all.'

'Well, make sure it happens. Get some dates down.'

'Obviously not now, though. Not until...'

I'm not even sure how I intended to finish the sentence. Until Erin's found? Until her body's been recovered from the ditch she may currently be lying in?

My face burns with fear. What the hell did Kieran do to her?

'The police are going to ask questions,' I say.

'About what?'

'That night at the hotel. You and me... Kieran and Erin.'

Marcus pulls a face. 'How would they even find out about that? It's irrelevant anyway. Is this what's making you unwell? You've got nothing to worry about.'

'You don't know that. They'll look into everything. Shit... it's all such a mess.'

Marcus sits at the table and looks at the plate of toast. 'Eat something, please.' He waits for me to take a bite. The toast tastes like cardboard, sticking to the roof of my mouth. 'Whatever's happened to Erin, wherever she is, it isn't your fault, Lou.'

'You need to go back to the Isle of Wight.'

'Oh yeah, just leave you while you're in this state?'

'You should be there. You've planned for months to be there. If we behave differently, we'll look guilty. The police are going to come here at some point.'

'All the more reason for me to stay.'

'No,' I argue. 'It's the exact opposite. If you're here when you should be away, we look suspicious. We need to behave normally. We need to be doing exactly what we would have been doing anyway.'

I barely recognise myself as I talk. I sound as guilty as I am, a desperate woman trying to cover the tracks of the chaos she's left.

'I still don't understand why you think the police would be interested in us.'

I close my eyes, put my head in my hands. The headache that started earlier has swelled into a migraine, pulsing at my temples with an intensity that's making me feel sick again. What the hell has happened to Erin?

'No one can find out about that night,' I tell him, putting a hand on his knee. 'Please, Marcus. They might think we're involved in her disappearance. We could lose everything.'

I hate the sound of my own voice. The sound of my own words. I sound self-absorbed, consumed only by the impact this might have on my own life. I should tell the police about me and Kieran, because then they might start looking closer to home. But surely that's where they'll look anyway? They always investigate the husband first.

'No one's going to find out,' Marcus tells me again, but hearing it repeated fails to make me any more convinced.

'Erin's missing. The police will look into absolutely everything. It'll come out if we're not careful, I know it will. Please... go back to work. For me. For us.'

The hypocrisy of the request almost chokes me. I know I have no right to be sitting here asking him to behave normally to save my skin. I no longer have the right to touch him as though everything between us is as it's always been.

'Please,' I say again. 'Go back tomorrow.'

The truth is, he's better off away from here. *I'm* better off with him away from here, at least until I can sort out the mess I've made of everything. If he finds out about Kieran, he'll confront him, could end up getting into trouble with the police. I've seen what he's capable of through his interactions with Cameron, so God only knows what he'd do to Kieran. I wish we'd thought harder about what an open marriage might do to us. How naïve it was of me to believe that no one would get hurt. How stupid I was to fool myself we could do what we did without consequence.

'If it's what you want, I'll go.'

'Thank you.'

'You should go and lie down,' he says. 'You really don't look well.'

When I go into the living room, the first thing I do is check my phone. A part of me still hopes to find a message from Erin: *All fine here – sorry, lost my charger!* If only. I think of the photograph they used for the television report of her disappearance, her beautiful face smiling back at me. There are no messages from her. No missed phone calls. When I go to her WhatsApp, it says she was last online on Saturday evening, before I saw her outside her house.

There are five emails waiting for me: three junk, one from someone at the council, the fifth from an account I don't recognise. Its name alone is enough to send a shiver down my spine: *iknowyourlittlesecret@gmail.com*. The subject line has been left blank. I open the message.

> Louise, you have until Saturday to transfer £500,000 to the account below. If the money hasn't been sent by 6 p.m., the attached video will be put online on Saturday night.

There's no sign-off – nothing to offer a clue as to who might have sent the email. There's just the attachment. I don't want to open it, but the threat of it being put online can only mean it's something embarrassing or incriminating, something I wouldn't want anyone else to see, and although I can't think what the footage might show, I know I can't just delete the email and ignore it.

'Do you want a cup of tea?' Marcus calls through from the kitchen.

'No. No thanks.'

With my breath held and fingers shaking, I open the attachment and press play on the clip. At first the image is blurred, the outlines of the moving figures distorted by what appears to be a low-quality recording. Then, regrettably, the video comes into focus. The room is instantly recognisable. Two people move into view of the camera as they stumble towards the bed, and as the footage unfolds, I watch in horror, already knowing how the scene plays out. The email's threat repeats now, a klaxon in my head. The thought of someone else viewing this sends bile rising to the back of my throat. I watch in disbelief, though I know it all to be real; muted by inertia as I am forced to relive those moments: Kieran and me having sex in his and Erin's bed.

TWENTY-TWO

I wake from a dream where I'm running from someone, the kind of dream where you can't gain any ground no matter how fast you move or how hard your heart hammers in your chest. I tripped and stumbled; I was just about to fall, but as with every fall in every dream, I never hit the ground. My heart still pounds. I can still hear my own breathing, ragged and uneven as though I'm still running.

'Louise.'

In the darkness, Marcus's hand finds mine. He's being too nice to me, more attentive than he's been in ages. It feels ill-timed and undeserved.

'It's just a dream. It's okay.'

His thumb rubs my knuckles. I feel my skin grow colder at the thought that I must have said something in my sleep, because how else would he know that I was dreaming?

I turn and reach for my phone on the bedside table, bringing the screen to life to see the time: 04.15. Shit. I always wake early, but never this early, and I know I'll pay for it by this afternoon when I'm made impatient by exhaustion.

'What were you dreaming about?' Marcus asks.

'I don't remember.'

'You mumbled something about a video.'

'Did I? God knows.'

Shit, shit, shit. I can't even trust myself when I'm asleep. I might have said anything, but I wouldn't remember it. I get out of bed, grateful that it's still too dark for Marcus to see me. He asks what the time is. He's never usually awake this early, and when he rolls back over, I take it as a sign that he's already forgotten about the video comment. I know him well enough to know he doesn't overanalyse things in the way I'm prone to.

I walk into the en suite, wondering how I'm going to manage to push through the day ahead. Whenever there have been things going on in my private life, school has always provided a welcome distraction. I've immersed myself in my work to avoid drowning myself in thought. Now, I'm not sure it's going to offer the same escape. I've never had personal problems that have reached this scale before. It feels as though I barely slept, my mind too active to seek any proper rest. Erin is missing. Kieran is responsible. That camera was set up in his bedroom. And now he's trying to blackmail me with footage that could end my marriage and my career.

I've no idea how Kieran would know about the inheritance money I've got stashed away, though I suppose it wouldn't be too difficult for him to have found out. My family's history is all over the internet, available to anyone who might choose to search our name. The fact that a substantial amount of the money my father stole was never given back is also common knowledge, and it's logical that it would have been passed down after my parents' deaths.

I step into the shower with a thumping headache, the kind I used to wake with regularly in my early twenties, morning after morning. It feels as though I drank two bottles of wine last night, and I wonder how I used to do it over and over again, relentlessly abusing my body in my pursuit of escape. It was a wonder I managed to finish my degree – and complete it with a good result – but I worked as hard as I partied, study and alcohol the means through which I tried to forget what I'd moved away from.

And then I found myself back here, just a town away from the place where I'd grown up. I rebuilt bridges with my mother. An English teaching post came up in another local school, at a time when permanent positions were difficult to come by. It was too good an opportunity to let pass by, so I swallowed my pride and moved back to the area, determined to prove that the legacy my father had left need not shape my future. I met Marcus. We built the kind of life I'd always dreamed of.

After washing my hair, I stay in the shower for longer than necessary, with the water turned too hot. My mind races with all the things I can't put into order or make sense of. I can't confront Kieran; he's too dangerous. The only way I might be able to do so is if I meet with him again at the school, but with Jasper already suspended, there's no reason for either of them to be there, and anyway, I can't risk a conversation that might expose my secret on school grounds. How can I look him in the eye and ask him why he's doing this to me when there's every chance that he's done something to hurt his own wife?

The inheritance left by my mother means I have the money. That's not the issue. But demands don't stop when someone gets what they asked for. I've no way of guaranteeing that if I part with the money, he won't just ask for more.

By the time I get out of the shower, Marcus is up and in the main bathroom. I go downstairs and put coffee on, then take two paracetamols. He comes down a while later and I make us breakfast, and we sit at the kitchen table together like any other couple on any ordinary morning. Except everything is as far from ordinary as it could possibly be, and the weirdness of it all sits between us like an uninvited guest.

'I don't need to go back,' Marcus says, pushing a lump of scrambled egg around his plate.

'You do. Everything needs to be normal.'

I hate myself for the way I sound. I've been trying to convince myself that Erin's disappearance is voluntary, and that she's doing this to spite Kieran, to make him suffer for his infidelity. For a short while, I've managed to distract myself with the thought, allowing it to cement itself in my mind as fact. But the truth is, Erin is likely in danger. Worse, it may already be too late. I picture her broken body lying somewhere, dumped from the car by Kieran after an argument about our one-night stand. The coffee in my mouth suddenly tastes like blood, tangy and metallic.

'I'm just a phone call away,' Marcus says. 'If you need me to come home, I can.'

I nod but say nothing. Every time I open my mouth now, I'm scared the truth will slip from my lips. He deserves the truth, and yet I know how bad it will now make me look. For all I know, Marcus might start to suspect that I've had some involvement in whatever's happened to Erin.

He pushes back his chair and comes over to me, crouching beside me. 'We're going to be okay,' he tells me, one hand on my knee. 'Everything is going to be okay.'

'And Erin?'

He looks as though he's going to say something, but then changes his mind. There's nothing he *can* say. He knows as well as I do that with every day that passes, the likelihood of her being found safe and well diminishes tenfold.

'This isn't your fault.'

My skin turns cold.

'You manage to find a way to blame yourself for everything. Wherever Erin is, you couldn't have changed the outcome.'

I feel my heart settle back in my chest, aware of how selfish it makes me. For a moment, I thought Marcus knew. 'You should get going,' I tell him, glancing at the clock. 'You don't want to miss the ferry.'

He lingers, reluctant to leave me while things are so unsettled, but eventually goes upstairs to fetch the suitcase he packed last night. It barely needed doing, still near-full with the things he'd brought home with him on Monday.

I wait for him to go, and then I leave for work. I manage to avoid people for most of the morning, dealing with emails in my office and postponing a meeting with one of the governors about a fund-raising event, asking the secretary to reschedule for after half-term. The morning is consumed with thoughts of Kieran and Erin and the email. I want to confront him about it, but I know I can't. It's too dangerous.

But I could go to see Jasper. He lives in the same house; he was there on Saturday night. He must know something.

I tell the secretary I've got a meeting at the council offices over in the next town and that I'll be back by the end of lunch break. My hands are shaking as I start my car, and the closer I get to Erin and Kieran's house, the wilder this decision seems. But I can't sit around and do nothing.

Kieran's car isn't on the driveway. I assume at first he must be at work, but surely any workplace would offer time off to someone whose spouse has been reported missing. Wherever he is, I know I don't have much time. I park the car in the side street where I parked on Saturday night, and when I go to the house, I bypass the front door, instead heading for the door at the side. Jasper is in the kitchen; I see movement through the gaps in the venetian blinds as he moves about, preparing lunch for himself.

When I knock on the door, I see him stop, but he doesn't come to answer it. I go to the window, and when he sees me, his face creases into a look of confusion.

'Two minutes,' I say. 'I just want to check you're okay.'

He moves quickly to the window and closes the blinds, blocking me from sight.

I knock again, knowing he won't come to the door. 'Please, Jasper. I just want to make sure everything's all right. Everyone's worried about you at school. We're here for you – I just want you to know that.'

Whatever Jasper might be, he's not an idiot. He knows that head teachers turning up at the homes of suspended students isn't standard practice, even in circumstances where a parent has been reported missing.

I stand at the door, not really knowing what I'm waiting for. He's never been prepared to talk to me before, and it seems a certainty that he's not going to now. I've already made too much noise out here, possibly drawing attention from neighbours. I shouldn't be here; I need to go. Yet I can't shake the feeling that Jasper must know something. He would have heard an argument. He might have seen a fight.

I just hope for his sake that he wasn't exposed to whatever Kieran has done to his mother.

TWENTY-THREE

By the time I get home from school on Wednesday afternoon, I have a message from Marcus.

Everything okay back home? I still feel guilty for leaving you x

I keep my response brief.

Everything fine. Nothing to feel guilty about. Keeping busy x

My brain works feverishly all the time now. I can't stop thinking that at some point, if the police find out about Kieran and me, or about the night Marcus and I shared with Kieran and Erin at the hotel, they will check our phone records. Every text exchange Marcus and I have had will be scrutinised for evidence of wrongdoing. So why would Marcus feel guilty about leaving me? And why am I already obsessing about alternative reasons to explain our exchange?

I go upstairs and get changed out of my work clothes,

straight into my comfiest pair of pyjamas. I go back downstairs for my laptop before getting into bed, pulling the duvet up over my knees. Once the laptop has come to life, I search for the television appeal that was aired on Tuesday evening. I watch again as the newsreader gives details about Erin's disappearance, the camera panning along a table where Kieran and Jasper are sitting alongside a female detective whose name is shown at the bottom of the screen as Detective Inspector Gemma Clarke.

'We are growing increasingly concerned for the whereabouts and safety of Erin Foster,' she begins, the waiting press falling silent as she speaks. 'Erin was last seen on Sunday morning by her husband after she left their home to go shopping. She was due to get on the nine forty-five a.m. train from Pelton to Bristol, but she never made it to the station. This is the last known sighting of Mrs Foster.'

The camera pans to the screen beside the table. Kieran doesn't turn his head, but keeps staring out at the audience, his eyes seeming to look nowhere. Next to him, Jasper has his head lowered, as it remained throughout the detective's speech. CCTV footage is played. It shows a street corner, a small café to the left, a bridge crossing a river to the right. I recognise the area, just a couple of miles from my mother's house. Erin comes into view, carrying a handbag on her shoulder. She waits by the kerbside for a gap in the traffic before crossing the road and heading across the bridge, disappearing from sight in the direction of the train station.

'This footage was recorded at nine thirty-two on Sunday morning,' DI Clarke continues. 'This bridge leads to parkland and the canal path, which is used by locals as a shortcut to the station. An eyewitness reports seeing Erin on the canal path at around nine thirty-five, so it's our belief that she did intend to go to the station as planned. With no further CCTV sightings of her at the other end of the high street, we can reach two conclusions. One is that Mrs Foster fell into the canal at some point between the bridge beneath Ealing Road and where the path leads into Crosshill Park. The second theory is that before reaching the top of Westbury Street, where the canal path comes to an end, she got into a car with someone.'

She was taken, I think – that's what this woman is really trying to say. There's a possibility that someone took her. My focus rests on Jasper. Putting him through this – making him sit there and listen to the theories that his mother has either drowned or been abducted – seems an unnecessary torture to inflict upon the boy. He may be wayward and disruptive, but in so many ways, he's still just a child. No one could imagine the thoughts that must be running though his mind in these moments.

'Divers have spent the day searching the canal,' she continues, 'but nothing has been recovered.'

At his father's side, Jasper flinches. It's so painful to watch that I want to turn the recording off, but I can't bring myself to do so. I need to see this through to the end. I need to see evidence that Kieran is somehow involved in whatever's happened to Erin.

'We are appealing for any witnesses who may have been on or near the canal path that day and may have seen Erin at some point that morning. Her husband, Kieran, and her son, Jasper, are deeply worried about her safety and are desperate for her to come home. Please,' the detective says, addressing her plea to the camera, 'if anyone knows anything about the whereabouts of Mrs Foster, you can contact us anonymously on the number shown below.' She glances to her left. 'Erin's husband would now like to say a few words.'

The camera pans in on Kieran, focusing on his tired face. He looks exhausted. I want to believe it to be true. I want to believe that the camera never lies and that the tension in his jaw and the shadows beneath his eyes are the result of panic, fear, grief... but I just can't. I keep thinking back to that email, knowing I should tell the police about it. If I tell them, they'll know exactly what kind of man Kieran is. What he's capable of. But in doing so I'll expose myself, and it will cost me far more than the money he's demanding.

He looks at the desk in front of him, at the prepared script from which he's about to read. Beneath the harsh lighting of the room where they're being recorded, the sweat across his brow is visible.

'Erin,' he begins, looking directly into the camera now, 'Jasper and I haven't stopped worrying about you since you didn't come home.' He pauses. His voice is already breaking. He appears on the verge of tears. 'We want you to know that we love and miss you, and that we need you back home with us safe and sound.' His words catch in his throat. When he returns his focus to the camera, he seems to look through it, communicating silently only with Erin, no one else in the room. He opens his mouth to say something more, but the words are strangled and evaporate before they're able to be heard.

He was going to say sorry, I think. He seemed to be on the brink of an apology. But was he apologising for Saturday night, or for something else? Something that may have happened since?

'Please,' he continues, 'if anyone has any information about Erin's whereabouts, please, please contact the police, no matter how small or insignificant you might think the information you have is.'

He sinks back in his seat, deflated. I pause the footage.

Is it possible that Erin might have gone with someone she knew? Gone willingly, without realising the danger she was stepping into? I imagine Kieran pulling up at the roadside where the canal path slopes back up towards the town, greeting her with a wave as she opened the car door. He might have surprised her, and why would she see anything suspicious in her own husband arriving to offer her a lift? She would have been happy to see him. Blissfully ignorant of the fact that little more than twelve hours earlier he'd been fucking me in their bedroom, in their home.

Either that or she wasn't ignorant. She knew. But had Kieran pulled up beside her and she'd not wanted to go with him, I know Erin well enough to know she would have screamed blue murder before getting in that car with him. Someone passing nearby would have been alerted to the fact that something was wrong.

I rarely use Twitter, or X as it's now named, though I have an old account I've never deactivated. I log in now, searching for hashtags using Erin's name. It doesn't take long to find people tweeting about the appeal. From behind their phone screens, it seems so many people are willing to say things they'd never dream of coming out with in real life.

That detective's lying. Been at the canal today – no divers down there #FindErin

Hate to say it, but I reckon she's been taken. That police-woman knows it as well #FindErin

Poor kid, being made to sit thru that. Surprised the police did that to him #FindErin

It's always the husband. First place they'll be looking. They know she didn't fall in that canal #FindErin

That husband looks guilty as fuck #FindErin

And so they continue. Speculation, accusation, trial by tweets. But I can't help thinking about that last comment. About how Kieran did look guilty. The sheen of sweat on his forehead. The look of panic in his eyes. I think back to his strangeness when he came to the school on Monday, when he could have just told me then that Erin was missing. I might have been able to help him. I might have been able to help Jasper.

I think of every case in which a partner or a parent has been caught out as the guilty party after filming a police appeal: the watering eyes, the stammered words, the faux-concern carefully delivered for the watching public. People who thought they could get away with it. Individuals brazen enough to flirt with the danger of exposing themselves, their narcissism stoked by the adrenaline rush of the attention offered to them in their apparent darkest hour.

Is this who Kieran really is? And does Jasper know it? I look at Jasper's stilled face on the screen on my laptop, wondering whether his silence is born out of fear of his father.

TWENTY-FOUR

I'm heading from the science block back to the main reception building when I see the police car in the car park. I can see there's no one inside it, which can only mean they're already over at reception, and I know they're waiting there for me. I straighten myself, adjusting my hair and taking a few deep breaths to calm my nerves.

When I go in through the main doors, two officers are sitting by the reception desk. They're both wearing plain clothes. I don't need the female officer to introduce herself: I already know who she is from the television appeal.

'Mrs Anderson? I'm Detective Inspector Gemma Clarke,' she says, flashing me her identification. 'This is DC Palmer. We'd like to talk to you about Erin Foster.'

'Of course,' I say, trying to sound as casual as possible. 'Come on through to my office.'

They follow me in and I close the door behind us.

'You're probably already aware that Mrs Foster has been reported missing?'

'I saw the TV appeal.'

'Her son attends this school, is that correct?'

'Jasper,' I say, feeling a lump of anxiety knot in my throat. 'He hasn't been here very long... just a couple of months.'

'Do you know Mrs Foster outside of a school context?'

Panic rises, constricting my airway. Her focus lingers on me for a little too long, and I feel my face flush though I've not yet said anything. I can't lie. Other people from the yoga class will have seen us together. There'll have been CCTV at the coffee shop and bar where we met up.

'Yes. We met when she started at the yoga class I attend in the leisure centre. We went for a drink together on a couple of occasions.'

'So would you describe her as a friend?'

The question feels leading. 'No. Yes. I mean, we don't know each very well. As I said, we just met for a drink a couple of times.'

Though I'm not explicitly lying, I'm not telling the full truth either, which I've always felt more or less amounts to the same. I've always been a useless liar. It was never something I aspired to be good at, although recent weeks would suggest a latent desire for the opposite.

'How long have been head teacher here, Mrs Anderson?'

'Five years.'

'And have you established good working relationships with your colleagues during that time, would you say?'

'Yes. Yes, I would. The school's improved results across the board are evidence of that, I think. But I don't see how any of this is relevant to Mrs Foster.'

The detective moves to the side of my desk and peers behind it, as though expecting to find Erin trussed up beneath my chair. She smiles when her eyes meet mine, and her focus is unsettling.

'So you've never had any other meetings with Mrs Foster

outside of your workplace?' she reiterates. 'Other than the yoga class and the two occasions on which you met up for a drink?'

'That's right,' I say, knowing that this time I've lied and there's no going back from that without an acknowledgement of the fact. 'I've never actually had any dealings with Mrs Foster relating to school. Jasper was suspended for a week, as I'm sure you'll already be aware, but it was his father who came here for a meeting with me about that.'

'Kieran Foster,' the male officer says, running a hand across his stubbled jawline. 'Jasper's stepfather.'

'Yes. He came to the school on Monday.'

DI Clarke eyes me steadily. I know what she's doing: watching me for any telltale signs that Kieran might be known to me as more than just the parent of a student here. Waiting to see if I lie about it in the same way I've just lied about Erin.

'And what about Mr Foster?' she eventually asks. 'Have you had any involvement with him outside of your workplace?'

'No,' I say resolutely, managing to shock myself with how apparently adept at lying I've become in such a short space of time. They know. They know about that night at the hotel.

DI Clarke's lips purse and she exhales as though blowing invisible cigarette smoke from her mouth. 'Interesting,' she says, in a voice that manages to sound anything but interested. 'You see, we've had a report that you were seen leaving the Fosters' house on Saturday evening.'

My chest swells, and blood pounds in my ears. Jasper. It could only have been Jasper. 'I don't know where the family lives.'

She studies me with an intensity that feels suffocating, while I sit here almost choking on the lie. I was there just yesterday, banging on the side door as I tried to get Jasper to speak to me. I understand now how innocent people come to make confessions for crimes they didn't commit, worn down by the pressure of the scrutiny. Although in this case, I'm not entirely innocent.

'The person who made the claim was adamant the female leaving Mr Foster's house was you.'

'Who is this person?'

'I'm afraid I'm not at liberty to disclose that information.' She smiles, but the expression is joyless. She's setting me up for a fall, hoping I'll trip myself up somewhere on my own lies.

'Why was Jasper suspended?' DC Palmer asks.

'Unfortunately, there was an incident with another student. We had no idea when Mr Foster came here on Monday to pick him up that his mother had been reported missing. It would certainly have explained Jasper's anger.'

'What sort of incident?'

'He threw a chair at another student. The matter's been dealt with.'

I see the glance that passes between the two officers, and this is all it takes for me to realise what I've done. Jasper has a history of angry outbursts. He's tall for his age, physically strong. They can't seriously be considering that he might be involved in some way in his mother's disappearance? Their focus is surely on Kieran. Nine times out of ten, it's the husband.

DI Clarke takes a deep breath, and just when I think she's about to hit me with some new revelation, she instead tells me that'll be all for now.

'If there's anything else you happen to think of,' she says, 'please let us know. We'll be in touch.'

I see them back out to reception and wait at the doors as they head towards the car park. The detective's words ring like an echo as I go back into my office, trying to ignore the attention the secretary gives me as I pass. *We'll be in touch.* She didn't believe me when I told her I've never had any involvement with

Kieran. In fact, her whole demeanour suggested she already knows more and was waiting for me to admit to something. If they haven't yet done so, it's only a matter of time before they search Erin's text history. After that, everything will begin to unravel.

TWENTY-FIVE

When I get home, the first thing I do before even taking off my coat is go to the fridge and take out a bottle of wine. A large glass disappears in record speed, numbing some of the sting from the day. That detective thinks I'm involved in Erin's disappearance. She knows I'm lying about my relationship with Kieran. The next time they question me, the truth is going to come out, one way or another.

I pour a second glass and take it into the garden, where I sit on one of the patio chairs. It's mild for February, climate change seemingly delivering exactly what was promised. I wonder where Erin is. I try not to think in too much detail about what might have happened after she was taken from that canal path – if that's even what happened. Surely if she was dead, her body would have been discovered by now. But not necessarily, I tell myself. Human remains are sometimes concealed for years – decades even. I shudder at the thought. I think of our night out just a couple of weeks ago, picturing Erin in that red dress she wore. She was so beautiful. So full of life and fun. If only we'd known what was just around the corner, we might have somehow been able to alter fate.

I hear my phone ringing from inside the house, breaking me from my thoughts. I ignore it, but when it starts to ring again after just a few minutes, I go in to see who it is. Maria's name flashes up from the screen. I wonder if she knows the police came to the school today. Someone would have seen them, and it never takes long for a rumour to circulate. A part of me considers letting it ring through to the answerphone again, but she's already called twice, which she never usually does. Whatever she wants to say, it'll only be brought up tomorrow, so I might as well deal with it now rather than risk it being aired among our colleagues.

'Are you home?' she asks brusquely.

'Yes. Is everything okay?'

'Can I come over?'

'Of course. I mean... what's this about? You're sure everything's okay?'

'Probably better we talk about it in person.'

She ends the call abruptly. I'd known there was something going on even before the police arrived this afternoon. Maria behaved strangely towards me at school today, barely making eye contact when we saw each other in the assembly hall and then again at lunchtime. I wondered whether I was being paranoid in light of everything else that's going on, but she's never avoided me like that before, and I know I didn't imagine it.

Half an hour after she calls, I hear her car pull up on the driveway in the space that Marcus's Audi has left. I get to the front door moments after she presses the bell, and when she steps into the hallway, she can hardly bring herself to look at me.

'What have I done?' I ask as soon as the front door is closed.

She reaches into her pocket for her mobile, taps in a passcode and swipes a few times in search of something. When she passes it to me, I feel my heart drop into my stomach.

'Tell me I'm seeing this wrong,' she says. 'Please.'

I know what she's going to show me before the phone reaches my hand. I don't need to look, but I see it all again anyway. So this is his plan: increase the pressure bit by bit until I give in to his demand for the money.

'I obviously know who he is,' Maria says, taking the phone back from me. 'His face has been all over the news.'

'Who sent you this?' I ask.

'I don't know. But judging by your reaction, I'm guessing you've seen it before.'

I can't say anything. There's no way of explaining this, not in any way that makes it acceptable. She follows me down the hallway to the kitchen.

'I'm assuming Marcus doesn't know about it?'

'No. But he knows Kieran. He knows Erin as well. It's... complicated.'

'More complicated than this?' she says, gesturing to the phone still in her hand. 'How's that possible?'

'Shall I put the kettle on?'

'It's that long a story, is it?' She sighs. 'I don't want tea, Louise. I just want to know what the hell is going on.' She throws me a death stare. In all the years of knowing her, I can't remember her ever looking at me in this way. I don't blame her for the reaction. She's a married mother. A decent person. She thought I was the same. God knows what she must think of me now.

'Is this why you were so weird about suspending Jasper?'

'What? No. Of course not.'

'How could you do this to Marcus?'

I sit at the table. 'I don't know. We've been having problems. I've been trying to sort them out.'

'By having sex with someone else? Sounds a good idea.'

'Well... funny you should say that.'

She frowns.

'Take a seat. I'll explain everything.'

And so I do, from meeting Erin at the yoga class to the four of us ending up together at the hotel. I tell her about Cameron and the break-in, about calling Erin and ending up over at their house. Unburdening myself of it all feels strangely cathartic, yet the relief is crushed by Maria's expected response.

'And now Erin is missing,' she says, exhaling loudly when I've finished. 'Jesus, Louise, this is a mess. What the hell were you and Marcus thinking?'

'I don't know. I mean, we weren't, clearly. Not properly. It seemed a good idea at the time.'

She pulls a face, the very thought of it foreign to her. 'Have you got feelings for him then? For Kieran?'

'Of course not.'

But the way she's looking at me says she doesn't believe me. I don't even believe myself. That instant connection I felt with Kieran was something I've not experienced since meeting Marcus. It was something more than just physical, and it's this that's made the guilt so much heavier.

'You're a useless liar.'

'Apparently not, it seems.'

Maria pushes her unruly hair from her face. 'The break-in was on Saturday, you said. Was that why you tried calling me?'

I nod. 'And then I tried Erin's phone. And Kieran answered.'

She sighs loudly. 'Do you know where Erin is?'

'No.' The suggestion smarts. 'God, Maria, what are you trying to say?'

'I'm not trying to say anything. You know me well enough by now: if I want to say something, I just say it.'

I rest my elbows on the table and put my head in my hands. 'The first I knew about Erin being missing was when I saw the TV appeal,' I tell her, using the same white lie I offered Marcus, not wanting her to know that I ran an internet search on Erin's name as soon as Maria left my office that day. Things look weird enough as they are already.

'Do you think she knows about you and Kieran?' Maria suggests, echoing my suspicions. 'What if she found out somehow? She might have seen this footage.' She brandishes her phone in front of me like a flick knife. 'He must have set the camera up before you got there. Unless...' Her face changes, morphing into an expression of disgust. 'You didn't know it was being filmed, did you?'

'Jesus, Maria, of course I didn't.'

She presses her fingers to her forehead, exasperated by my stupidity. 'You don't know anything about this man, Louise. He could be dangerous. Erin's disappearance...'

'Anything you can think of, I've already thought of it.'

We sit in silence for a while.

'I wish I could understand why you did it,' she says eventually. 'But I don't. This just isn't like you at all.'

She's right. It *isn't* like me, or at least it wasn't until recently. I've just no idea how to explain any of it without alienating her further. Maria is my closest friend. There's already so much I risk losing; I don't want to lose her too. Just a month ago, everything looked so simple. If I could go back in time and warn myself of the mess a few hours would lead to, I would scream at myself with all the breath in my lungs, imploring myself not to be such an idiot. If only.

'None of this was meant to happen.'

'No shit.'

Maria stands and walks to the window, looking past the sink and out into the garden. 'Do you think Kieran's done something to hurt Erin?'

'I didn't want to think so, but it's the only thing that makes sense. The police will find out soon enough. They always look to the husband first.'

'Have you spoken to them about any of this?'

'And risk losing everything? If I tell Marcus, I lose my marriage. If anyone else gets hold of that video of me and Kieran, I'll lose my job. No other school will touch me. I love teaching, you know that. It's the only thing I've ever managed to get right.'

'You'll excuse me if I don't react to the self-pity,' she says, her tone scathing. For the moment, she hates me, and I don't blame her. She's a good person. She's been married for almost two decades now, to a man she met at university. They have two teenage sons who have grown into hard-working, well-mannered young men. Maria's moral fibre is made of strong stuff.

'What do I do?' I ask her. 'Everything's such a mess.'

'I don't know,' she admits. 'But I don't want to be dragged into any of it. Jesus, Lou – if anyone finds out I had this footage and did nothing with it, that I didn't tell anyone, I could lose my job as well. It's not just you this affects any more.'

'I'm sorry. I am so, so sorry. I never meant for you to be involved.' I pause. 'He's trying to blackmail me for five hundred grand.'

She turns to me, her mouth open. 'What the *fuck*? And Marcus knows nothing about this?'

'We have separate bank accounts,' I tell her, wondering whether half a million would be enough for Kieran, and he'd leave me alone if he got it. 'There's no need for him to know anything.'

She laughs bitterly. 'You still think you're going to be able to hide this from him? Best of luck with that. You need to come clean. You might not have much choice – if I've been sent a copy of that video, how long do you reckon it'll be before it lands in Marcus's inbox? Tell him. It'll be better coming from you, trust me. Things might be horrendous for a while, but your marriage can be fixed. The same won't apply to your career. Save one of them while you've still got a chance. Christ, Lou, if this guy's capable of blackmailing you, it's not exactly hard to imagine he's also capable of hurting his wife. You need to be careful.' She looks at her watch. 'I've got to go – I've got to pick Freddie up from football practice.'

I stand up quickly and reach for her arm, but she pulls away from the physical contact. I feel her rejection like a burn.

'Please, Maria. Please don't mention any of this to anyone. I just need a bit of time, that's all.'

'You don't have time.' She shakes her head, closes her eyes for a moment as though doing so might erase everything we've just talked about. 'For everyone's sake, Louise, just sort this mess out somehow.'

TWENTY-SIX

It's the last day before the February half-term holiday, and I have never been more grateful to see a break from school arrive. Maria has organised an open evening for parents to view the work of her A level art classes – a realism project they've been working on since the autumn term. As much as I'd like to be able to, I can't avoid going. It wouldn't look good just weeks before an inspection if I failed to turn up to an event that so many parents will be attending, and I know Maria can be relied upon to remain professional, despite her current feelings towards me.

Display boards have been set up around the hall, tables arranged ready with plastic glasses and paper plates for refreshments. A couple of the sixth-form girls have spent the afternoon baking cupcakes over in the food technology department, and they're due to put them out before the parents arrive. Maria is setting up a tea urn at the end of the table, her back to the door so she doesn't see me when I come in.

I browse the first set of displays, admiring what even I, as someone who knows nothing about art, can appreciate as being above-average talent for a group of seventeen- and eighteen-year-olds. The project has focused on life drawing, and some of the portraits are postgraduate standard. The students have worked hard on honing their craft, but I know much of their success is down to Maria and her teaching. I feel a pang of sadness for what's happened between us, the echoes of last night's conversation ringing in my ears. For years now Maria has been one of my closest friends. She's always been someone I can rely on to offer advice on any troubles, and I hope I've been the same for her. But not any more.

'I didn't hear you come in,' she says, by way of a frosty reception.

'This work is so impressive.'

'They've worked hard.'

'And not just them. You too.'

She doesn't say anything. It must seem to her that I'm trying too hard, offering compliments in search of forgiveness, when the truth is I just want things to be normal again. But with Erin's disappearance and my night with Kieran lingering like invisible phantoms in the space between us, it feels that nothing will ever be normal again.

I turn to the doors to make sure we're still alone. 'I'm so sorry, Maria.'

'Sorry isn't going to help find Erin.'

She can't make me feel any worse than I already do. I have barely slept in almost a week. The guilt is eating me alive from the inside out, a parasite that's growing bigger as it thrives. I've lied to Marcus. I've lied to the police. When I look in the mirror, I don't recognise the person I am any more. I don't know why I expect Maria to.

'Let's just keep things strictly business, shall we?' she whispers. Her attention turns to the door, where a group of sixth-formers have gathered. 'I don't want to talk about this again until you've sorted everything out.'

She walks away, not giving me a chance to respond. I

wonder how she thinks I'm supposed to sort everything out: such a simple instruction yet so seemingly impossible to do. I'm just grateful it's half-term next week, that I'll have more time to try to make sense of what's happening. Though I have little over twenty-four hours left in which to transfer the blackmail money. The more time that's passed, the more I've tried to convince myself I'll be able to find a way around this without exposing myself to the shame of that video becoming public viewing; yet now, with Saturday looming, I realise how naïve I've been to believe I might maintain any element of control.

Maria ushers her waiting students inside. Moments later, a couple of girls carrying trays of cupcakes follow them in.

'Wow,' Maria says, going to help them. 'They look amazing. There's my diet out the window.'

Parents begin to filter in. I greet people in the way I'm expected to, polite and professional, gushing about how hard the students have worked and how proud we are of their achievements. But I hear my words differently to how they must sound to everyone else. Strained. Forced. False. Standing here making small talk with the parents of young people whose education I've been entrusted with, I feel a total fraud.

I move around the room once the welcomes are over, grateful for some space and time in which I don't have to talk to anyone. I make my way in a semicircle around the display, and when I come to the final piece, I stop dead in my tracks, the breath sucked from my lungs.

The pencil drawing is huge, the subject's face taking up the entire canvas. The detail is so incredible that it's impossible not to be captivated by the work once it's caught your attention, from the individual strands of hair to the light that's reflected in the eyes. Yet it's not the skill of the piece that keeps me transfixed. It's the subject herself. The little girl with the unusual eyes and the sad smile. Once again I'm face to face with the image of Iris.

Stuck to the bottom right corner of the canvas is the photograph from which the drawing has been copied. The colour close-up shows the girl's pale blue eyes, her light blonde hair; her youthful, unblemished skin highlighted by the sunshine that strikes her face.

'She's incredible, isn't she?' one of the mothers says beside me. 'A natural talent. To think she only started drawing during the first lockdown is quite something. Toby said she's applied to the Royal College of Art in London. Her heart's set on it, apparently.'

I can't say anything; any possible response is trapped in my throat. I can't make sense of what I'm seeing. Does Beth, the student who produced this drawing, know Jasper's family? Is this a tribute to his sister?

'Well,' I finally manage, 'they'd be mad not to take her. This is really something special.' I remind myself where I am. Why I'm here. 'Toby's work is very accomplished too. Mrs Gatland told me he's really developed technically over the past six months.'

I scan the room for Beth, finding her chatting with Maria near another student's display.

'Excuse me,' I say to Toby's mother. 'I just need to ask Beth something.' I leave her admiring the drawing of Iris. Beneath my dress, my skin feels slick with a nervous sweat, a strange panic rising in my chest.

Beth and Maria are talking about London: Maria is saying something about one of the galleries Beth must visit when she gets there, but the words bubble over me like I'm hearing them from underwater. She stops when she notices me standing beside them, there but not.

'Everything okay?'

Her tone could cut through glass. God, she hates me. I understand it. I understand the pressure I've inadvertently placed on her by asking her to keep my secret; by expecting her to risk her own career in a bid to save mine. I just wish it didn't have to be this way.

'Your portrait drawing is beautiful,' I say to Beth, forcing a smile. 'Really incredible.'

'Thanks, miss.' Her face breaks into a beam. Beth is a lovely girl: bright, inquisitive, talented. She has a great future ahead of her. She's one of those characters who, even at this tender age, you can see will go on to make sensible choices and not fall into the trappings of bad decisions that lure so many young people during their teenage years and early twenties. I feel a sudden and strange surge of envy. Nostalgia. I long to go back to a past that never really existed.

'Is it someone you know? The little girl in the picture.'

She shakes her head. 'I just found her photo on the internet. I wanted someone with unusual eyes – they're gorgeous, aren't they?'

A prickle itches across my skin, travelling up my arms and down my spine.

'Yes,' I manage. 'Striking. Whereabouts did you find her?'

I feel Maria's attention burn on my face.

'Just Google Images, I think. An advert for something.' She sees Toby's mother standing by the portrait and waves to her. 'Do you mind if I just go and say hello?'

She leaves Maria and me alone, awkward in the unspoken question that waits between us.

'What was that all about?' she finally asks. 'You're behaving really strangely.'

'I'm not,' I say defensively. 'Anyway, I thought you said this wasn't the place?'

She shakes her head and leaves me to go and talk to another student who's standing with her father near the tables of cakes. I watch Beth and Toby's mothers chat, their faces animated as they discuss Beth's artwork. I feel sick. There must be a simple explanation. Perhaps Iris was a child model, and Erin just never mentioned it. She was certainly a beautiful little girl. Maybe her sad story was featured in a magazine or news article somewhere.

'Mrs Anderson,' someone says, my focus still caught on the drawing.

I turn at the sound of my name, expecting to see one of the parents wanting my attention. Instead, Detective Inspector Clarke stands beside me, DC Palmer waiting just behind her. The room has fallen silent as one by one the parents and students notice the presence of the police.

'Shall we go somewhere quieter?' DI Clarke suggests. They follow me out into the corridor. I can just about manage to shut out everyone else, but I can't ignore the look Maria gives me as we pass.

'Is there any news about Erin?' I ask as soon as we're away from the doors of the hall. 'Do you know where she is?'

The detective eyes me with a look I'm unable to read. I'm unsure whether she wants to arrest me or offer me a chair and a cup of tea. Whatever they're here for, it was never going to be good news.

'This isn't about Mrs Foster, I'm afraid, Mrs Anderson. It's about your brother. I'm very sorry, but Cameron's been found dead.'

TWENTY-SEVEN

I'm barely able to drive home through the blur of tears that near-blinds me. It's gone 8 p.m. by the time I close the door behind me, and when I do so, all I'm able to picture is Cameron standing in this hallway a week ago, so dejected and beaten by the world that he looked as though all he needed in that moment was for someone to just put their arms around him and hold him. I could have been that person, but I didn't do it. Now, I would give anything to go back and do things differently.

He was right about one thing, at least. Bad things happen when you least expect them.

I manage to finally get hold of Marcus, after trying to call him three times in the car. He falls silent when I tell him about Cameron. For a moment, I wonder whether he's been cut off.

'Marcus?'

'I'm sorry,' he says. 'I just... I can't believe it. God, Lou... I'm so sorry.'

'I was still at school. The police turned up, and I thought...' I stop myself before mentioning Erin; before telling him that I thought they'd come to question me again about her disappearance.

'What happened?'

'He was found at the bottom of the stairs in his flat. He didn't turn up for work, apparently. Someone went over there when he didn't answer any of their calls. A colleague identified him.'

'I didn't know he had a job.'

'No. Nor did I until recently.'

It saddens me just how little I knew about my own brother's life, although I suppose it was always going to end up the case that we would drift in different directions. But we had a chance at reconciliation. It was there, and we both let it go.

'Are you okay? I mean, I know you had your differences, but he was still your brother.'

I don't know how to answer. I feel numb. It isn't real. For all the years I spent dreading a phone call to tell me something had happened to Cameron, I didn't expect this now.

'Louise?'

My phone alerts me to a waiting call, and I look down to see Maria's name on my screen.

'Maria's trying to call me,' I tell Marcus. 'Do you mind if I speak to her? She was there at the school when the police came.'

'Yeah, of course. I'm coming home as soon as I can get a ferry, okay?'

'You don't have to.'

'I'm coming home, Louise. Go and speak with Maria.'

He ends the call and I answer her.

'Look, I was thinking,' she says. 'Marcus is away at the moment, isn't he?'

'Yeah, but it's fine. Honestly, Maria, I'm okay.'

I'm lying. She knows I'm lying. I'm about as far from okay as it's possible to be. I keep thinking about Cameron in that flat on his own. Dying alone. Lying at the bottom of the stairs, injured but still alive, just needing someone to turn up to help him. The hopelessness of it all. The despair and desperation.

Might there have been a chance for his life to be saved? Had someone been there with him... had there been a chance for him to make a call... As in the aftermath of my mother's death, I torture myself with a succession of what-ifs, knowing none of them can change the reality of what's happened.

'I'm going to come over,' Maria says. 'If you're okay with that, obviously.'

I don't want to be alone. Yet I know what Maria thinks of me at the moment, and I don't want to have to spend the next few hours sitting beneath the shadow of her disapproval.

'I'm okay,' I tell her again. 'So much has been said...'

'None of that matters. This isn't about Kieran.'

His name manages to turn the air around me cold. I realise how naïve I've been. How stupid. I allowed myself to get caught up in a fantasy that didn't exist, with a person who wasn't real.

'I'm going to go and pick up some food,' Maria says.

'What about the boys?'

'James is with them. They're probably having a gaming night. They won't notice I'm not there.'

I thank her, grateful that I won't have to be alone for the next few hours. The last thing I want to do is sit alone in my silent house.

Once the call is ended, I go straight upstairs and shower. I stand beneath a flow of water that's too hot, crying at the memory of Cameron and the toad he shed tears over all those years ago when we were just kids, wishing I could somehow rewind time and undo all the things that caused his life to spiral downward. At some point I stop feeling anything, and when I get out of the shower, my thighs and stomach are scorched red with the heat. I dress in a pair of leggings and a sweater and go downstairs to make a cup of tea I know I'm not likely to drink. I sit with it at the kitchen table, my mind numbed beneath the weight of everything.

The doorbell sounds and I go to let Maria in. She follows

me down the hallway without speaking and puts a carrier bag of shopping on the kitchen table.

'It's just a ready-made lasagne. I figured you wouldn't want much, but you need to eat something.'

'Thank you.'

Maria and I have never had the kind of tactile friendship that involves hugs: neither of us is really that type of person. Yet now she comes over to me, reaches out and puts her arms around me, my body rigid against hers. The contact doesn't last long before she pulls away, but it's enough to convey the silent message that to some extent, at least for now, she forgives me.

'You need something stronger than that,' she says, gesturing to the cold cup of tea left untouched on the table. She moves between cupboards, searching for alcohol. 'Go and sit on the sofa,' she instructs me. 'I'll put the lasagne in the oven. You look white as a sheet.'

I do as she tells me, too tired to put up any resistance. She comes in a few minutes later with a shot of whisky in a tumbler.

'Here. Drink this.'

I hate the stuff, but I take it from her anyway. She sits beside me, and I'm grateful for the company.

'I just don't get it,' I say eventually. 'I saw him a week ago. Everything seemed fine. I mean, he was still angry with me about the inheritance money, but there was otherwise nothing wrong with him. He hadn't been drinking. He'd got a job too. Maybe he was telling the truth when he said he was sorting his life out.'

'But then he trashed your house,' Maria reminds me. She's the only person other than the police and Marcus that I've spoken to about it.

'I know,' I say, but I can't explain to her that something just feels wrong in my gut. 'Someone else must have been with him. Someone did this to him.'

I can't escape the way she looks at me. I take a gulp of the whisky and it burns my throat as it slides down to my stomach. I put the glass down and wipe my wet eyes, leaving a smudge of mascara on my sleeve.

'You don't know that, Louise. A lot's happened recently... you mustn't let your mind run wild. Will there be a post-mortem?'

My body flinches at the words. 'I assume so.'

'I'm sure it'll be confirmed as an accident.' She looks at me, gauging my reaction to her words. 'I'm sorry. I just don't want you to torture yourself with this. It isn't your fault.'

Maria knows about the guilt I've carried with me since my mother's death. We've spoken about it at some length; more so, in fact, than I've probably spoken to Marcus about it. She watches me as I drain the rest of the whisky, my face contorting with the strength of the alcohol.

'Let me see how that food's getting on.'

She puts a hand on my shoulder before going back into the kitchen. No matter what she says or how she might try to reassure me, I can't escape the feeling that Cameron's death is somehow my fault. These past couple of weeks have shattered everything I thought I'd known about my marriage and myself. I am capable of more destruction than I ever imagined possible. Perhaps, at the wrong time and with the wrong set of circumstances, we are all capable of destroying what we love the most. But I can't use that as an excuse for the havoc I've wreaked. I've inadvertently dragged Maria into the mess I've made, and though I can't make sense of how I may have done the same to Cameron, it feels too much of a coincidence that his death should occur now.

I wish I could tell him how sorry I am. How sorry that I wasn't there for him when he needed me the most.

I get up and go into the kitchen, not wanting to be alone with my thoughts. Maria is standing near the sink, chopping fruit.

'I'll stay until Marcus gets back. I don't think you should be alone.'

My stomach churns, the heat of the whisky still burning my insides. 'Why are you being so nice to me? I don't deserve it.'

She sighs. 'You're my friend, Louise. I don't have to agree with or like everything you do.' She slides a pile of strawberries from the chopping board into a bowl. 'When are you going to tell Marcus?'

When, I think. Not if.

'I don't know.'

We talk more while the lasagne cooks through before eating at the kitchen table, though I barely touch what's on my plate. It feels wrong to even think of eating when Cameron is lying cold somewhere. I imagine his body covered with a sheet on a steel table, or in one of those drawers you see in films and TV shows. It would be easier if I hated him, but I just can't bring myself to.

When we're finished, Maria insists on clearing the table and loading the dishwasher. We return to the living room, where we sit with the television on, the sound muted to a low mumble that barely breaks the silence, and we speak intermittently, both of us avoiding further mention of Cameron.

'I wonder why Kieran and Erin moved Jasper to a new school in his GCSE year,' Maria muses.

'I've wondered the same. Seems very unfair on him. I assume one of them had a job offer they couldn't turn down, although you'd think they might have delayed it by a few months for his sake.'

'What does Kieran do?'

'For work? I've no idea.' I realise with a sense of shame that I never asked too much, happy to keep him as the fantasy he'd become inside my head.

'What about Erin?'

'Nursing. I'm not sure what type, to be honest. Children's unit, I think.'

Maria's top lip curls as she thinks. 'They didn't mention her job on the TV appeal. I mean, there's no reason why they should, I suppose.'

I think of the drawing of Iris I saw in the school hall yesterday evening. With the news of Cameron's death coming so soon afterwards, I've not had time to consider why the child's image may have been available online.

'I feel sorry for Jasper,' I say. 'It explains what happened on Monday. The poor kid must be traumatised.'

'Yet someone encouraged him to sit in front of all those cameras. Seems a bit odd, don't you think?'

The same thought has occurred to me, but I didn't dwell on it. Perhaps Jasper, for reasons known only to him, chose to be there that day. But I can't imagine why he'd have wanted that.

'Where shall I sleep?' Maria asks. 'I'm happy to have the sofa, but I don't want to get in your way.'

'The bed's made up in the spare room. I'll get you a towel.'

I use it as an excuse to get out of the living room for a few minutes, a feeling of claustrophobia having set in. Upstairs in the bathroom, I realise I'm sweating beneath my clothes. I get a towel from the cupboard and stop at the mirror, reluctantly taking in the sight of my heavy eyelids and sallow skin. For a moment, I see my brother in my reflection.

Maria stays until Marcus arrives home the following morning. He comes straight to me with open arms and pulls me into his chest, and neither of us says anything for a moment, the enormity of what's happened hovering above us, drowning us in the weight of its shadow.

'I got back as soon as I could,' he says. 'The bloody ferries...'

'It doesn't matter. I'm okay.'

Maria stands in the living room doorway, looking at her feet.

'Thanks for staying with her,' Marcus says.

'It's fine.' She turns and goes back into the living room, unable to maintain a façade in the way that has apparently been second nature to me. Despite everything that was said last night, I know all too painfully what she still thinks of me. She can't bring herself to look at Marcus, knowing that she's also inadvertently lying to him.

'Come here,' he says, pulling me close again. 'I am so, so sorry, Lou.'

I break away when Maria comes back into the hallway, her mobile phone in her hand.

'She won't want to think about it at the moment,' Marcus says to her, 'but don't let her try to get out of that weekend you're planning.'

My heart lurches in my chest. The silence seems to stretch an age as Maria looks at me and then back at Marcus. 'Weekend?' she finally says.

'Louise mentioned a spa or something. She could really use the break.'

'Oh,' Maria replies flatly, realising she's been unknowingly roped into another of my lies. 'That. Of course.'

She goes to the banister where she left her coat and bag, and after putting her shoes on, she leans in towards me, moving close to my ear. 'Tell him,' she whispers. 'Or I will.'

TWENTY-EIGHT

After Maria leaves, Marcus makes breakfast. I can't face even the thought of food, but I sit with him at the kitchen table and force a piece of omelette into my mouth, the smell of the eggs making me feel sick. The coffee tastes bitter and acrid, everything tainted by my guilt. Maria is right. I'm going to have to tell him everything. It needs to come from me.

'What happens now?' he asks, his attention on his phone. 'Are you going to have to make the funeral arrangements?'

A piece of mushroom gets stuck in my throat and I dislodge it with a drink of water.

'You okay?'

I wish everyone would stop asking me that.

'Yeah. I just... I hadn't thought that far ahead.' This much is true. But with both our parents gone and Cameron estranged from his ex-wife, responsibility for arranging the funeral will fall to me. It's the last thing I feel I can face.

'There's something I need to tell you.'

Marcus pushes his phone to one side. He looks different from just a few days ago: a little greyer at the temples; a little more tired around the eyes. I'm about to bring his life crashing down around his ears, and I hate every inch of myself for it.

'What is it?'

His eyes remain fixed on me, expectant.

'Something happened when you first left for the Isle of Wight,' I finally manage. 'It was the night I tried to call you. The night I came home and the house had been trashed.'

'I knew something wasn't right when we spoke,' he says quietly. 'What is it? What really happened?'

'Everything I told you was true. Cameron had been here on the Friday. But on Saturday...'

'What?' Marcus urges. 'What happened on Saturday?'

I pause, bite my bottom lip, realise now that there's no getting out of this, not this time. 'I went to Erin's house.'

He waits for the punchline. 'Okay,' he says slowly. 'And...?' His eyes narrow. 'This was before she went missing, right?'

Heat rises in my chest, my skin aflame. I see the possibilities of what I'm about to confess to him pass across his eyes. The thought that I might know something about her disappearance. That I've been hiding it from him and from everyone else for this past week.

'I didn't see her. She was out with her sister.'

Confusion plays out on Marcus's face.

'I saw Kieran,' I say, before I have a chance to swallow the words back down, burying them for good this time.

For a moment, there's no reaction, Marcus appearing to have already cast the name and the person to a far-flung corner of his mind where it no longer bears any relevance to his life. Or at least it didn't until Erin went missing. I watch as the penny drops – less of a coin, more a ten-mile-wide meteorite. I see his face fall, the colour draining away as he realises what's yet to come.

'What is it?' he eventually says. 'What have you done?'

But I can't speak. Because beneath it all, I must be the same as my father. My mother. All of us spun from the same cloth. A coward.

He shakes his head, not wanting to hear what I've not yet articulated. Not wanting to believe it.

'I don't understand.'

It all comes out in a flood. Cameron being here on the Friday night. Coming back from my mother's the following day to find everything in a state of chaos. Trying Marcus and Maria's phones, but neither of them being available. Trying Erin's phone, and Kieran answering.

But I hear it all as I know Marcus must: just a string of excuses for a responsibility I don't want to accept as mine alone.

When I've finished speaking, he remains silent.

'Marcus.' I reach across the table and put a hand on his arm. 'I'm so sorry.'

He shoves my hand away. 'Don't. Just don't. We said we wouldn't do this. We said we'd be honest with each other.'

His chair scrapes back across the kitchen tiles. I follow him into the hallway.

'I'm trying to be honest with you. That's why I'm telling you.'

'A week on!'

'Where are you going?'

'Anywhere. Don't try to follow me. Please.'

He slams the door behind him. I go into the living room expecting to see his car pulling off the driveway, but instead I see him head away from the house on foot. At least, I suppose, that means he must be planning on coming back.

I drop onto the sofa, deflated and defeated. I wonder whether he's able to contact Kieran in any way, but I'm pretty sure he doesn't have his phone number or know where he lives. Why would he? And surely he wouldn't go to the house to confront him anyway, although I've seen him angry before, the day he confronted Cameron.

I go to the kitchen for my mobile, which is plugged into its charger next to the microwave. I plan to call him, to ask him to come home, but then I spot his phone, left on the windowsill above the sink. It's locked. I don't know his passcode; I've never felt the need to know it before. That day I checked his phone weeks back, it had been left unlocked.

My eyes are blurred with angry tears: for Cameron, for Erin, for Marcus. For myself. I stand in the kitchen, Marcus's phone in my hand, and try to work out what his passcode might be. Because something in my heart and head feels wrong. I'm suddenly desperate to see if he's been messaging Lucy again, maybe to justify my own awful actions and remind myself why I suggested an open marriage in the first place. I tap in the date and month of his birthday, but it doesn't work. Then I try my own. With only one attempt left at finding the right four digits, I rack my brain for combinations that are of any relevance to him. Nothing comes to mind as an obvious option, so in desperation I tap *1234*. The screen throws out colour as it comes to life.

When I go into his messages, the first ones I see are from me. Then there's Pete and another man he works with. I keep scrolling, waiting to see Lucy's name, but before I get to hers, another stops me in my tracks. Cameron. I check the date. Wednesday. The day before my brother died. Yet he hadn't spoken to Marcus since the day of my mother's funeral – or so I thought.

When I open the thread, there's just one message, from Cameron to Marcus.

Tell Louise or I will.

There are no other messages before or after this, so anything that might have come before or after has been deleted; either that or Marcus never responded to this message. Not by text, at least.

I feel myself grow cold. I lock the phone and return it to the windowsill, not wanting Marcus to know that I've been looking at it. I don't want him to know that I've seen that message from my brother. I knew something didn't feel right. I leave the kitchen to go and find my car keys, almost crying out in shock when I find Marcus standing in the hallway. I didn't hear the front door. We stand in silence for a moment, neither of us knowing what to say. My heart beats painfully in my chest; I don't want to believe what that message might suggest.

'Was he better than me?' he asks eventually, an age seeming to have passed between us.

'Don't,' I say, glancing at the sideboard where my car keys are sitting.

'Does Erin know about it?'

'I don't know. I don't know anything any more.'

He hesitates, deliberating over what to say next; where we go from here. 'I just don't understand.'

Nor do I, I think.

'I wish we'd never gone to that hotel.' It's the wrong thing to say, but the first thing that falls from my mouth. I realise the implication: that I'm trying to deflect blame, suggesting that if we'd never made the decision to spend the night with another couple, I wouldn't have had sex with Kieran last Saturday. Yet it's the truth. That night at the hotel set off a seemingly unstoppable chain of events.

And now my brother is dead, Erin is missing, and I can't escape the feeling that the two things are somehow inexplicably connected.

'So do I.' His eyes remain fixed on me, and I feel almost dizzy beneath the pressure of his attention. 'I always knew there was a chance something like this would happen. I mean, I never wanted to think about it, obviously, but we both knew we were taking a risk. I should have been prepared for it.'

'It's not your fault. We were supposed to be transparent. Honest about everything.'

'Then why did you do it?'

The truth of this is probably far more complicated than even I realise. Years ago, back before I met Marcus, I started seeing a therapist. I needed someone I could talk to – someone who didn't know me and wouldn't judge because they didn't care about me. For the first time in my life, I could be completely honest about how I felt and what I thought, without fear of rejection or scorn. By the time our sessions ended, she knew more about me than probably anyone else in my life ever had, and it occurred to me then that the kind of knowledge she'd gained was the kind that could prove dangerous if left in the wrong hands. I know what she'd make of all this. She'd likely think that on some subconscious level I'm still afraid of commitment; that even after a decade with Marcus – ten years that have been happy and secure – I can't bring myself to trust in this life, because it isn't one I've ever felt I deserved. I'd never fully committed to anyone before him, my longest previous relationship having lasted just a little over a year. Maybe my mother was right about me after all.

'Louise?'

But I can't give him an answer. All I can think about is that message from Cameron on his phone.

'Tell me what happened,' he urges.

I say nothing, unsure which parts he means. Tell him how I ended up at their house? He already knows that. Surely he doesn't want to hear what happened once I got there.

'Where did it happen?' he prompts me.

So I tell him everything – from going over to the house and spilling a cup of tea on myself to being upstairs in the bathroom, Kieran there with me. I watch Marcus's expression change, flitting through an entire textbook of emotions until I end my narration before the point at which he needs to know no more.

After purging myself of the details, all that remains in my head are those words.

Tell Louise or I will.

'You called Erin's phone after Cameron had been here?'

I nod.

'So it was because of him, then? If he hadn't been here and trashed the house, you never would have ended up at Kieran's, is that what you're saying?'

'I just didn't want to be on my own. I was hoping I'd be able to get hold of you or Maria, but—'

'So it's my fault then?'

'That's not what I'm saying.'

Until I find out what Cameron meant by that message, Marcus and I have no space to be talking about Kieran. But I don't want him to know I checked his phone. I have no idea how he might react.

'Cameron said there was something you needed to tell me. What is it?'

Marcus's eyes darken, his brow furrowing. 'What are you talking about?'

'When he came here that night,' I lie. 'He said there was something I should know. Something you needed to tell me. When I asked him more, he said I should speak to you about it.'

My heart pounds as I hold his gaze, not wanting him to see through the fabrication I've had to invent on the spot.

He sighs. 'He went to the house. Your mother's house. This was weeks ago now – that man who lives over the road saw him loitering in the garden and called me. It was a weekday so he knew you wouldn't be available.'

'Why didn't you tell me?'

'You had enough on. There was nothing for you to worry about. I went over there... I dealt with him.'

'What do you mean, dealt with him?'

Marcus tuts and looks away.

'You hit him, you mean?'

'Look, Lou, it was nothing – he was making more of it than it—'

I don't get to challenge him further on what really happened, or why Cameron was at the house in the first place. Marcus is interrupted by the doorbell. Through the frosted glass of the front door, a figure stands waiting. Somehow I already know who it is before Marcus reaches for the handle and opens the door.

DC Palmer greets us as though we're friends he hasn't bumped into for a while. 'Mrs Anderson. Mr Anderson.' He turns his focus to me. 'We'd like to talk to you some more about your brother, if we could.'

'She's grieving,' Marcus snaps, his face too close to the officer's; his anger fuelled by what's just happened between us. 'Whatever it is, it can wait.'

Palmer looks past him, ignoring his words.

'Mrs Anderson, it's probably best we do this down at the station.'

TWENTY-NINE

'What's this about?' I ask, not moving from where I stand. I'm going nowhere with them until I know why they're here and just what it is they think I'm involved with.

'It's about your brother's death.'

'What about Cameron's death?' Marcus asks.

'New evidence has come to light,' DC Palmer says. 'We've reason to believe Mr McNally's death may not have been an accident.'

The words punch me in the gut and I lose my balance. I feel a hand on my arm, keeping me upright.

'What new evidence?' Marcus presses. His fingers close more tightly around my arm, holding me in place. *Tell Louise or I will.* The rush of blood to my head has reduced the sounds around me to a muffled cushion of noise, like trying to listen to a conversation on land from three metres below water.

'As I said,' DC Palmer says, 'it's probably best we do this at the station.'

The police agree to Marcus driving me there, sparing me the humiliation of being taken away from my home and past my neighbours' houses in a police car. They've said nothing about an arrest, but I don't rule it out. Whatever this new evidence is, one thing seems clear: the police suspect foul play. In the passenger seat, I sit with my hands in my lap, watching my fingers tremble. I think again of Cameron alone in that house, picturing him at the bottom of the staircase. Now my brain places Marcus beside him, standing over my brother's dying body, waiting there to see him take his final breath.

'Ask for a duty solicitor,' Marcus tells me. 'They should offer one, but if they don't, make sure you say nothing until one arrives.'

'I need to know what happened,' I say shakily, barely able to get the words out. 'What did you do to him?'

Marcus looks crushed when I turn to face him. 'I hit him, Lou. I'm sorry. It was just once, just to send him on his way. He was threatening to take you to court, to get solicitors involved. He said he was prepared to destroy you to get his hands on that inheritance. He said some awful things about you, Lou. Personal things. I think he'd taken something. I wasn't going to just stand there and let him talk about you like that.'

'And then what happened?' I ask quietly.

'He left.'

'And that was the last time you saw him?'

Marcus's attention moves from the road to me. The implication of my words sits between us like an undetonated bomb. 'Yes. But I knew he wouldn't leave it there. That's why I reacted like I did when you told me he'd been to the house. Jesus, Louise, you don't think I was involved in his death, do you?'

But I don't know what to think, so I say nothing, and we don't speak again until we reach the station.

'You don't need to wait for me,' I tell him as we pull into the car park. He ignores me, parking in a free space and cutting the engine.

DC Palmer is standing by the reception desk when we enter the building.

'You can wait here,' he says to Marcus, gesturing to a row of seats beneath a pinboard of addiction self-help advice and posters urging people to hand in their knives.

Marcus opens his mouth to object, but I raise a hand, urging him to leave it.

I follow the detective through a set of double doors and down a corridor. He pushes a door open and ushers me into a small square interview room that contains nothing more than a table and four chairs. DI Clarke is sitting in one of them, waiting for me.

'Good morning, Mrs Anderson,' she says, standing. 'Thanks for coming in.'

I look from her to the other officer and then to the recording device sitting on the desk.

'Am I under arrest?'

'No. We just need to talk to you some more about your brother, straighten out a few details.'

Straighten out a few details. I've no idea what that means, or whether it should worry me.

'What's happened? What happened to Cameron?'

'Some of your brother's injuries are incompatible with a fall. We've reason to believe someone else was with him before he died.'

I look from one officer to the other. 'Someone killed him?' As soon as the question leaves my mouth, I remember Marcus's words. They think I was involved. They think I killed my own brother.

'I'd like a duty solicitor,' I say.

DI Clarke glances at her colleague with a look that may as well be an eye-roll, as though by asking for a solicitor I'm indirectly confessing my guilt. 'That can be arranged,' she says.

DC Palmer takes his cue and leaves the room. DI Clarke's attention doesn't leave my face.

'You must be in a state of shock still,' she says.

'Yes.'

'Would you like a cup of tea while we wait? Coffee?'

'No thanks.'

Taking the hint that she's not going to get any more from me while it's just the two of us here, she falls into silence. I'm not sure which is worse: the questions or sitting here in this soundless room with the weight of her stare on me. I've done nothing wrong, I want to tell her. I just want to go home.

This is one of those moments when I no longer feel like the forty-four-year-old woman I am. I'm transported to a sensation of childlike helplessness, like being nine years old and lost somewhere foreign, abandoned without a familiar face in sight. I can hear the pounding of my own heartbeat; I can feel the blood rushing in my ears with the adrenaline that floods to my brain. I want to run in the way I could as a child, without a sense of self, free of any care, yet I can't remember how it feels to be without restraint. They're rare, these moments, but when they hit, they hit hard. I felt this way in the moments after hearing my mother's diagnosis. I'd felt it years earlier, as a teenager, my father's face on the television in my student house, the news of his sentencing running across the bottom of the screen in a red banner alongside a weather warning of snow and the announcement of the birth of David and Victoria Beckham's first child.

'Are you okay?' DI Clarke says. Her expression of suspicion has morphed into one of mild concern.

'Fine.'

We wait for what feels an age before DC Palmer returns with another man, who introduces himself as Leighton Brent, the duty solicitor. I'm left on my own for a while as he speaks with the detective in another room, and when he returns, he's alone. He informs me that the interview will be recorded and advises me to stick with the facts.

'As we said earlier,' DI Clarke reiterates upon her return, 'we'd just like to ask you some more questions about your brother, Cameron McNally, and about your relationship with him.'

'I haven't had much of a relationship with my brother for years.'

'And why is that?'

I take a deep breath, trying to clear my mind of all the debris flying loose between things that have happened over these past couple of weeks and the things that are decades old, long-ago unchangeable.

'Our father was sent to prison when we were teenagers,' I say, wanting to keep the explanation as brief as possible. 'He was charged with blackmail and extortion and was given a fifteen-year sentence. He died of a heart attack before he became eligible for parole. His arrest affected Cameron and me in different ways. I moved to university before his trial. I rarely went home after he'd been sentenced. Cameron fell in with some destructive influences and got himself into some problems.'

'What sort of problems?' asks DC Palmer.

'Addiction. Drink, drugs, gambling.'

'That must have put an immense pressure on your relationship,' DI Clarke says leadingly.

I wonder when Leighton bloody Brent is going to say something, or whether he's even going to bother speaking at all.

'I tried to help him. I offered him money when I had it. I met up with him and tried to help him change things.'

But he didn't want to change, I think. And no one can change unless they want to.

DI Clarke continues to study me, looking for signs of guilt. 'You've already admitted to us that you and Cameron argued about the inheritance money.'

'Yes,' I say, my voice shaking. 'I told the officers who came to the house last weekend after the break-in.'

'But the house wasn't broken into, was it? There were no signs of forced entry.'

'Yes, I know, but... however he got in. The spare key. I don't know. My point is, I told the police about the argument that day. I had nothing to hide then, and I've nothing to hide now.'

Except you do, Louise. You have plenty to hide.

'Where were you on Thursday evening, Mrs Anderson?'

I look from one to the other as I feel my heart deflate in my chest.

'I loved Cameron. We may not have always agreed on everything, but he was still my kid brother.'

'That didn't answer the question.'

I lick my dry lips and try to order my thoughts. 'I was at work until just gone five o'clock. I went home, where I took a call from one of my colleagues, Maria Gatland. She's an art teacher at the school. She came over to my house shortly after she called, at around six fifteen.'

'Is that normal? For her to come to your house?'

'We've been good friends for years now, going back to before I started working at Eastbridge. We met on a training course. She's been over to the house on plenty of occasions, so yes, it's nothing unusual.'

I realise how defensive I sound – almost aggressively so. I try to relax my shoulders, make myself appear less tense, but it's a difficult thing to do when the police are indirectly accusing me of murdering my own brother.

'Your husband sent your brother a text message on Sunday evening,' DC Palmer says, referring to the paperwork in front of him. 'Do you know what it said?'

'No.' I think of Cameron's solitary text on Marcus's phone, still not knowing whether any other communication had taken place before or after it.

'"Stay the fuck away from Louise",' the detective reads from the sheet in front of him. '"Speak to her again and you're a dead man." Is your husband prone to violence, Mrs Anderson? Or making threats against other people's lives?'

'What? No! Not at all. It was just words. Cameron had just damaged our property. It was intimidating... I felt violated. Marcus would have said it to warn him off, that's all.'

But he's not long ago admitted to hitting Cameron just a few weeks back, I remind myself.

'Seems a bit of an extreme response, though, don't you think?'

'Yes. No. I mean, it wasn't the first time Cameron had done that sort of thing. He turned up at our mother's funeral drunk and high. There was a bit of a fight... It was nothing.'

'There was a bit of a fight but it was nothing,' DI Clarke repeats. 'Well, which one was it, Mrs Anderson? Was it a bit of a fight, or was it nothing? It can't have been both.'

The police are digging Marcus a hole and I realise I'm pushing him towards it.

'You should invite Mr Anderson into the room if your questions relate to him,' Leighton Brent says, finally contributing to the interview, though not in a way that's helpful to anyone, least of all Marcus. 'Do you have any evidence to suggest Mrs Anderson was with her brother at his home on Thursday evening?'

DI Clarke exhales through her nose. 'What time did your colleague leave your house on Thursday, Mrs Anderson?'

'By seven thirty.' I realise what the implication is. It wasn't late: there would still have been time for me to get to Cameron's house. 'I haven't seen Cameron since a week yesterday. I had no reason to hurt him. Despite everything he'd done to destroy his life and his relationships, I still loved him. He was upset about the inheritance, but it was never going to go to either of us. The money may have been signed over to me, but I didn't plan to keep it, and Cameron knew that. It's blood money.'

I stop talking for a moment, worried I may have said too

much. Yet the silence only prompts me to keep talking, because I've done nothing wrong and I need to prove it. 'My father hurt a lot of people,' I explain. 'That money... it was never my family's. I didn't want it. My brother didn't have quite the same view on things. I don't think he really cared how it had come into our father's hands, as long as it ended up in his. It wasn't right. My mother obviously knew that too. If you want a motive for murder, you won't find it with me. We didn't have the best of relationships and I've never made a secret of the fact. But I had no reason to hurt him. If you're thinking of the inheritance as a motive, it was all in my name anyway.'

'A reason for your brother to hurt you then?' DI Clarke says. 'Unless, of course, someone stopped him before he could do anything more.'

I've said too much. She means Marcus, and I know they'll be looking to him for questioning next. I should have followed the example of Jasper Healy and Callum Benton: teenagers who've kept their mouths shut in the face of accusation. The more I speak, the more I appear to be implicating my husband.

But what if there's good reason to? a voice in my head taunts me.

'If Cameron had wanted to hurt me, he would have done so when he came to the house last Friday. There was no one else there. Marcus was away. It would have been the perfect opportunity.'

We sit in silence for a moment while the detectives muse over my words and I silently regret each one, berating myself for being so naïve that I believed for a second I could single-handedly remove myself from the suspicions of the police using reason alone. The truth is, I may have made everything so much worse for myself.

'Is Mrs Anderson going to be arrested today?' Leighton Brent asks.

'No. But there are likely to be further developments over

the next few days as the investigation continues, so we'll be in touch again at some point.'

I want to ask about Erin. I want to know whether anything has been found, or if anyone has come forward since the television appeal. But I can't ask about her without drawing further suspicion to myself. I should have told the police about the blackmail while I had the chance, but doing so now would be throwing a hand grenade into an already fragile chaos in which I've no possibility of coming out well.

The duty solicitor walks with me back through the waiting area, offering nothing of any help on the way. Marcus is pacing the room; he stops when he sees us, relief passing over his face as he realises that I've not been arrested.

'What did they say?' he asks once we're in the car, waiting for privacy before he starts a conversation.

'They think someone was with Cameron on Thursday. They don't think it was an accident.'

Marcus starts the engine. He looks grey as he reverses the car out of the parking space and heads towards the exit, barely looking in my direction as he waits for a gap in the traffic before pulling out onto the main road.

'What do you mean?' he finally asks.

'Well, they didn't say explicitly, but...' I can't bring myself to say the word 'murder', but I don't need to. Marcus doesn't need it spelled out.

I take my phone from my coat pocket and check my emails. Three junk. One from the person I've been expecting to hear from.

I open it. There's no greeting, just a single sentence that punches me in the gut.

A polite reminder: you have until 6 p.m.

THIRTY

Marcus barely looks at me as he drives towards home. I tell him I've got a terrible headache, the lie falling as easily from my lips as they all seem to these days, without me having to do much thinking about them. As I'd hoped, he offers to stop and pick me up some paracetamol from the supermarket, and I give him a list of three or four extra things we need, just to buy myself a bit more time while he's in there.

Once he's out of the car, I log on to my online banking. I transfer five hundred thousand pounds from the savings account it's been sitting in for months to my current account, watching the numbers on the screen change as though they're meaningless. Five hundred thousand pounds. It's a small fraction of what my father managed to extort from his employees and colleagues during his reign of greed, and yet looking at that figure on the screen now, its life-changing quality seems unthinkable. Within these next moments, this intangible sum has the ability to make or break a life, depending on what I do next.

Five hundred thousand pounds is a fortune. Even though it isn't mine, it doesn't deserve to go to a person who's found a way to threaten everything that means most to me in this world. A lump solidifies in my chest. This is what my father did to people. All those years he extorted money from his colleagues using blackmail and threats of violence, this is how he made his victims feel. I was seventeen years old when his crimes were first exposed. To my mind then, and still now, the life I'd led until that time had been a lie. My father was a fake and a fraud. And as for my mother, Cameron and me, we were all guilty by association.

I search my emails for the account details my blackmailer sent me. Kieran can have it – every penny. I don't care about the money. I'm not sure I even care about my marriage any more. All I care about is finding the person responsible for my brother's death. I care about saving my career. I care about finding Erin and discovering what really happened to her last weekend.

I tap the account details into my phone, followed by the figure I want to transfer, then press the button to make the payment. For a moment, nothing happens, just a buffering line that signals something's in progress. Then I see an exclamation mark, with a note that tells me I'm exceeding the amount I'm able to transfer.

Panicking, I edit the details to one hundred thousand, but again I get the same response. I try fifty, but get the same again. My heart rate begins to increase as I wonder how I'm going to get my hands on the money. It's Saturday afternoon: the bank in town just a mile or so away closed at midday.

I keep trying, eventually managing to transfer twenty thousand pounds. It's a wonder the app let me continue trying after so many attempts, but I'm grateful at least that I've managed to send over something. Checking the shop doors in case Marcus is already heading back out to the car park, I go into my emails and quickly tap out a message.

20K sent. It's all the banking app would allow me to transfer
in one go. Will have to send some more tomorrow, or can get
to bank on Monday. Please wait – you will get the money.

Just moments after I press send, I see Marcus near the ATM
machines, carrying a plastic carrier bag. I feel my phone vibrate
as he gets into the driver's seat.

'Bottle of water and some paracetamol in there for you,' he
tells me, handing me the bag.

'Thank you.'

I take two tablets as he makes his way out of the car park. I
turn in my seat, angling myself so I'm able to read the reply to
my email without Marcus catching a glimpse of it if he happens
to look over. At first, I see no message – just a list of email
addresses. I don't need to look closely to recognise them. Several
belong to my colleagues at school. Then there are PTA
members, parents, education officers from the council; followed
by addresses I don't recognise, though the names of local papers
and media outlets make it obvious the type of people they
belong to and just what the sender of this email plans to do
to me.

At the bottom is the message.

I'm not fucking about. If I don't get the rest of the money
within 24 hours, this list gets the video.

'Are you okay?' Marcus asks.

'I need to go to my mother's house.'

'Now?'

'There's something I have to pick up.'

'Can't it wait? We need to get home. We need to talk.'

If only he knew the true extent of just how much we should
talk. Briefly I think about telling him. He might be able to help
me. But he doesn't have that kind of money sitting around to

give me, and I know that if I tell him about the blackmail, he'll want to see the video. He may think now that he's prepared to forgive me for my night with Kieran, but if he watches that footage, I know he'll change his mind. There'll be no going back from it.

'I won't be long,' I tell him. 'I just need to find something.'

'What?'

'Just some documents for the solicitor. He needs them before the house can be put up for sale.'

Lying, I suppose, is just like anything else: the more of it you do, the easier it becomes. The better you get at it. The more it becomes second nature.

'It's Saturday, Lou. Whatever it is, you won't get it to him before Monday anyway. It can wait.'

'It can't.' I open the car door while we're moving. Marcus swerves, veering into the opposite lane as he yells at me to close the door.

'What the fuck are you doing?' he shouts.

'Take me there or I'll take myself.'

He eyes me as though I've lost my mind, but he takes the next left turning and heads towards Pelton, muttering his frustration beneath his breath.

Years ago, not long after my mother was diagnosed with dementia, she told me that my father had hidden some money in the house. She said it in such a way as to suggest that she wasn't talking about a twenty-pound note; she meant serious money – money the police had managed to miss despite their various searches of the place. A part of me wrote off her words as soon as she'd spoken them: she had just received life-altering news, and her memories of my father and her life in that house were all tainted by his crimes. I mentioned it to Marcus once, and he believed there could be truth in her claim. He was right: my father was guilty of so much that the idea of him hoarding money in the house was entirely credible when stacked against his vast back-catalogue of crimes. I often wondered how frequently my mother must have dwelled on how different her life might have been had she made other choices: if she'd married someone else, or if she'd left my father while Cameron and I were still young. Either way, I didn't pay too much attention to what she told me. I didn't want to hear about that money; I didn't want to know. But I still recall her mentioning something about a jigsaw.

When we get to the house, I tell Marcus I'm not sure where my mother kept the documents. I know I'm clutching at the most desperate of straws: if the police were unable to find that money, and if it was here the whole time I lived here as a teenager, I'm not sure why I'd even contemplate how a quick ten-minute search could lead me to the secret stash my father hid all those years ago. But this is what I am now: desperate. And it's worth a go before I spend the rest of the evening panicking over a plan B.

'I won't be long.'

I leave him in the car while I go into my mother's house, planning to head straight for my old bedroom. I was always more of a jigsaw and board game child than Cameron ever was, so it seems the most logical place for the money to have been hidden. The floorboards creak as I hurry upstairs. In the wardrobe, I hunt through old shoes and bags, in wonder at the things my mother held on to for all these years. When my search proves fruitless, I look beneath the bed for a loose floorboard. The notion is lunacy, my imaginings stolen from the books I've read, but my optimism is prepared to believe that in these next few moments, anything might be possible.

There's an odd smell in the bedroom. It's too strong to be damp or mould; it smells almost like decay, something rotting somewhere, and as I continue my search, the odour makes me feel nauseous. After emptying the contents of every drawer and cupboard onto the carpet, I head downstairs to the living room.

My mother's things still lie everywhere: blankets thrown over the backs of chairs, books shoved chaotically onto shelves, framed photographs gathering dust on every available surface. I go to the cupboard in the corner and start pulling things out frantically, searching for a jigsaw puzzle among the stash of crap my mother accumulated over the years: sewing patterns she would never complete, recipe books she would never use, board games no one has taken the lids off since 1995.

Once again, my search yields nothing but clutter.

'Please, Mum,' I say aloud as I get up from the carpet. 'Send me some kind of sign.'

I wait there like an idiot, as though my plea might be received from beyond the grave and prompt one of the paintings on the wall to wobble or a book to fly out from the shelving unit: some supernatural pointer to a hidden safe embedded within the brickwork behind the woodchip wallpaper.

'Louise!'

'Shit,' I mumble, almost stumbling over a pile of junk as I make my way to the living room door. Then something catches my eye. Something coral-coloured fallen down the side of the armchair. I reach to pick it up. It's a scarf. I don't remember ever seeing my mother wear it, although she never really went anywhere, especially not in her later years. I put it to my face and breathe in the scent of her, a perfume I don't recognise still trapped in the fibres of the cotton.

'What are you doing?'

I throw the scarf over the arm of the chair as Marcus comes into the room. His face changes when he takes in my appearance, flustered and red-cheeked.

'Are you okay?'

I know I look terrible. Nausea churns in my stomach, as though I might throw up over the carpet at my feet, with no control over myself. 'Not really. I'm not feeling great.'

'We need to get home. This is ridiculous – it can wait.'

I pause for a moment as I try to work out what to do for the best. He isn't going to be put off, and I can't look for the money while he's here in the house with me. Perhaps I could wait until tonight, until he's asleep, and then come back here to search. If he wakes to find me gone, I could use Maria as an excuse, feigning some kind of emergency.

'Come on,' he says. 'It's bloody freezing in here.'

I follow him through to the kitchen and out of the house, locking the kitchen door behind me. In the car, he starts the engine and turns the heating up.

'So what are you going to do?' he asks.

'About what?'

'The solicitor,' he says impatiently.

I can barely bring myself to look at him. I feel sick at the thought of that email reaching the local education authority, and I still have a headache over the revelation that Marcus might have been with Cameron just a few weeks ago. I wish he had told me. If he'd told me, I wouldn't now be thinking the worst.

Speak to her again and you're a dead man.

THIRTY-ONE

I go straight upstairs for a bath when we get in, using the excuse of my headache to get some time alone. Earlier I couldn't look at Marcus because I felt so guilty. Now I can't bring myself to look at him because I don't know what to think about his fight with Cameron. Did he go over to Cameron's on Thursday to finish what had been started? The more I think, the worse it becomes. My thoughts grow darker, and Marcus appears more and more guilty.

But we said we would be honest with each other, and he has been. If he was responsible for Cameron's death, he wouldn't have told me about the fight at my mother's house. He could have feigned ignorance when I asked him what Cameron had meant when he told me I needed to speak to my husband. He could have made an excuse; said he didn't know what he was talking about.

When I get out of the bath and go back into the bedroom, a towel wrapped around me, Marcus is sitting on the bed waiting for me.

'How's your head?'

'Still banging.'

He pats the duvet next to him, and I sit beside him, my entire body tensed. I love this man, I remind myself. I trust this man.

But my mother loved my father. She trusted him in everything... until she had reason not to.

'None of this is your fault,' he tells me again, a mantra to pull myself from the cyclic destructive thoughts he knows I'm prone to. 'Cameron made plenty of enemies. Whatever happened, there wouldn't have been anything you could have done to stop it.'

He puts a hand on my leg, pushing aside the towel. His fingers slide up my thigh.

'I can't,' I say, putting a hand on his arm, gently pushing him away. 'Too much has happened.'

He leans in and kisses me. 'I forgive you. What happened with Kieran... it was as much my fault as yours. I shouldn't have pushed for that night at the hotel. You had doubts, but I encouraged you to ignore them. I just want to forget any of it ever happened, okay? I just want to go back to being us.'

He kisses me again, and this time I relent, closing my eyes and letting his tongue find mine. Everything about it feels wrong, though. I picture Kieran, and Marcus senses my body stiffen as I pull away.

'Are you okay?'

No. I'm not okay. Nothing is okay. I can't trust you. I can't trust myself.

I pull the towel around me, covering myself. 'I'm just not feeling great.'

'It's not surprising.' He puts his arm around my shoulder, drawing me close. 'I'm so sorry about Cameron. We didn't see eye to eye, but I know you loved him. I should have told you about what happened the other week. I'm sorry.'

I say nothing, just let him hold me. I don't know what time it is, but it feels later than it probably is. I wonder whether

Kieran will really allow me the extra twenty-four hours to find the money, or if that attachment is already sitting in a dozen inboxes, waiting to be opened first thing on Monday morning.

'There's some wine in the fridge,' Marcus says. 'Shall I get us a glass?'

'Not for me.'

'Cup of tea?'

I nod, and he slides from the bed. I watch him as he leaves the room. The tension at my temples tightens, the thought of my brother's body lying at the bottom of a staircase returning like the details of a nightmare, taunting me with its irreversible truth. And then another image fills my mind, sudden and intrusive: Erin's naked body lying in a ditch, her grey skin dappled with frost. The cool marble of her complexion appears in high definition, every detail of her exposed to my mind's eye, and a rush of bile floods my mouth. I hurry into the en suite and throw up into the toilet.

'Lou?'

Marcus comes into the bathroom and crouches beside me. He runs his palm up and down my back.

'You're okay,' he says soothingly. 'Everything's going to be okay.'

He puts an arm around me and guides me back into the bedroom, rearranging the pillows so I can sit up to drink the tea he's made.

'I meant to tell you – I won't be going back to the Isle of Wight. The production company has found someone else to take my place.'

I lower the mug from my lips. 'I'm so sorry.'

'What are you sorry for?'

'I know how much this job meant to you.'

He waves his free hand, dismissing my apology. 'It's nothing. There'll be more work, it doesn't matter. Nothing matters except making sure you're okay.'

He climbs onto the bed beside me, and I put my tea on the bedside table so I can curl myself into him, resting my head on his chest. He plays absent-mindedly with my hair as we sit in silence for a while, absorbing the enormity of everything. I finish my tea and feel my eyes growing heavy, exhaustion dragging me towards the grip of sleep. When I edge down the pillows, trying to get comfortable, Marcus slides down beside me and pulls the duvet over us. He lies on his side, his face close to mine, and runs his finger along the length of my arm, slowly up and down. His touch feels barely there, my skin somehow absent from my body.

'Close your eyes,' he tells me, his voice somehow two rooms away, though he's right here beside me. 'It'll all be over soon.'

THIRTY-TWO

The first thought I have as my mind drags itself into consciousness is that I can't open my eyes. My lids are weighed down by an unseen force, with a pressure behind them that feels like the tug of a migraine. My second thought is of Marcus. Marcus and Cameron together at my mother's house. I picture their argument; Marcus hitting my brother. Cameron hitting his head as he fell. Was this really what happened? Or did it happen somewhere else, more recently than Marcus has admitted to? Just because I didn't know where my brother was living doesn't mean Marcus didn't.

The bedroom is a blur as I manage to peel my eyes open. Everything seems out of focus, like a camera homed in on a single tiny detail, so small I'm unable to make it out. My head screams as I turn onto my back. It feels like the worst of hangovers, yet I didn't touch a drop yesterday. I reach out a hand, feeling the sheet on his side of the bed. Marcus isn't here.

I don't know where I left my phone. It isn't on the bedside table, and when I lean over to check the carpet beside the bed, I'm almost sick with the pressure that floods my brain. This is unlike anything I've ever known; not like any hangover I've ever had. Then the evening comes back to me, rushing in on a wave of memory. I didn't drink wine. I only had a cup of tea.

It'll all be over soon.

I hear his voice as though he's still here in the room with me, and the echo of his words startles me. The mug left on the bedside table crashes to the carpet as I push back the duvet and haul myself from bed, my brain shaking in my head as I try to steady myself. Nothing makes sense. Marcus. Kieran.

The money.

I think about the email that was sent to me yesterday. I've no idea what time it is, but whatever the time, I'm running out of hours to find that money. I should have known already that I wouldn't be able to make such a large transaction in one go, but I was so consumed with thoughts of Cameron and Kieran and Erin and Marcus that it just didn't occur to me. I left everything until the last minute, as though it all might just disappear if I ignored it for long enough. I haven't been able to think straight, and that's never applied more so than this morning.

Marcus couldn't have sent that email, I think. He was sitting beside me in the car when I received it.

Have he and Kieran been working together this whole time? Did Erin somehow find out what they were plotting, and is this the true reason for her disappearance? If Marcus was capable of killing Cameron, he wouldn't have thought twice about hurting Erin.

I feel nauseous as I stumble around the end of the bed. The room seems to shift as though I'm on a boat, and the floor sways beneath me.

There was something in the tea. For whatever reason, Marcus wanted me out of it. Either that, or something worse.

I go into the en suite, shaky on my feet. I use the toilet before splashing cold water over my face, then dress with difficulty, my balance failing me as I try to pull on a pair of leggings. There's no noise from downstairs. From anywhere in the house.

Marcus isn't here. With still no idea what the time is, I go downstairs in search of my phone. The clock on the kitchen wall tells me it's 10.15 a.m.: the latest I've overslept in as long as I can remember. I would never sleep for this long unless I'd been spiked with something, and the only person who could be responsible for that is Marcus. The thought makes sickness surge in my throat, and I dash for the downstairs toilet, a gush of tea and bile leaving me in a fountain.

When I've gained enough strength to haul myself up off the bathroom floor, I find my phone in my coat pocket and try his number. It goes straight to answerphone. I go back upstairs to the smallest of the bedrooms, furnished as an office but rarely used by either of us. In the desk drawer, I search for our passports, finding mine straight away. But Marcus's is gone. I drop into the swivel chair, trying to make sense of what's happening. It's difficult to even try to think straight when my head is pounding and another rush of sickness is threatening to wash over me.

Have I been emailing Marcus this whole time? We had a prenup. I never doubted his intentions, but I wanted everything to be done properly, and he's always known how I felt about the blood money I knew I'd be likely to inherit. There was no chance of my mother leaving any of it to Cameron, so I knew the responsibility of getting rid of it somehow would be left with me. Marcus never showed any interest in that money. As far as I knew, his feelings towards it were the same as mine: that it was dirty money, useless for anything other than being put towards something good. We've talked about where it might go; how it might finally be used to do something positive after all this time. He could have emailed me yesterday, while he was sitting in the waiting area at the police station, while I was being interviewed. Is *iknowyourlittlesecret@gmail.com* him?

I'm sick again, this time barely making it to the bathroom. When there's nothing left to come up, my stomach burns from retching. My heart burns with betrayal. Marcus has been lying to me this whole time. He's been blackmailing me. But that would mean he knows about the video of Kieran and me together; that he already knew all about that night. Marcus. Kieran. They must have plotted this together. I can't begin to even process the possibilities.

I return to my phone, finding Maria's number. She answers after just a couple of rings.

'Where are you?'

'I'll give you one guess.'

I can hear the background noise: the shouting of inaudible words and the high-pitched scream of the wind. She's at a football match with one of the boys.

'Is James there with you?'

'Yes. What's going on?'

'I can't drive. I'll explain later. But I'd rather tell you everything in person than over the phone.'

There's a long pause. Maria doesn't want to get dragged into any more of my drama, and I don't blame her for wanting to keep a distance. I've lied to her as much as I've lied to everyone else. As much, apparently, as I've been lied to.

'It's Marcus,' I tell her, when she doesn't offer a response. 'The blackmail.'

I wait as she processes the information. 'Christ, Louise,' she finally says. 'Where are you? Are you at home? Is he there with you now?'

'No. I don't know where he is. His passport's gone.'

I hear her sigh as she battles with the internal dilemma of whether to keep herself out of any potential trouble or help me. 'Fuck,' I hear her mutter, and this alone is enough to let me know just how far I've pushed her. Maria rarely swears. 'Give me half an hour.'

I am so grateful in this moment to have a friend like her: someone who has watched me make my worst mistakes but is prepared to put our differences aside when I need her the most. I know I don't deserve her loyalty, but I am thankful all the same.

As promised, a short while later I hear her car pull up onto the driveway. I go outside before she has time to get out of the car, and climb into the passenger seat beside her. Her eyes narrow when she takes in my appearance: the dark circles around my eyes, the bloodshot whites; the greasy hair scraped back into a too-tight ponytail.

'He spiked my drink,' I say as I pull the car door closed.

'Marcus?'

'He gave me a cup of tea last night. I woke up feeling like crap. But I've never felt *that* crap.' Maria is the only person other than Marcus who knows the details of my past. I've trusted her enough to confide in her about what happened to me after my father's crimes were exposed, so she knows about the drinking and the partying. She knows how much it took for me to drag myself out of that place, to give myself the kind of life I'd told myself for years I didn't deserve.

But perhaps I was right to begin with. Maybe I never deserved it, and that's why we're sitting here now, having this conversation.

'Everything is so complicated,' I tell her, fastening my seat belt. 'But now his passport's gone, I know he sent those emails. He must have set up an account in a false name. He's been planning this for ages.'

I think back on those early days of our relationship, when I trusted him with so much of myself and my history. He was the first person in years I'd felt an instinctive connection with, instant and undeniable. Most of the men who'd entered my life had come and gone in brief succession. Some had accused me of being unfeeling. Others had seen an opportunity for a bit of fun in which nothing was expected of them, and they'd left as soon as they'd grown bored, neither party caring when the spark fizzled and burnt out. But it was different with Marcus. I trusted him. I wanted more from him than just the physical escape so many men before him had brought with them, and so I let him in, and he stayed, and I loved him for the non-judgemental way he just listened for so many hours without passing comment.

I'd not felt that same instinctive connection again until I met Kieran.

All those conversations, all those hours... all the attention Marcus showed me during the early months of our relationship looks so different now, with the benefit of hindsight. I've no idea how long he's known Kieran, but it must surely be longer than I've known Erin.

'Are you sure?' Maria asks, though her expression suggests she's as certain as I am. A missing passport means only one thing. 'How did he get that footage, though?'

'Kieran. They must have been plotting this together. That night the house was trashed... maybe it wasn't Cameron. There was no sign of a break-in, was there? I told the police he must have got his hands on the spare key. But what if it was Marcus?'

Maria puts the gearstick into reverse, but she doesn't move the car. 'Where are we going?'

'Kieran's house.'

'That's madness,' she says, cutting the engine. She leans forward, arms resting on the steering wheel.

'Please. Hear me out. I can't let them both just walk away from all this. At least one of them knows what's happened to Erin.'

Every time I speak her name, a tide of guilt floods over me. I can't escape the feeling that no matter what's happened to her, it needn't have. The feeling that she is collateral damage in this awful situation, and that I might have changed things somehow if only I'd acted differently.

'I owe it to her to find out the truth.'

Maria's expression darkens as she looks at me. 'Do you think it was Marcus who hurt Erin?'

'No. Yes. I don't know. Kieran maybe. Both of them. I just don't know.'

'This is all such a mess,' she says, sitting back and folding her arms across her chest. 'It's been a week now. Do you think she's...'

She can't bring herself to say the word 'dead'. But I've thought it endlessly, a loop that's gone around and around in my head, taunting me. Erin's disappearance... Cameron's death. Cameron's murder. The thought that my brother might not in some way be connected to all this seems too much of a coincidence. Perhaps no one was meant to get hurt, but they got in the way somehow.

'I thought Kieran was behind the email. I still do. But Marcus is the only person who knows how much money was left to me in my mother's will. Marcus and Cameron.'

'So you think they argued over the money?'

'Maybe. It seems to make sense, I suppose. Either that or Cameron had somehow found out what Marcus was up to. Please, Maria. I need to stop them leaving.'

She sighs and starts the engine. 'You've no idea how dangerous Kieran might be.'

She's right: I don't. But I fear that whatever happens next, I might be about to find out, and I have no other option left than to face the unknown head-on.

THIRTY-THREE

When we get to Kieran's street, I ask Maria to stop the car at the end of the road, not wanting to risk either Kieran or Jasper seeing me before I get to the house.

'I'll wait here for you.'

'Don't,' I tell her. 'You've done enough.'

'He could be dangerous, Louise – I'm not just going to leave.'

There's no point in trying to argue with her about it; Maria is headstrong, and the most loyal person I've ever met. I tell her not to let herself be seen; the last thing I want is for Kieran to know she's here and for her to get dragged further into this mess.

As I did the last time I came here, I go around to the side door. I pass Kieran's car on the driveway, so I assume he must be home. The curtains in the front window are closed, which seems odd for early afternoon. At the back of the house, the kitchen blinds are open. The room is quiet, no one there. I knock on the glass of the door. There's no sound at first, but when I knock again, I hear voices from inside the house.

Kieran comes to the door. He's wearing scruffy jogging

bottoms and a hoodie, and the grey bags beneath his eyes betray his lack of sleep.

'What are you doing here?'

'Where is he?'

His eyes narrow. 'Where's who?'

'Marcus. Don't bullshit me, Kieran, please. I know what's going on.'

Behind him, Jasper appears from the hallway. He's dressed in pyjama trousers and a T-shirt with the name of some band I've never heard of. He's been crying, his eyes red-rimmed and bloodshot. When he sees me, he looks at the floor, embarrassed by his appearance.

'Are you okay, Jasper? What's he done to you?'

Kieran's jaw stiffens. 'What do you want?'

'Marcus,' I say again. 'Where is he?'

'How the hell would I know?'

'I know everything,' I tell him, trying to steady my voice and hide my fear. 'I know you've been sending those emails. I know Marcus knows about the footage. How long were the two of you plotting this?' I almost ask him what he did to Erin, but with Jasper standing just behind him, I can't bring myself to do it. Whatever's happened to his mother, he shouldn't be subjected to the truth of it like this.

'What footage?' Kieran asks, his eyes narrowing. 'I have no idea what you're talking about.'

It's then that I hear it. The sound comes as though I'm hearing it from a dream, or some distant memory long forgotten and resurfaced. Her laughter tinkles from the living room, haunting.

'Erin.'

I barge past him, sidestepping Jasper as I push open the door, almost stumbling over the chaos littering the floor: the albums and photographs, greetings cards and memory boxes. The paraphernalia of a life.

'Jay,' Erin's voice says lightly. 'Say cheese.'

Her face fills the television screen. Behind her, Christmas tree lights glitter, and when the camera pans away from her, the focus moves to a small child sitting amid a mess of ripped-up wrapping paper and cardboard boxes, his smiling mouth smeared with chocolate and his eyes lit with the excitement of Santa's visit. Little Jasper, no more than three years old.

I look down at the floor. An entire life is played out among the photographs and memories: a wedding day, a birth, parties, festivities, sports days. Erin is everywhere I look. Posing in a long white dress on a newly mown lawn. Lying in a hospital bed with a red-faced newborn scrunched at her chest. Sitting at a table laid for Christmas dinner, a paper crown on her head and a goofy expression stretched across her beautiful face.

Kieran and Jasper are behind me, but I can barely bring myself to look at them.

'I'm sorry,' I mumble, ashamed at the way I've intruded on such an intimate moment.

Kieran reaches for the remote control and pauses the video that's still playing on the television. Erin's face is paused on the screen, her image frozen mid laughter.

'Jasper, do you mind going upstairs?'

'But...' He falls silent, though I don't see whatever look is passed between him and Kieran.

'Please, mate. Just five minutes.'

Jasper glares at me. I can't blame him for the reaction, though I've still no idea just how much he might know. He huffs and mutters something beneath his breath, but turns and heads up the stairs. I don't hear a bedroom door sound, so I assume he's on the landing, listening in on us.

When I look at Kieran, I no longer know what to believe. This past week, I have feared him more than anyone, believing him to be responsible for the disappearance of his wife. I've thought him guilty of trying to blackmail me. Now, amid the scene I've walked in on, everything is changed. Yet people are capable of living double lives, seeming to be one thing while really another.

He moves into the living room and pushes the door closed behind him. 'I just want her home,' he says, close to tears.

My breath catches in my throat. I can't let my guard down; I might still be right. He may still be all the things I've feared. People are capable of anything, given the wrong set of circumstances.

'Why have you come here looking for Marcus?' he asks.

The answer clogs at the back of my mouth, choking any sound. I don't know where to start or how to explain anything.

'Louise. Why are you looking for Marcus?'

I stare down at the floor, at the montage of images surrounding me.

'Where's Iris?' I ask, scanning each photograph in turn. There isn't a single image of her. I can't imagine that even in the bleakest depths of grief, anyone would be capable of removing a child from their family history, deleting her from memory as though she'd never existed.

I've barely thought of Iris since Friday evening. The news of Cameron's death sent everything else scattering to the far corners of my brain. Now I can once again make no sense of what I saw on Friday, or Beth's explanation for how she'd come by the child's photograph.

Kieran's eyebrows knit. 'Where is she?' I repeat.

'Don't you think I wish I knew?' His face alters, the greyness beneath his eyes seeming to seep through to the rest of his skin. 'Do you think it was me? Do you think I did something to her?'

'I don't mean Erin,' I say, no longer knowing what to believe. 'I mean Iris.' I sweep a hand across the air, gesturing to the images laid out before us. 'Where is she?'

Kieran's eyes narrow. 'Who's Iris?'

THIRTY-FOUR

The temperature between us seems to drop several degrees. I came here believing the worst of Kieran, yet it's now the case that he's wary of me.

'Erin told me you had a daughter together. Iris. She said she died when she was six years old.'

Kieran's jaw tightens with my words, his face locked with something that might be anger, might be grief.

'She told you that?'

'There's no Iris, is there?'

My whole body tenses when he moves towards me. I brace myself for an assault, but it doesn't come; instead, he drops onto the sofa, his head in his hands.

'Why would she tell you something like that?'

'You've never had a child together then?'

'Jasper was four when I met her. It wasn't long after that.' He gestures to the television screen. 'She was a single mum holding down two jobs. She told me she'd had a traumatic birth with him, that she'd almost died during the delivery. She made it clear early on that she could never go through another labour, and I was fine with it. If it was a choice between children and her, I chose her.' He lowers his hands from his face. 'Why the fuck would she make up something like that?'

To get me close, I think. To make herself seem vulnerable, in the same way she found me, still thick in the grief of losing my mother. Inventing Iris gave us a shared experience, a common ground of loss upon which she could build our friendship.

But I don't say any of this aloud. Kieran wants answers, but I'm not the person to offer them.

'I don't understand why she'd say something like that. You must have got it wrong.'

'I didn't get anything wrong. She showed me a photograph of a little girl. Blue eyes, like yours. She asked me never to mention her to you. She said you were still devastated by her death.'

Kieran's face is shadowed with anger. We find ourselves unexpectedly in the same scenario, confronted with the fact that our spouses aren't the people we believed them to be.

'But why?'

'I don't know. I suppose Erin's the only person who can answer that.'

'I think she saw the socks you left here,' he says, avoiding eye contact with me. 'I found them later on Saturday night, but she'd already been upstairs by then. She was a bit quiet with me, but I thought she was just tired. She'd been quiet a lot recently, way before she met you. We'd been arguing. Nothing I ever did seemed enough for her. When she didn't come back from Bristol on Sunday, I thought she was doing it to make me suffer, to pay me back for what we'd done. But it went on too long. She wouldn't do that to Jasper. Someone's hurt her, Louise. And no matter what happened between us, it's my job to protect her. I wasn't there for her. When she needed me most, I...'

He stops dead as a realisation falls upon him.

'Marcus. You came here looking for Marcus. Do you think he's done something to her?'

'I don't know,' I say, when what I really mean now is yes.

Kieran stands and heads for the door.

'Kieran,' I say, grabbing him by the arm. 'Stop just a minute. Please. We don't know where he is. We need to work out what the hell's going on, and maybe then we can work out what to do.'

He needs to know about the blackmail. He needs to know about the footage of us together, because if he's not responsible for it, that only leaves one other person.

'Are you and Erin in an open marriage?' I ask.

I think back on how nervous he seemed in the hotel room that night, and how it struck me as odd for someone who apparently did this kind of thing all the time. I'd hoped he'd take charge, that he would defuse my own anxiety, but we were just as uncertain as each other, neither of us sure how to behave in circumstances that were so unusual for us both.

Now, looking back at the memory, it looks entirely different. He was as nervous as I was because we were both at the same place. Neither of us had been there before. Neither of us knew how to react to the situation.

'What?'

'Erin told me you'd had an open marriage for years.'

His eyebrows knit together again as he tries to make sense of my words. 'She'd been distant for ages. I felt like I was losing her. I suggested counselling, but she wouldn't consider it – not for herself and definitely not for the two of us together. She was going to leave me. But then you came up in conversation. She started talking about non-monogamy, all this stuff about how she'd read it could save relationships. She told me you'd planted the idea with her. That you and Marcus were "living the life-style",' he says, raising his fingers to make inverted commas. 'I thought you'd done it all before. I wasn't convinced by the idea, but Erin wanted it, and I'd have done anything to keep her.'

He falls silent. Unless Kieran is an Oscar-worthy actor, the evidence of Erin's lies is stacking in a pile in front of us. She played us all for idiots, weaving a story at different angles, altering it each time to suit her audience. But what I don't know is why she did it.

'I thought it was you who'd been sending those emails.'

'What emails?'

Kieran sits quietly while I tell him about the footage of the two of us, and the blackmail demands that followed. It's only when I've finished my explanation that I remember Maria is still sitting outside in her car, presumably worrying about me. I get out my phone and text her.

I'm fine. I'm safe. Kieran isn't involved. This is all Marcus.

I press send, and the message is opened instantly.

'But how the hell could a camera have been set up in my own bedroom without me knowing about it?' Kieran asks, surely already knowing the answer. There's only one person who could have been responsible.

'I thought the two of you were working together. But it wasn't you and Marcus, was it? It was Marcus and Erin.'

'And now she's gone,' he says quietly. He stands, his face fixed in a grimace as he retrieves his phone from the windowsill. 'I'll fucking kill him.'

'Wait,' I say, putting a hand on his arm. 'We need to think this through logically. We don't even know where he is. His passport's gone.'

Kieran pulls away from me and goes to the living room door. When he opens it, he's greeted by Jasper, who's been standing in the hallway, presumably having heard everything. He looks from Kieran to me and back again, mistrust in his eyes.

'I'm so sorry, Jasper,' I say. 'I never meant for any of this to happen.'

'Where is she?' he asks Kieran, ignoring my apology.

'I don't know.'

Kieran moves past Jasper to get his car keys from the hallway table. Above it, jackets and bags hang from a row of coat pegs. One of Erin's handbags is hooked at the end of the row, resting on top of a green silk scarf.

'I'm coming with you,' Jasper says.

'No you're not. You stay here.'

'I'm not a little kid, you can't tell me what to do any more. She's my mother.'

'I think I know where she is,' I say quietly, the words barely audible.

Kieran turns sharply to me. 'What?'

I go to the row of coats and move Erin's handbag aside, feeling Kieran and Jasper's eyes upon me as I reach for the scarf and pull it to my face. I breathe in its scent, the smell of Erin's perfume still trapped within the fibres of the silk. Yesterday afternoon floods back in a rush of senses. My mother's house. The living room. The scarf on the carpet at the side of the chair. The perfume I didn't recognise, believing myself to have forgotten its scent.

'Louise,' Kieran pleads with me, desperate for an answer.

'You need to take me there. I know where Erin is.'

THIRTY-FIVE

After we've left Kieran's street, I realise I didn't check to see whether Maria's car was still there at the end of the road. I check my phone now, seeing the reply she sent just after I'd messaged her.

Please stay safe. I'm not going anywhere.

I tap out a message, needing her to know my location should anything go wrong.

On way to my mother's house. Too much to explain. I think Marcus took Erin there.

I add the address and press send. I've spoken to Maria about my mother's place many times, but though I've described it, she's never been there and doesn't know where it is other than in Pelton.

I think of the smell I noticed there yesterday. Something rotten and decaying. The smell of death. Bile rises in my throat. Kieran catches my eye as he turns onto the main road that links

Eastbridge with Pelton. With the colour drained from my face, I think he's able to read my thoughts. He knows what we're about to find.

I turn to Jasper in the back seat. 'You have to wait in the car. My husband could be dangerous.'

He glares at me, but I see the glint of tears in his eyes, and my heart breaks for this boy who is in so many ways still a child.

'Fuck your husband,' he says, the words shaking. 'And fuck you.'

Kieran's eyes stay fixed to the road, and I turn back to the windscreen, telling him where he needs to head next. The roads become narrower and the greenery denser, and when we turn into the lane that leads to my mother's house, I feel sick with the promise of what we might find. My own naïvety tears at my chest. I was there just yesterday, with Marcus, and Erin was somewhere there too, so close to us without me realising. The root of all the bad things was standing in front of me the whole time: there in my home; there in my bed.

I see my husband's car before we reach the house. Kieran pulls onto the driveway, blocking Marcus's only exit route, and is out of the car before I've even had a chance to unclip my seat belt.

'I know you hate me,' I say to Jasper, 'and I don't blame you, but please, stay here, for your own safety.'

He ignores me, not so much as making eye contact as he undoes his seat belt and gets out of the car. I do the same, running to catch Kieran up, trying to stop him before he reaches the front door. 'Please stop Jasper from going in there. Please, for his sake.'

Understanding what I'm trying to communicate, Kieran stops. Neither of us knows how long Erin has been here, or what Marcus may have done to her. I see the sickness that has settled on his face, his skin tinged with an unearthly green tint. He turns back to Jasper and grabs him by the arm, pulling him back down the driveway as the boy shouts out in protest. I hurry to the back door, which I find unlocked. When I rush through to the kitchen, Marcus is sitting at the table with his back to me, the room bathed in a strange silence, as though he knew he'd be found and has been sitting here waiting for us.

'How the fuck could you?' I ask him, my voice trembling.

He doesn't bother turning to me, too much of a coward to grace me with any kind of response. There's nothing he could say to me now, though. Nothing could ever explain why he's done the things he has, and no attempt at redemption could even begin to put right the wrongs he's caused so many people. I look at the back of his head, contemplating the circuitry of him. So many times I have wondered what it would mean to be able to see his thoughts. Now I'm grateful in some ways to have been ignorant of the things that make him tick.

I wonder why he's back here when he's had the chance to leave. Surely by taking his passport from the house, that was what he was planning.

My attention is drawn to the floor beneath his chair, where I notice a dark patch staining the floor.

'Marcus?'

He doesn't move, and when at last he speaks, the sound is little more than a gurgle. I step tentatively towards him, scared that he's trying to trick me into some kind of trap. I keep him at arm's length as I move around him, seeing now the way he's slumped back in the chair, one arm lolled to his side. He has his eyes open, and when he sees me in his peripheral vision, he tries to turn his head towards me. He mumbles something else, and this time I hear my name. It's then that I see the handle of the knife sticking out from his side.

'Shit.'

I search for something, anything, to staunch the flow of blood. In one of the drawers I find a pile of tea towels, and I take one and try to press it to the wound, but with the knife still embedded in his body, he cries out in pain as I knock the handle.

'I don't know what to do,' I say, as Kieran appears in the doorway. 'Call an ambulance.'

He just stands there for a moment, unresponsive to a scene that for both of us is completely unexpected.

'Kieran! Call 999!'

His mobile clatters to the floor as he fumbles in his pocket. Marcus groans something, but I can't make out what he's trying to say. It sounds like 'hex' or 'ex', but each time he opens his mouth, the attempt at the word becomes weaker.

'Try to stay still,' I tell him. 'Don't speak any more.'

'Where is she?' Kieran says, moving around the table to face Marcus, who by now is barely able to keep his eyes open. 'What have you done with her, you bastard?'

Marcus strains to focus, turning to me and reaching for my arm. He pulls me closer, his blood transferring from his sweater to my sleeve. His breathing is ragged, his throat gurgling again as he tries to force out the words.

'Hex,' he says again. 'Ex.'

I crouch beside him and urge him to stay awake, because no matter what he's done, he can't die like this. We all need too many answers. He doesn't deserve to leave without first telling the truth.

'What did I do to you?' I ask him, not expecting a reply. 'Other than love you and give you everything.'

Kieran stands there watching us, still not making any move to unlock his phone. He wants to let Marcus die, to let him suffer for whatever he's done to Erin.

'Please, Kieran,' I beg him. 'Don't be this person. If you stand here and let him die without doing anything to help, you're no better than he is. Jasper needs you to do the right thing. *I* need you to do the right thing.'

He looks at me, then sighs before sliding a thumb across his phone screen and tapping in his passcode. He moves to the back door, where he can get a better signal.

'Put the phone down.'

My body freezes at the sound of her voice. I'm still crouched beside Marcus, my focus on the stab wound in his side and the blood that's pumping through the tea towel and between my fingers. A chill snakes through me, running down my legs and reaching my toes. When I look up, Erin is standing in the door that leads through to the hallway, a second knife gripped in her hand.

THIRTY-SIX

When I turn to the back door, Kieran is standing there frozen. He looks as though he's seen a ghost. His eyes don't move from Erin while he convinces himself she's real. That she's really alive. A rush of emotions flood his face within mere seconds: relief merged with confusion, merged with betrayal, merged with fury. Erin looks far from the perfectly polished, glamorous woman I've known these past couple of months, although I suppose squatting in a stranger's house would have the same effect on anyone.

'Just let him go,' she says.

'Erin.' Kieran's voice is little more than a whisper.

'What's she told you?' she asks, talking about me as though I'm not here. 'It's all lies, Kieran, I swear. He's been keeping me here, locked upstairs. I managed to break free before he arrived earlier. It was self-defence.'

I look pleadingly at Kieran, wondering whether he's going to believe this bullshit. He knows now what a liar Erin is: Iris, the open marriage, all of it. He knows the deceit she's capable of.

'She invented a dead daughter to get my sympathy,' I remind him.

'Shut the fuck up,' Erin warns between gritted teeth.

'There she is,' I say. 'There's the real Erin.'

Marcus reaches for my arm and digs his fingers into my sleeve, still trying to communicate something.

'Did you set up that camera in our bedroom?' Kieran asks her. 'Or are you going to blame that on him as well?'

'He made me do it.'

He laughs bitterly, and I feel relief in my chest that he's no longer going to be fooled by her. 'I've never known anyone able to make you do anything, Erin.'

Her lips thin. 'Look at me,' she implores, ignoring my presence again as she appeals to her husband. 'He tried to blackmail me. He's kept me hostage. I've been terrified.'

'How did you know Louise would be at the house that night?' he asks, paying no attention to the fabricated version of events she's concocted in an attempt at a get-out clause.

'The break-in,' I remind him. 'It wasn't Cameron. It was Marcus. He knew I wouldn't want to be in the house on my own. It was all set up to get me over to your place.'

'No one forced you,' Erin said. 'You were quick enough to open your legs back up for him.'

I look at Marcus, incredulous, wondering what happened to the man I once knew; doubtful now that the person I believed him to be had ever really existed. I think of him trashing our living room in my absence, all the while focused on the warped plan he and Erin had in place to stage her disappearance. Her death. When I look back at Erin, a stranger in the doorway, I'm sickened with myself for ever being taken in by this woman's apparent charm. All the stories she constructed about her marriage. All the vulnerabilities she presented to encourage my sympathy; all the lies she spun to make me believe we had so much in common. Of course we did. We had Marcus. And who better to learn about me from than the person who knows me better than anyone.

'Shut up,' Kieran tells her.

'Aww,' Erin drawls, tilting her head to one side and smiling with a complete lack of sincerity. 'He's defending you. How cute. You two should get together.'

'Why did you join that yoga class?'

'Mindfulness,' she says, rolling her eyes.

I think back to the day I saw her, that first evening she came to the yoga session. Memories of our later conversations come back in snatches: the talk of marriage and family and life. The thought that she went to that class with the intention of targeting me makes me sick at my own naïvety.

'I thought you were a friend. I trusted you.'

'Some friend. Do you always go around shagging your friend's husbands?'

'What about you, Erin? Were you sleeping with Marcus?'

'Only until he gave me what I wanted,' she answers smugly. 'Poor thing, he really seemed to believe we were going to be together. Start a new life with your inheritance. Or so he claimed. All bullshit, I suppose. He's always been a liar. It's a shame about the rest of the money really, but never mind. You're going to need it to live on now your career's in tatters.'

The email. The list of addresses she threatened me with. She's already sent it.

She smiles with satisfaction, proud of the destruction she's wreaked upon my life.

She steps closer, the knife still poised. 'So where is it?'

'Where's what?'

'The rest of the cash. Marcus told me it's here somewhere. You didn't think I'd stay in this dump for any other reason, did you?'

I glance at Kieran, still in the doorway.

'Do *you* know?' she asks him, reading more into the look than was there.

'No one knows,' I tell her. 'I don't think even my mother knew where it was. Do you think if she did it would still be lying around here? I'm not even sure of the amount. You could have spent the last week searching for a fifty-pound note for all I know. Is that why you stabbed him, Erin? Because he couldn't give you as much as you wanted?'

'No, Louise. It's you who's failed me there.'

Everything that happens next happens so quickly. Erin surges towards me with the knife held at arm's length, aiming it at my stomach. But it never makes contact. Behind her, without any of us realising he's somehow gained access to the house, Jasper lunges for her. He swings a table lamp at her head, knocking her sideways, and the knife clatters to the floor.

I grab it before she's able to get her hands back on it. She groans on the floor, dazed and injured, no idea yet who her attacker was.

'You were going to leave me,' Jasper yells, his voice cracking. 'You were going to take her money and just fuck off without me.'

He heard everything. All those truths that were spilled here and in his living room, he heard them all. He knows about the blackmail. He knows about the footage of Kieran and me. But worse than anything he's had to listen to is the newly gained knowledge that his mother put him through the worst kind of ordeal imaginable, allowing him to believe that she had been murdered.

Erin puts a hand to her head and moans as she twists herself around to look at him. 'That's not true. I was going to come and get you. You were coming with me.'

'Bullshit.' He disappears back into the hallway and reappears with a passport in one hand and his mother's handbag in the other. 'No sign of *my* passport in here.'

She tries to stand, using the oven door handle to heave herself up from the floor. There's blood on the side of her face now, smeared from the blow to the head delivered by her son.

'There were things I needed to sort out first,' she says, desperately trying to keep Jasper on side. 'I was going to find us a home. A proper one this time... just the two of us.'

'Stop lying to him.' Kieran comes further into the room, closer to Jasper. I hear sirens somewhere in the distance, and so does Erin. 'You were never planning to come back, were you?' he continues. 'Were you going with him? Was that the plan?'

The knife shakes in my hand as I feel Marcus clawing at my arm once again. I look him in the eye, the colour of his irises fading, the life draining quickly from him now. The sirens grow louder, but they're not going to get here in time.

'Hex,' he mouths, unable now to produce a sound.

Erin looks from her husband to her son, torn between a lie and a truth she doesn't want to admit to.

'Ex,' Marcus moans. A trail of blood dribbles from his mouth to his chin, and despite everything he's guilty of, I wish it didn't have to end like this. I wish we could go back and alter everything.

The sirens are growing closer. Maria, I think.

Erin steps towards Jasper, but he recoils from her. 'Jay,' she says, her voice soft and persuasive. 'Come with me.'

Marcus's fingertips dig into my arm with the little strength he has left. His words echo in my head, and for the first time I hear exactly what he's trying to tell me. I look at Erin. Dark hair. Almost exotic-looking. Everything that Marcus once described.

I feel the breath sucked from my lungs as I realise who she really is, here in front of me this whole time.

Hex. Ex. Lex.

Alexis.

Erin is the ex-girlfriend who broke Marcus's heart. My words are strangled in my throat as I look from him to Jasper.

The boy is fighting back tears. Here, with them both in the same room, the similarities between them are undeniable. The colour of their eyes. The shape of their noses. I think of the photographs I've seen of Marcus from when he was younger, and one in particular springs to memory. Seventeen-year-old Marcus sitting on a friend's dad's sailing boat, a fishing rod balancing on his knee as he squints in the sunlight. If I had it here with me now and I held it up beside Jasper, it would be like holding up a mirror through time.

It's been in front of me all these weeks, if only I'd been able to see it. Jasper is Marcus's son.

THIRTY-SEVEN

The sound of the sirens gets closer. Erin repeats her plea to her son, urging Jasper to give her another chance and leave with her now. He is torn between her and Kieran, his head telling him to stay where he is, his heart drawn towards the mother he has loved and grieved.

'You let him think you were dead,' Kieran says, his voice ice.

'I did it for you,' Erin tells Jasper, giving up on the lie that Marcus has been holding her here against her will.

They start to argue, but their voices are crushed beneath the weight of everything that presses on my skull, deafening me. All I can think of is Marcus. All the lies. All the years given to a person I've never known. I crouch beside him, the rest of the room disappearing.

'Help is coming,' I say. 'They'll be here soon.'

But his eyes are closed, and I don't know if he can hear me. I should hate him. But in this moment, I can't feel anything.

'How long have you two been planning to take that money?' I hear Kieran ask.

'I never planned anything. It was Marcus, all of it.'

'Have you been having an affair?' Jasper asks, his face screwed up at the prospect of it.

'No! Don't be ridiculous. It was never like that. Jay, please... you've got to believe me.'

But Jasper doesn't have to believe anything his mother tells him, and the expression of resentment on his face says he doesn't. I don't think Kieran believes it either.

I think of Marcus and Erin together in that other bedroom at the hotel, while Kieran and I were further along the corridor. How stupid and naïve we both were, seduced by an idea sold to us by a pair of liars – both unaware that while we were trying to save our marriages, our partners were plotting to rip us off and leave us. They must have been sitting in that room laughing at how easy it had all been.

I feel as though a weight has been dropped onto my chest, the air being slowly crushed from my lungs. All this time, Marcus has known about the video. He already knew about Kieran and me. He made me talk through the details of everything that happened last Saturday evening; he played the part of victim, all the while already knowing what I'd done. He acted like a betrayed husband when the truth was that he was guilty of a betrayal far worse than I could ever have imagined him capable of. His performance was entirely believable. He watched me grovel and beg for forgiveness while in the thick of his plot to blackmail me out of the money he knew I resented being in possession of. For a moment, I feel as though I can't breathe. This man I married is a stranger to me.

'How long have you known him?' Kieran asks. 'And don't give me any shit about meeting him through Louise.'

I look up from Marcus. 'Kieran,' I say, hoping the warning will be heard in my voice. He looks at me. I shake my head, not wanting to utter another word and give anything away. Jasper doesn't deserve any of this. He doesn't deserve to find out the truth like this.

The sirens sound as though they may already be on the lane. Their wail pierces the air.

'We've got to go now,' Erin says, putting a hand on Jasper's arm.

'I'm not going anywhere with you.'

With time running out, she's forced to make a choice, and once again she decides to leave her son behind. She bolts for the back door. Kieran chases after her. Jasper stands close to Marcus and me, frozen for a moment. Then he turns to us. 'This is all your fault,' he says coldly, his eyes filled with tears. His focus moves between us, and I've no idea which one of us he's accusing.

There's the sound of tyres on the gravel driveway, engines being cut, doors being slammed. Jasper glances anxiously at the back door through which his mother has not long ago left, then turns to the hallway and leaves the way he came in, choosing not to follow the woman who opted to abandon him.

There are voices at the back door. A paramedic enters the kitchen, closely followed by a second. They hustle and bustle, filling the kitchen with movement and noise.

But here in our silent bubble, just the two of us, Marcus has fallen heavy in my hands, his face grey and lifeless.

'It's okay,' I hear a voice say, the words muffled as though I'm being suffocated. 'We'll take over from here.'

I move aside, gently lowering Marcus's body to the cold tiled floor as he slides lifelessly from the chair. The paramedics crouch to attend to him. But it's too late. He's already gone.

THIRTY-EIGHT

I'm sitting in the living room when the doorbell rings. The whole house has been stripped of any trace of Marcus: his toothbrush and razor gone from the bathroom, his clothes pulled out of the wardrobe, his photos taken from the frames, now left standing empty. I've removed all evidence of him as though in doing so I might erase his memory. It's been the only way I've been able to cope with the last couple of weeks without feeling as though I might lose my mind. I can't stay here, not after everything that's happened. But while I'm suspended from work pending an investigation, I've little other choice. It's this place or my mother's house, and that's only recently been released from its status as a crime scene.

I go to the door expecting to find a delivery driver there: since Marcus died, I've tried to avoid going out when possible. I've ordered groceries online and there's been little else I've needed. As promised, Erin sent that video footage of me and Kieran to the list of addresses in her email. As a result, it'll be quite some time before I can show my face in town again.

When I open the door, there's no delivery driver on the

doorstep. Instead, it's Kieran. 'Are you okay?' he asks, before I've said anything.

I shrug. Telling him I'm fine seems pointless. Talking to him about any of the million and one things that have been crashing into each other in my brain for these past weeks is equally pointless.

I step aside to let him into the house, and once the door is closed he takes me in his arms and holds me to him, neither of us speaking. He's the first to pull away.

'How's Jasper doing?' I ask.

'He's okay. Physically, at least. I don't really know much more. He won't talk to me.'

He follows me into the living room.

'Do you want a cup of tea or anything?'

'No thanks. Look, Louise... I'm sorry about Marcus.'

I feel my jaw tense. 'I'm not.' But of course I don't mean that, and Kieran knows it. Whatever my husband was guilty of, I would never have chosen for things to end this way. I just wish he'd had the decency to leave me, if that was what he wanted to do. Fighting me for that money through the courts would have shown greater respect than what he willingly chose to subject me to.

'I loved him. I loved the person I thought he was, anyway.'

'I know you did. I loved Erin just as much.'

'Have you been to see her?'

Erin hadn't made it far from the house before the police caught up with her. She'd tried for a while to maintain the story that Marcus had been holding her captive there, but it wasn't long before the lies began to unravel.

He shakes his head. 'I can't speak to her. I just... I wouldn't know where to start. Not yet, at least.'

I sit on the sofa, Kieran takes the chair opposite.

'Marcus must have mentioned her,' he says. 'I mean, before all this.'

I nod. 'Early on. You know, in those first months of getting to know each other, when you talk about your exes.'

'Do you think he knew about Jasper?'

I shrug. 'I don't know. I don't think Marcus ever told the truth about anything. Half the work trips he'd been on over the past couple of years turned out to be productions that had never taken place.' I laugh bitterly. 'I've found out quite a lot over the past two weeks.'

As the details of Marcus and Erin's blackmail plot have unfolded, so too have the lies he told to make himself unavailable to me. I have no idea where he really was during some of those fictional work trips, and can only assume that for at least some of them, he and Erin met to plan. Perhaps they had sex during that time; maybe they didn't. Only Erin is able to share those details now, yet whether she will is something I've still to find out.

'I'm so sorry, Louise.'

And so am I, I think. Because in another life, at another time, there might have been something between Kieran and me. We might have had a chance.

'You don't deserve any of this,' he adds.

But perhaps that's where he's wrong. Over these past couple of weeks, I've been haunted by the thought that maybe everything that's happened is some kind of retribution: the long-awaited payback for the sins of my younger years. Either that, or I'm paying for my father's crimes, our family's fate for each of us to suffer as a result of what he did.

'Are you going to tell Jasper?' I ask.

So far, the details that have been unearthed during the police investigation have been kept from the boy. Whether it remains that way I imagine is now up to Kieran. Unless, of course, he makes the choice to one day visit his mother.

'This is why I'm here, really. I mean, I wanted to see you, to see how you are. But I need your advice too.'

'I'm not sure I'm the best person to offer that.'

'What would you do, though? Do you think he should know?'

'I don't know. Maybe, one day. But he's got so much already on his shoulders. He's just lost his mother. He's coming to terms with what she did. He's survived for sixteen years without Marcus. He doesn't need to know about him now.'

'I should have seen it somehow. I should have known she lied about Jasper's father.'

'How could you have possibly known that? You can't blame yourself. None of this is your fault.'

Kieran presses his fingertips to his temples. He looks so tired. I'm sorry now for ever having thought him guilty in any way.

'How did Erin convince you to move here?' I ask. 'She must have been pretty persuasive.'

Kieran knows now, as we all do, that their move to East-bridge was nothing more than a stage in Erin's plan with Marcus. He must feel such an idiot to have listened to her lies and fallen for them, in much the same way I was influenced by Marcus.

'About eighteen months ago she lost her nursing job. She told me they were making cuts, but I don't know any more whether that was true. I can't be sure of anything now. She was unemployed for a while after that. She kept talking about how a change of scenery might do her good, be a fresh start for the three of us. Eventually I came around to the idea. I tried to get her to consider other places, but she always came back to this area. She reckoned the country air would be good for her.' He laughs bitterly, annoyed at his own naïvety.

'What did she tell you about Jasper's father?'

'That he died of cancer before Jasper was born. That it all happened quickly, within months of his diagnosis. I asked about his parents or siblings – I thought Jasper might still see his grandparents. But she told me he'd been raised by a single mother who'd recently died and that he'd been an only child. I should have asked more questions. I should have made sure I got more answers.'

'She used the illusion of grief to seduce you. She did the same to me, with Iris.'

Kieran looks crushed. Like me, he never really knew the person he was married to.

He stays on my sofa and I tell him everything. With Marcus's death and Erin's arrest, there's been no time yet for us to share the details of what happened before the day we met. I explain about the conversation in the café that day, when Erin told me about their marital problems and how they'd finally got themselves back on track by opening up their relationship to other people.

'We were having problems,' he admits. 'But they'd started before we came to Eastbridge, and the move here was one of the things that was supposed to help us. She was more depressed than I'd ever seen her. She said she just needed to get away.' His face changes, the enormity of his wife's lies fully realised now as they stack up in an invisible pile between us. 'I loved her. I'd have done anything to make her happy. That's why I agreed to what we did. And then when you came to the house that Saturday...' He lowers his head, not wanting to look at me. 'The guilt ate me up. And all that time...'

I think of all the things Erin said about Kieran when I met her in the cocktail bar that night: how he was the person she went home to; the person she shared her secrets with; the person she loved. I don't want to pity him, not when he and I are in so many ways the same.

'What happens with you and Jasper now?' I ask.

'I've always tried to treat him like he was my own, tried to be the father he never had. He was four when I met him. It wasn't easy, and I've not always got it right, but I'd do anything for that kid. And I want to do the right thing now.'

'Then don't tell him,' I say. 'But it has to be your choice, Kieran, not mine.'

'I don't like to think of lying to him. It feels no better than what his mother did.'

'This is different. Some lies are there to protect people. That's all you'd be doing: protecting him.'

Kieran closes his eyes for a moment, lost to thoughts he doesn't share with me. 'I'm so sorry about your job,' he says when he opens his eyes.

'I can't do anything about Jasper's exams now,' I tell him, not wanting to get into the details of my suspension with him. 'Not with things the way they are. I've spoken to Maria about it, though, and she's going to chase it up with the relevant people. He should get mitigating circumstances.'

'He'd be better off redoing the year, I think.'

'Possibly.' Yet I wonder just how much Jasper's mental health will be affected by everything that's happened over these past months. I always sensed that beneath the bravado, he wasn't the boy he wanted the world to believe he was. And then he saved my life. Had he not attacked his mother that day, there's no doubt in my mind Erin would have killed me.

'Has he forgiven you?' I ask. 'For us?'

The *us* sits awkwardly in the air between us for a moment.

'We've not really spoken about it much,' Kieran says. 'He gets the gist of it... he's not an idiot.' He glances at his phone, looking for the time. 'I'd better get going. I don't like leaving him on his own for too long.'

He gets up, and I go with him into the hallway. I nearly tell him to send Jasper my best, but I doubt this will be well received. He probably wishes we'd never had to meet: that he'd never come to my school; that his family had never moved to this town.

Kieran reaches for the front door handle. 'I'm sorry,' he says suddenly, before he's opened it. 'I told you to come over to the house that night. I encouraged it. I shouldn't have done it. I just wanted to see you, but it was wrong. If I hadn't...'

'You weren't to know she'd set that camera up before she left. If I hadn't gone to the hotel that night... if I hadn't confided my problems to Erin. If I hadn't gone to that yoga class and we'd never met. We could do this all day. She left her mobile in the house that day knowing I'd try to call her after the fake break-in. Knowing that I'd speak to you. She set the trap, Kieran. We just walked into it.'

After he's gone, I go outside and sit looking across the lawn. The gym at the bottom of the garden stands unused, though I suppose that was always the case anyway. I wonder how many conversations with other women Marcus had on the evenings he spent down there alone, feigning the need for a workout to alleviate the stresses of the day. It would be naïve of me to believe that Erin was the only other woman in his life. I wonder how many video calls were made before he returned to the house and came upstairs to our bedroom, continuing in the pretence of our farcical marriage as though we were just any normal couple.

I spent my childhood living with a man who was capable of the worst of deceptions. Years later, I chose someone equally manipulative. Even in my friendships, it seems I've leaned towards the destructive, unknowingly drawn to people who would cause nothing but harm. I suppose it's true what they say: that we gravitate towards what we know, seeking comfort from the things that are familiar to us.

THIRTY-NINE

In the weeks that follow Marcus's death, the police begin to piece together the history that united him and Erin. Transcripts of their text conversations are dissected and scrutinised, a post-mortem of a blackmail plot, and it turns out that everything Erin promised him in return for the money he would help them acquire – a life together and the family he'd never had – was nothing more than bait. She didn't love him now, but she might have loved him then, back when Erin Foster was Alexis Healy.

All those conversations Marcus and I shared in the early days of our relationship have come back to me over these past few days, the forgotten details resurrected from the haze of a honeymoon period that now feels a lifetime ago. Alexis was his first real love; they'd lived together for a while, but the fairy tale had come to an abrupt end when he'd found her in their bed with another man. It had devastated him for years afterwards, during which he'd shunned even the thought of another relationship. Until he met me, that was. At least that was what he told me. Now it's a case of his word against hers.

I request to visit Erin; there are things left unsaid that need to be spoken, even if only by me. There are obviously questions

I'd like to ask her, and there are answers only she can give me. But I know she's unlikely to offer them, so it comes as a surprise when I get a message to say she's agreed to see me.

Since police arrested her less than a mile from my mother's house, Erin has been remanded in custody at a local holding prison. She apparently hasn't said much to anyone, still thinking she can keep the truths of the past concealed. But there's still the truth of Cameron's death to be revealed, and I fear that Erin's silence is a stand upon the only thing she retains any kind of control over. Perhaps the fact that she's agreed to see me is an indication that she may be prepared to talk, though I won't hold my breath. It's more likely that she wants to taunt me with whatever she knows – to mock me with the fact that she's the only person who can tell me what really happened that night.

I've never been inside a prison before, but it turns out the portrayal on modern crime dramas is pretty accurate. I'm searched, and my belongings are put through an airport-style scanner before being left with a member of staff. When I go into the room where Erin and I are to meet, I'm expecting the kind of set-up I've seen in those same dramas: an open room furnished with nothing more than tables and chairs. I expect other people to be here, other detainees waiting to meet with family or partners, so when I'm ushered through the door by a male guard, I'm surprised to see just one table – more like a police station interview room than a prison meeting place. Erin is already here, sitting with her back to me.

Even from behind, she looks different. The hair that was always so immaculate is dishevelled and greasy, and there are the first signs of grey roots. Her shoulders look even more slender than they did before, and the confidence she wore has been replaced with a slouched posture that emits defeat. It seems that every mask slips eventually.

She doesn't turn at the sound of the door, though she must know I'm here, just behind her. The guard motions to the chair opposite her and reminds me that we have twenty minutes. It's probably far longer than we'll need.

I sit down without speaking.

'What do you want, Louise?'

'You and Marcus. I just want to know the truth.'

'For what purpose?'

I shrug. The fact is, I don't really know myself why getting these answers seems so important, not when there are so many other things of which I know I'll remain ignorant. But perhaps this is it. Certain details of my father's crimes went to the grave with him. Cameron died in circumstances that no one other than Erin may ever know about. Marcus had more than his fair share of secrets, but with Erin still here, there's a chance I can learn at least some of them.

'I met him when I was nineteen. He was eight years older than me. The age gap didn't matter to me, but my family weren't too happy about it. Anyway... things moved quickly. By the time I was twenty, we were living together. I felt safe with him. He adored me. When I was with him, he made me feel as though nothing else mattered, that it was just him and me against the world. I'm sure he probably made you feel the same.'

The person she describes is exactly the Marcus I met. Things moved quickly between us too. It just felt right. But I probably now know more than she realises. His lies about being in the Isle of Wight were the same for a fabricated work trip to the Lake District, as well as the festival he never went to last summer. He even sent me photographs from that one, letting me know how bad the weather was. I can only guess that he may have been with Erin on those occasions too.

'They've got a word for it now that never existed back then,' she says. 'Love-bombing. Sound familiar?'

'Did he know about Jasper before this year?'

This is the question that has burned me more than any other, but I fear I already know the answer. I think back on all those conversations we had about starting a family; about the concerns I raised that he actively and enthusiastically agreed with, all the time knowing he already had a son. He'd never shown up for that one, so how could he be expected to for another?

'He knew as soon as I found out I was pregnant. I was twenty-two. But I already knew by then he was a liar. I'd found messages on his phone from other women, and there'd been things sent to the flat. I was so young and naïve that I thought a baby might put things right between us – that once he knew he was going to be a father he might grow up and change his ways. Instead, he said we weren't ready. He said he didn't want a child. He asked me to get an abortion.'

I say nothing. I think of the conversation with Marcus in the kitchen that day, when I told him I'd found out that Kieran and Erin's son was a student at the school. He must have realised then that it was Jasper – his own son – yet he maintained a façade of ignorance, keeping to the script that he and Erin had written and rehearsed between them.

'So he left?'

'Yep. We'd been renting, so it was oh-so-easy for him to just walk away. I sent him photographs of Jasper after he was born, but I never heard anything back. He never sent so much as a birthday card.'

'He told me he'd found you in bed with another man.'

Erin's lip curls into a sneer. 'Of course he did.'

'And then the two of you just met up again by chance after all those years?'

Erin forces a smile. She knows I'm not an idiot. There would have been no opportunity for her and Marcus to pass through one another's lives by coincidence. One of them planned and instigated the meeting, and I'd be prepared to gamble everything she didn't manage to take from me on that person being Erin.

'It's really easy to find out your family's history. It makes for interesting reading, too. You know even up until about five years ago, the relatives of your father's victims were still trying to find legal loopholes to get back the money he was never made to repay. It had to be somewhere, didn't it? Presumably still with his wife. I was sorry to hear about her suicide, by the way. The guilt must have eventually become too much. You poor thing... you've lost so many of your family. Everyone now.'

If we were alone – if there wasn't a guard by the door and we weren't inside a prison room – I'm not sure what I'd have been capable of in this moment. The look in Erin's eyes as she sits staring at me, a smug expression stamped on her deceitful face, says there's more she could tell me. Did she have some involvement with my mother before she died? Did she somehow manage to resurrect the past, breathing fresh life into my mother's guilt and pushing her towards the decision to take her own life? It seems impossible, but then these past couple of months have proved if nothing else that anything is possible. That everyone is capable of anything given the wrong, or right, set of circumstances.

Marcus may have been a liar and a cheat, but I'm still unconvinced he was capable of murder. He may have fought with Cameron that day at my mother's house. He may have punched him. But the woman sitting across from me now: she's the cold-blooded one. She stabbed Marcus without a second thought, and I know she would have done the same to me had Jasper not intervened. There was never any evidence that Marcus was at Cameron's flat the day he died. Presumably because he was never there. Erin was.

'It was you,' I manage, my words barely a whisper. 'I thought Marcus had killed him... but it was you, wasn't it?'

Erin smiles but says nothing. She's not going to, not while there's a guard standing at the door and this meeting is more than likely being recorded. Bile rises at the back of my throat.

She may never face justice for what she did to my brother, but I'll make sure she more than pays the price for killing my husband.

'Did you or Marcus manage to persuade Cameron to go to my house the night before the "break-in", as well?' I ask, making inverted commas with my fingers. 'He was the perfect decoy, wasn't he?'

It seems too much of a coincidence that Cameron had been there that Friday, just before Marcus had staged the break-in at our home. Erin smiles and says nothing. She isn't going to give me the answers I want, but I know that somehow, she orchestrated all of this.

'I called a friend that evening,' I tell her. 'Before I tried your phone. If she'd answered, I would never have ended up at your house. That video would never have existed. What then?'

'There was always a plan B,' she says simply.

I swallow hard, not wanting this woman to see any evidence of my emotions. 'So you made contact with Marcus, and what? He just agreed to your plan without question?'

'People don't change, do they? Not really. He was still thinking with his dick and his pocket. And my gosh, he talked about you and that inheritance money a lot. How you needed your head looking at for thinking you shouldn't keep it. How he'd been an idiot for agreeing to sign that prenup.' She sits forward and rests her arms on the table. 'Two things Marcus always loved more than anything else – sex and money. And I was able to offer him both.'

Behind the table, I sit on my hands. My nails dig into the backs of my legs, willing my reaction not to spread to my face. I don't want to give her the satisfaction.

'Did he think the two of you were going to get back together?' I ask.

'He pretended he did. But we were just leading each other on. He told me he wanted to atone for abandoning Jasper as a kid. Such a load of bullshit. We just served a purpose for one another.'

'So where did Cameron come into all this?' I ask, finding it hard to speak my brother's name. 'What had he done to you, Erin? Did he know about your plan?'

Over these past weeks, without work to go to and in the silence of an empty house I no longer want to be in, I've had plenty of time to think about the circumstances in which my brother might have come to end up in the sorry mess made by my husband. When he told me to watch my back, I misinterpreted the warning. Now, I wonder exactly what and how much he knew. Perhaps Erin approached him first, thinking she'd be able to use him to extort the money from me. Or perhaps Cameron found out about her and Marcus's plan and threatened to expose them. The truth may never be revealed, but of one thing I'm sure: despite everything he was guilty of, my brother never deserved to be dragged into this mess.

'He'd seen us together. He had no idea who I was – just assumed I was another of Marcus's extramarital projects, I suppose. Marcus confronted him, told him to keep his mouth shut. They fought.'

'I know,' I say, thinking of the text message Cameron had sent to Marcus, threatening to tell me whatever he'd known. I watch the smug smile fall from her face. 'Marcus told me.'

I hold her eye until she looks away, then make a point of glancing at the guard.

'You found out where he lived, didn't you? You went there to finish what you knew Marcus wasn't capable of. My husband may have been many things, but he wasn't a murderer. He didn't have it in him. But you do, don't you? You've already proved that. I'll find the evidence, Alexis. I don't care how long it takes.'

The confident, self-assured woman I met at that yoga class all those weeks ago has vanished. If only for the briefest of moments, I get to see this version of her: intimidated, uncertain; vulnerable, even. But it can't and doesn't last for long.

'Why did you agree to see me today?' I ask.

'Just to make sure that you know,' she says, leaning across the table to hiss the words at me. 'He cheated on you with me. I let him do it a couple of times, just to keep up the pretence that we had a future together. There were likely many more women. How well did you really know your husband, Louise?' She sits back, a satisfied grin stretching across her face. 'You might want to get yourself checked out.'

I allow her a moment to enjoy what she seems to perceive as a small victory. Marcus played quite an impressive double bluff: a man apparently so scorned by a cheating ex-lover that no future woman could ever imagine him capable of doing the same. I realise now just how fooled I was by his casual charm; by his ability to face life with a humour I believed to be a form of self-defence. But his façade was never constructed to protect himself from the harm that others might cause him: it was a shield used to disguise the damage he himself was capable of inflicting.

'Why do you hate me so much?' I ask her. 'We're both victims of Marcus here, aren't we... according to your own assessment of him. We have so much in common. You don't hate me, Erin. You hate him. You hate what he did to you. What he didn't do for Jasper. And now you're here, about to serve a sentence for his murder. Perhaps you'll get out before you're old, perhaps not. Whenever it is, your husband will be long gone. Your son won't want to know you. As he gets older, he'll look back on what you put him through and the lies you told him, and the more time he has to think about it, the worse it'll come to look. You'll be dead to him. Do you still see yourself as victorious in some way?'

I push back my chair, its legs screeching sharply across the tiled floor.

'You've got nothing to go back to either,' Erin says snidely. 'Your cheating husband's dead. So's your brother. Your teaching career is over. Your life's no better than mine.'

'Maybe not,' I say with a shrug. 'For now. But I've got time and freedom. I can rebuild.' I push the chair beneath the table, leaving things as I found them when I arrived. 'Enjoy your four walls.'

After collecting my belongings, I can't get out of the prison quickly enough. I stop the car at the first opportunity, at the end of a residential street where a children's playground sits to my left, its colourful metal climbing frame and helter-skelter slide in stark juxtaposition with the imposing towers of the prison opposite. I watch a little girl around six or seven years old push her brother in a swing, the little boy's laughing face tilted up to the sky. Their mother stands to the side, taking photographs on her phone. I see myself and Cameron, my mother, the three of us somewhere in another life, in a different universe, and I sit behind the steering wheel and cry for all the things we might have been.

FORTY

My parents' attic is home to so many of my childhood toys that when I finally manage to pull myself up through the loft hatch it's like stepping back in time. There's an old plastic kitchen I remember getting for Christmas when I was seven, and in the far corner is the rocking horse Cameron inherited when I grew too big for it. I wonder how my parents even managed to get it up here.

In the opposite corner is the space where Erin slept, a duvet and pillows fashioned in a makeshift bed beneath the eaves. She apparently chose to stay up here rather than in one of the bedrooms just in case I made an appearance at a time I wasn't expected. No doubt Marcus made the decisions with her, gauging the days and times I'd be most likely to come to the house.

The smell I noticed from downstairs in my mother's bedroom is even worse up here. Erin must have felt sick living among it for that week. To think that at one point I considered the possibility that it was human remains – her remains – hidden somewhere in the house, left to decay. A bluebottle hums around the naked bulb hanging from the ceiling, two more crawling the wallpaper just to the side of me.

I pull my scarf up over the lower half of my face as I begin to root through the bin bags that have been shoved through the hatch then left forgotten. I find clothing and baby blankets, old hats and scarves; records bought by my mother then packed away when CDs became more popular. Marcus was right about one thing: one of those companies that comes in and clears everything out would be easier. Though he'd never have had a chance of getting his hands on that cash if I'd gone through with the idea.

As my search continues, I find a loose floorboard. When I pull it up, the stench hits me in the face like a slap – the putrid odour of rotten meat – and two dozen more bluebottles fly out at my face. I bat them away before turning on my phone's torch and angling the light to search the dark space. There, wedged beneath the floorboard and apparently unable to escape from where it became trapped, is a dead rat.

In my hand, my phone starts ringing. Maria.

'How are you doing?' she asks.

'I'm okay. Just chilling up in the attic with my new rodent friend.'

'What?'

'Never mind.'

There's a silence so long I wonder whether we've lost connection. The signal in my mother's house is poor at the best of times, but up in the attic it's terrible.

'You don't have to pretend to me, Louise.'

During these past few weeks, Maria has proved herself once again to be the best friend a woman could ask for. She's stuck by me through the scandal of that video footage being exposed, and I know she's defended me to her husband, despite James having every right to be furious with me. I knowingly led her towards danger the day I asked her to drive me to Kieran's house, but she did it anyway, and if she hadn't, things might have turned out so differently.

'You still haven't given me that date you're free for dinner,' I remind her, ignoring her comment. 'Or, you know, a takeaway, seeing as I can't show my face anywhere.'

'I don't want dinner.'

'You saved my life. You and Jasper.'

I keep thinking about what might have happened had Maria not called 999 that day. Erin had a knife. She'd already stabbed Marcus. She was capable of anything.

'Exactly. And you're planning to repay me with chicken balls and a bag of prawn crackers.'

'Absolutely not true. I was going to throw in some spring rolls as well.'

'Okay, well in that case, which night are you free at the weekend?' Maria laughs, but then falls silent again. 'Have you got a date for the funeral yet?'

'A week Thursday.'

Once again, I think for a moment that connection has been lost. 'I'll be there with you,' she says eventually.

'You don't have to do that.'

'Louise? You still there?'

'Sorry. Don't think my signal's great.' I inch across the attic floor, moving to try to get a better reception. 'Can you hear me?'

'I can now. Look... I wrote to the teaching council.'

'You shouldn't have done that.'

'It probably won't change anything,' she says apologetically. 'But it's worth a shot, isn't it?'

My union has assigned someone to represent me while the teaching council holds an investigation into my professional conduct, but I don't hold out hope that much will go in my favour. I'll never be able to return to Eastbridge Comprehensive, so the best I can hope for is finding work as a teacher elsewhere, somewhere no one knows me. But I know that what's happened will follow me wherever I go. Perhaps a clean break from the profession will turn out for the best.

'Thank you. For everything. Let's do the weekend.'

'Louise?'

But she can't hear me again, and seconds later, she ends the call. It's then that I notice it. A panel in the wall where the ancient wallpaper doesn't quite line up. I run my fingertips along the join, and when I reach the corner, it feels loose. I push gently against the panel, but it yields only slightly. Then I pull my hand back, smacking my palm against it, and the small section of wall falls in on itself.

Inside the darkened space that's revealed, there's a stack of boxes. Jigsaws. Old Christmas scenes: snow-covered churches and chocolate-box villages decorated with lights and trees. Pictures of harbours and lighthouses with so much sea you'd need the patience of a saint to finish the puzzle. I reach for them, taking each out in turn. The first four contain plastic bags filled with jigsaw pieces. But when I open the fifth – the lid showing a painting of two Labrador puppies nestled in front of a roaring fireplace – I'm met with something quite different.

The money is wrapped tightly in bundles, each secured with an elastic band. A quick scan suggests there are about fifty bundles. I take one out. Fifty-pound notes. The old ones – no longer even legal tender. I flip through it, not counting the notes properly, just guessing at how much is here. There must be around fifteen hundred in this bundle alone. The box must hold upwards of seventy-five thousand pounds.

The irony of this money being here all this time, just behind the wall, while Erin hid out metres away, doesn't pass me by. I drop the bundle of notes onto the rest. I picture my father here all those years ago, cutting the panel into the wall. Pasting over it, hoping the cracks wouldn't show. Maybe this was his rainy-day money; the cash he planned to come out to once he'd served his time. Had Erin known about it, she could have left without ever having to see or speak to Marcus again. Though I'm not sure any bank would even take it. How does anyone change this amount without some awkward questions?

Perhaps there's still a way to do it. The children's hospital in Bristol received a substantial transfer from my account just a couple of days ago, prearranged with the bank, and the weight lifted from my shoulders felt immeasurable. At last some good may come of the destruction my father wreaked all those years ago. But I've another plan for this money: one I decided upon while Marcus lay dying in my arms. This is for Jasper's future. Between them, his mother and father destroyed any chance of him getting decent results from school, and the next couple of years are going to be dictated by the chaos of their legacy. But it doesn't have to be for ever. Once he's old enough to be responsible with it, this money will be in a trust fund waiting for him, to give him a chance at the start in life his parents squandered for him. Three decades on, the saga written by my father might at last conclude with some kind of happy ending.

A LETTER FROM VICTORIA

Dear Reader,

I'd like to say a huge thank you for choosing to read *The Open Marriage* – if you enjoyed it and would like to keep up to date with all my latest releases, just sign up at the following link. Your email address will never be shared, and you can unsubscribe at any time.

www.bookouture.com/victoria-jenkins

This has certainly been a different kind of writing project for me, and it was exciting to tackle a subject that's never been featured in any other of my books. As with so many plots, the idea started with a simple 'what if' question: what if one decision destroyed someone's life? It's a concept that's been used in psychological thriller stories countless times, but the idea of an open marriage and its possible consequences offered so many potential plot routes. I knew I wanted my main female character to be a head teacher: a respected woman with professional responsibilities, with a career where any controversy in her personal life would carry far more risks than other jobs. She and Jasper were my first characters, though in my early plans it was going to be she who ended up saving his life, not the other way around. One of the things I love about the writing process is how a book, once started, can seem to develop a mind of its own and take you places you'd never intended it to lead.

I *love* writing female baddies, and Erin was a great character to develop. The way in which she seduces Louise into the proposition of embarking on an open marriage – as well as duping her husband at the same time – was a lot of fun to write.

I hope you loved *The Open Marriage*; if you did, I would be so grateful if you could write a review. I would love to hear what you think, and it really does make such a difference in helping new readers to discover my books for the first time.

I love hearing from readers – you can get in touch with me on social media.

Thank you,

Victoria

facebook.com/victoriajenkinswriter
x.com/vicwritescrime
instagram.com/vicwritescrime

ACKNOWLEDGMENTS

The biggest thank you to all the brilliant staff at Bookouture – it is crazy to think we are now on book fourteen! Thank you to Jenny Geras for continuing to support my writing, to Noelle Holten, who always promotes my books with such enthusiasm, and to all the other members of the team who help to make my ambition of writing full-time a real-life dream-come-true. In particular, a massive thank you to Claire Simmonds, who took the first draft of this book and transformed it from a brain-dump of jumbled ideas into something I could be proud to put my name to. It has been so much fun working with you on this story.

As always, a massive thank you to my family, who continue to support me and my writing. To my gorgeous girls, who still don't think I really have a job, and to my husband, who might catch up with reading these books eventually. I couldn't bring myself to write a dedication to someone for a book titled *The Open Marriage*... too weird. Instead, this book is for the readers: for everyone who has bought a copy of one of my books, borrowed a copy from a friend or a library, downloaded, rated or reviewed – it means more than you know. Thank you.

PUBLISHING TEAM

Turning a manuscript into a book requires the efforts of many people. The publishing team at Bookouture would like to acknowledge everyone who contributed to this publication.

Audio
Alba Proko
Sinead O'Connor
Melissa Tran

Commercial
Lauren Morrissette
Hannah Richmond
Imogen Allport

Cover design
The Brewster Project

Data and analysis
Mark Alder
Mohamed Bussuri

Editorial
Claire Simmonds
Jen Shannon

Copyeditor
Jane Selley

Proofreader
Liz Hatherell

Marketing
Alex Crow
Melanie Price
Occy Carr
Ciara Rosney
Martyna Młynarska

Operations and distribution
Marina Valles
Stephanie Straub

Production
Hannah Snetsinger
Mandy Kullar
Jen Shannon

Publicity
Kim Nash
Noelle Holten
Jess Readett
Sarah Hardy

Rights and contracts
Peta Nightingale
Richard King
Saidah Graham

Made in the USA
Monee, IL
02 July 2024

61125665R00163